"A SEXY STRANGER ASKS ME TO FOLLOW him on a Brazilian beach," she mused, tapping her finger against her lips. "To accept or not to accept."

He placed his drink in the sand and leaned into her personal space. Her nipples hardened at the welcome heat bathing her exposed skin. *Oh, yes, closer, please.*

"You strike me as the kind of woman who can more than handle herself, Leela. Take a chance and live a little. This life is all about passion, and sometimes the best experiences occur between two people who hardly know one another."

She shivered as he boldly brushed his mouth over hers.

Such a tease, and yet sexy as fuck. And his chocolate gaze said he knew it too.

Balthazar thought himself the master of sex, but what he failed to realize was he'd just met the mistress of sexual arts. One crook of her finger would have him on his knees begging for more, and yet, he wanted to play.

All right. She'd indulge him for the afternoon and see where it went. Because if anyone understood this game, it was Leela. She invented it, after all. Over five hundred years before his birth.

She slid the straw between their mouths and took hold of it with her teeth. His gaze fell to her lips as she sucked the liquid slowly, her throat working with each swallow. Yes, her oral skills were well perfected and trained, and she demonstrated her knowledge thoroughly before finally setting the glass down beside his.

"Show me what you intend to win, B."

IMMORTAL CURSE SERIES

ELDER BONDS

USA Today Bestselling Author

LEXI C. FOSS

Copyright © 2018 Lexi C. Foss

Editing by: Outthink Edits, LLC

Cover Design: Covers by Julie

Cover Photography: Zachary Jaydon

Cover Model: Daniel Rengering

Series Logo: The Font Diva

Interior Digital Art Paintings/Illustrations: Covers by Julie

Published by: Ninja Newt Publishing, LLC

Print Edition 2.0

ISBN: 978-1-7325356-2-6

To Allison - For convincing me this was a good idea, constantly navigating through all of my insanity, reading until early hours of the morning, talking me off the ledge and being a fantastic friend.

To Dan - This book is partially your fault. B is shamelessly thankful about that, too.

ELDER BONDS

AN IMMORTAL CURSE COLLECTION

A NOTE FROM BALTHAZAR

Dear Reader,

This is not your typical book.

For those new to me, I'm Balthazar, but you can call me B.
I'll be your guide on this journey through the Immortal
Curse world, along with my best friend, Luc. Together,
we'll provide you with ample insight into our history, lives,
and relationships. Don't be surprised if you learn a few
things along the way, especially in the bedroom.

Some suggestions for the newbies:
- Review my glossary of terms, as they might prove
  useful.
- Check out the character profiles; I wrote them
  myself.

There'll be a chat after each story because some of us will
be reading these for the first time. Hopefully, we'll keep
spoilers to a minimum, but you never know.

All right, we're ready. Remember to have fun, stay
hydrated, create a morning-after pack, and indulge a little.
Passion is life.

Love always,
B

B's Glossary

IMPORTANT STUFF PEOPLE SHOULD KNOW

Fledglings (noun): The love children of an Ichorian male and a human female, who have not yet experienced rebirth. Very rare since the Ichorians decided to make this illegal.

Hydraians (noun): Extremely good-looking beings who excel in the arts of sex. They also have an Ichorian father and a mortal mother and have died at some point, only to wake up the next day immortal.

Ichorians (noun): Bloodsuckers who descend from who knows what. Don't call them vampires. They frown upon that.

Immortals (noun): Beings who don't die (easily).

Seraphim (noun): Angels. More on that later.

B's Glossary

SOME TERMS YOU MIGHT SEE

Arcadia: Killer nightclub in New York City. I mean that literally. Definitely don't recommend a visit.

Blood Laws: The Ichorian response to the Treaty of 1747. Thou shall not consort with Hydraians, thou shall not knowingly create a Fledgling, and thou shall not do something else that's important, but who likes rules anyway?

Catastrophic Relief Foundation (CRF): An organization that claims to be all about humanitarian missions but is really a front for a group of elite soldiers who hunt and kill immortals.

Conclave: Scary. As. Fuck. Ichorian governing board.

Elders: The oldest of the Hydraians. There used to be five, but we're down to four—Alik, Jayson, Luc, and me.

Nizari: Assassins who hunt Fledglings. Most of them are retired because they did their jobs a little too well.

Nizari Poison: A green liquid used by the Ichorians to kill Fledglings. Not cool.

Sentinel: CRF super soldiers with a hubris complex.

Treaty of 1747: A false armistice that essentially allows Hydraians and Ichorians to live in harmony so long as they don't go anywhere near each other. Yeah. You're as skeptical as I am.

"You realize all of these are improper definitions, yes?"
—*Luc*

———

"Shh… Let's not scare them yet."
—*B*

CHARACTER PROFILES ACCORDING TO BALTHAZAR

"You might want to sit down for this."
—*B*

Aidan

Nicknames: None

Nationality: Sumerian

Age: Over four thousand years old

Immortal Classification: Ichorian

Maker: Unknown

Siblings: None

Children by Conception: Lucian & Amelia

Ichorian Progeny: Anya, Clara, Issac, Nadia, and Jonathan (by "adoption")

Immortal Talents: Intelligence/Omniscience

Relationship Status: Polyamorous with Anya and Nadia

Sexual Preferences: Open to all experiences and training opportunities

Favorite Position: All of them

Favorite Quote: *"More importantly, when did you cross the path of a Seraphim?"* Aidan *asked, drawing everyone's attention. "They're the only beings powerful enough to create something like this."*
Blood Laws, chapter 18

Pancakes or Waffles: Crêpes

Alik

Nicknames: None

Nationality: Babylonian

Age: Over three thousand years old

Immortal Classification: Hydraian — Elder

Maker/Father: Cyprus

Siblings: None

Immortal Talents: Mental Torture & Telepath

Relationship Status: Not interested

Sexual Preferences: Enjoys sex without expectations

Favorite Position: One where he doesn't have to look into his partner's eyes

Favorite Quote: *"You all know I would sacrifice anything to bring her back, but that doesn't belittle our bond. We're brothers and always will be, but love, true love, surpasses all the rules. Including those implied by our history."*
Blood Heart, epilogue

Pancakes or Waffles: No preference

Amelia Wakefield

Nicknames: Asset

Nationality: English

Age: A few centuries old

Immortal Classification: Hydraian

Maker/Father: Aidan

Siblings: Issac Wakefield (Half brother on maternal side), Lucian (Half brother on paternal side)

Immortal Talents: Humanoid Shapeshifting & Cerebral Knowledge Transfer

Relationship Status: Taken by Tom Fitzgerald

Sexual Preferences: Kinky at heart, but won't admit it out loud because she's a lady

Favorite Position: Tom on his knees

Favorite Quote: *"Make me forget, Tom." Her fingers wove through his hair, pulling him closer. "Help me forget everything." Forbidden Bonds*, chapter 12

Pancakes or Waffles: Equal-opportunity breakfast lover

Astasiya Davenport

Nicknames: Stas, Aya

Nationality: Montanan?

Age: Twenty-four human years

Immortal Classification: Hydraian

Maker/Parents: Sethios? Caro? Uncertain at this time

Siblings: None

Immortal Talents: Verbal Persuasion & Unknown

Relationship Status: It's complicated with Issac Wakefield

Sexual Preferences: Too young to be decided; will follow up in a century

Favorite Position: See comment above regarding sexual preference

Favorite Quote: *"Her demon was a billionaire playboy who masqueraded as a murder scene detective. Because that happened in real life."*
Blood Laws, chapter 2

Pancakes or Waffles: Pancakes

Balthazar

Nicknames: B, God, Oh My, Lover, Love, Fuck, Harder; the list is endless

Nationality: Sex God; Aegean

Age: Experienced

Immortal Classification: Hydraian — Elder

Maker/Father: My father didn't stick around to introduce himself

Siblings: None

Immortal Talents: Mindreading & Emotion Manipulation

Relationship Status: Polyamorous

Sexual Preferences: The more the merrier

Favorite Position: Read on to find out

Favorite Quote: *"Because in three thousand years, I've never seen you regard a woman the way you do Lizzie. And I am determined to give that back to you."*
Blood Heart, chapter 25

Pancakes or Waffles: Pancakes

Eli

Nicknames: None

Nationality: Aegean

Age: Over three thousand years old

Immortal Classification: Hydraian — Elder — Deceased

Maker/Father: Unknown

Siblings: None

Immortal Talents: Death by Touch & Super Strength

Relationship Status: Former Love of Amelia Wakefield

Sexual Preferences: Amelia Wakefield

Favorite Position: Worshipping Amelia

Favorite Quote: Not Available

Pancakes or Waffles: He always fancied crêpes like Aidan; I miss him dearly

Elizabeth Watkins

Nicknames: Lizzie, Red

Nationality: American?

Age: Twenty-four human years

Immortal Classification: Seraphim by genetic mutation

Maker: Jonathan Fitzgerald's mad scientists; birthed from the womb of Lillian Watkins

Siblings: None

Immortal Talents: None at the moment

Relationship Status: Engaged to Jayson

Sexual Preferences: Whatever Jayson tells her to do; submissive (to an extent)

Favorite Position: Still deciding

Favorite Quote: *"Jayson Masters,"* she chastised. *"You cannot throw a party without food!"* She shook her head. *"What time are you expecting people?"*
Blood Heart, chapter 9

Pancakes or Waffles: Waffles

Ezekiel

Nicknames: Kiel, Zeke, Assassin

Nationality: Babylonian

Age: Over three thousand years old

Immortal Classification: Ichorian — Lead Nizari Assassin

Maker: Osiris

Siblings: None

Immortal Talents: Tracing (he's like a little bloodhound teleporter)

Relationship Status: Married to his knives

Sexual Preferences: Violence

Favorite Position: Standing in a pool of blood and misery, lover of sarcasm founded in truth, and cryptic as hell

Favorite Quote: *He chuckled. "A myth, I assure you, but a similar concept. Try not to use that term too loudly outside our glass walls, though, darling. My kind do not take lightly to being compared to vile creatures of the night—our ancestry is much lighter."*
Blood Heart, chapter 13

Pancakes or Waffles: Blood

Issac Wakefield

Nicknames: Issac does not do nicknames (except for one person)

Nationality: Pompous. English. Ass.

Age: Only a few centuries old; he's a baby, really

Immortal Classification: Ichorian

Maker: Aidan

Siblings: Amelia Wakefield (Half sister on the maternal side)

Children by Conception: Wouldn't that be a sight?

Ichorian Progeny: Mateo & Tristan

Immortal Talents: Visual Manipulation

Relationship Status: It's complicated with Stas Davenport

Sexual Preferences: Playing hard to get (by pretending to resist me), alpha, enjoys biting, kinky minded

Favorite Position: One where he's in charge

Favorite Quote: *"I could do this all night, Aya." A nickname he created just for her. He was surprised the first time he said it, unused to nicknaming anyone, but it suited her. She was his Aya, and he intended to keep her for as long as fate allowed.*
Blood Laws, chapter 16

Pancakes or Waffles: Pancakes

Jacque

Nicknames: None

Nationality: European mix

Age: About a century old

Immortal Classification: Hydraian

Maker/Father: Unknown

Siblings: None

Immortal Talents: Teleportation & Minor Pyrokinesis

Relationship Status: Free-loving

Sexual Preferences: Up for whatever

Favorite Position: Seems to have a penchant for swings

Favorite Quote: *"Then you would be really displeased to know that I almost teleported to Luc's side just to see if I could nab him, but I chose to come back here and report instead. Shall I go try now?"*
Blood Heart, chapter 27

Pancakes or Waffles: Waffles (traitor)

Jayson

Nicknames: Jay, Jedrick

Nationality: Babylonian

Age: Over three thousand years old

Immortal Classification: Hydraian — Elder

Maker/Father: Artemis

Siblings: None

Immortal Talents: Metal Manipulation & Facial Distortion

Relationship Status: Engaged to Elizabeth Watkins

Sexual Preferences: Dominant

Favorite Position: All of them

Favorite Quote: *"I thought my yearning for you was a passing infatuation, just as the others who came before you were, but the desire grew with each day until I couldn't deny it anymore. And so I broke the rules, and tasted you, but, God, Liz, it wasn't enough."* His grip tightened as he pressed his forehead to her stomach. *"I don't think it will ever be enough."*
Blood Heart, chapter 28

Pancakes or Waffles: French Toast (because he's a rebel)

Jonathan Fitzgerald

Nicknames: John, Doctor Fitzgerald

Nationality: Scandinavian

Age: Several centuries old

Immortal Classification: Ichorian

Maker: Unknown—adopted by Aidan

Siblings: None

Immortal Talents: Lie Detection

Relationship Status: In love with himself

Sexual Preferences: Fuck if I know

Favorite Position: Probably something sadistic

Favorite Quote: *"I think we should play a game and find out just how far this infatuation goes,"* he mused. *"Would you like that, Lizzie? To learn Jay's true feelings?"*
Blood Heart, chapter 21

Pancakes or Waffles: Not relevant

Leela

Nicknames: Drawing a blank, but she sounds playful

Nationality: Great question

Age: No clue

Immortal Classification: Hmm. I'm not even sure why she's on this list? Do I know a Leela?

Maker/Father: ?

Siblings: None?

Immortal Talents: Unclear

Relationship Status: Hopefully, single, or at least open to experimentation

Sexual Preferences: Me? Maybe?

Favorite Position: Unclear; I'll investigate and report back

Favorite Quote: *"I don't belong here."* — Now

Pancakes or Waffles: Why does Brazil ring a bell?

Lucian

Nicknames: Luc, King, Hydraian King

Nationality: Nordic

Age: Nearly four thousand years old

Immortal Classification: Hydraian — Elder

Maker/Father: Aidan

Siblings: Amelia Wakefield (Half sister on the paternal side)

Immortal Talents: Intelligence/Omniscience & Sensation Manipulation

Relationship Status: Very single

Sexual Preferences: Anything and everything, but prefers women

Favorite Position: All of the above, and below, and in between

Favorite Quote: *"Pancakes are flat and shapeless, while waffles are geometrically delicious."*
Forbidden Bonds, chapter 16

Pancakes or Waffles: Waffles

Osiris

Nicknames: Not applicable

Nationality: No idea

Age: Ancient

Immortal Classification: Ichorian

Maker: Unknown

Siblings: None

Children: Sethios (maybe?)

Ichorian Progeny: Ezekiel, Lucinda, and possibly Sethios (circumstances are unclear)

Immortal Talents: Verbal and nonverbal persuasion

Relationship Status: Loves death and torture

Sexual Preferences: Pretty sure he needs to get laid more often; might put him in a better mood

Favorite Position: One of ultimate power

Favorite Quote: *"I daresay I am most pleased to make your acquaintance, Astasiya. Here I've spent the last few decades waiting to create a new protégé to replace my broken one, just to find that what I needed already existed. You."*
Blood Heart, chapter 27

Pancakes or Waffles: Paint either in blood, and he'll eat them

Sethios

Nicknames: Seth

Nationality: Babylonian

Age: Uh… old. Four thousand years, maybe?

Immortal Classification: Ichorian, but recent events have led me to question this

Maker/Father: Osiris

Siblings: None

Children: Astasiya Davenport (Unproven)

Immortal Talents: Hypnosis

Relationship Status: Has a tendency to break his sexual mates

Sexual Preferences: Sadist

Favorite Position: One that gives him ultimate control

Favorite Quote: Hasn't spoken a whole lot recently, considering Osiris wired his mouth shut, so… none?

Pancakes or Waffles: Does he even eat food? Pretty sure he lives on blood

Stark

Nicknames: Stark

Nationality: American (maybe)

Age: Looks to be about twenty-six or twenty-seven human years

Immortal Classification: Sentinel—Human-Soldier Hybrid (maybe)

Maker/Father: Unknown

Siblings: Unknown

Children: I really hope not

Immortal Talents: Stoicism (That's a talent, right?)

Relationship Status: Needs to get laid

Sexual Preferences: Doesn't seem to have one

Favorite Position: Probably the missionary type

Favorite Quote: *"Not everything is black and white,"* was his *cryptic reply. "Go ahead and shower when you feel up to standing. I'll find your clothes."*
Forbidden Bonds, chapter 2

Pancakes or Waffles: Doesn't strike me as the picky type

Tom Fitzgerald

Nicknames: Arrogant Ass, Arse, Sentinel, Fitzgerald

Nationality: American

Age: Twenty-seven human years

Immortal Classification: Hydraian

Maker/Father: Jonathan Fitzgerald

Siblings: None

Immortal Talents: Perfect Aim & Lie Manipulation

Relationship Status: In love with Amelia Wakefield

Sexual Preferences: Amelia Wakefield

Favorite Position: Amelia restrained/bound in some way with him in control

Favorite Quote: *"Shoot me,"* he urged. *"If it's what you need to do, then do it."*
Forbidden Bonds, chapter 11

Pancakes or Waffles: Likes food generally, so will eat either

THE ELDERS

"This is the story of how I met B, and as you can imagine, it took place a long time ago. Languages are fascinating, especially the way they evolve. If this story were told in its original format, no one in this day and age would understand it. The same concept applies to the sciences, time comprehension, and certain terminology with no equivalent today. So I've taken the liberty of translating it to something a little more current. Enjoy. Bring waffles."

—Luc

CHAPTER ONE

Luc

Around 1500 BC

Three women.

No, make that four. Or was that a man? Luc lifted his head to eye the human using his thigh as a pillow but couldn't tell the gender.

Oh well.

As much as Luc favored a pleasurable tumble between the sheets, he really needed to move. His father wanted to meet for a morning meal, and the climbing sun indicated that hour was fast approaching.

He stretched his arms and found a fifth mortal above his head. Nice breasts, supple waist. Ah yes, he had enjoyed her mouth around his cock. Her name, however, escaped him. She likely never even gave it. None of them did.

Luc sighed. All right. Time to dismantle the human pile.

He shifted subtly at first, dislodging the two brunettes from his abdomen, then the blond from his leg—male—and rolled over the dark-skinned woman who had snuggled into his side.

None of them woke.

Luc smirked. At least they were well satisfied. He wouldn't have it any other way.

Pulling on his signature blue robes, he tied it off with a bronze-laced sash, ran his fingers through his hair, and stepped outside. The sun warmed his exposed arms and neck and highlighted the coming day.

Gorgeous.

He padded barefoot along the path to his father's current home and waited outside against a tree. A breeze from the nearby sea calmed the air, soothing Luc to his very soul. These were his favorite hours, the ones where no one disturbed them. Catering to the humans' beliefs that he and his father were gods was cumbersome indeed, but necessary.

"Good morning," his father greeted as he exited in a similar outfit. The humans commonly mistook them for twins because of their similar physical ages, long blond hair, and matching green eyes. Luc had about four inches on Aidan's height, and his facial traits were graced by his mother's beauty, but they could otherwise pass as brothers.

Their uncommon heights, charming looks, and supreme intelligence lent to their nicknames as the "Divine Twins." The sapphire robes they always wore only added to their notoriety. They were worshipped, cherished, and frequently bedded by whoever was brave enough to ask. Not a bad life.

"Morning," he returned. "Another beautiful one at that."

"I'm not certain of that." His father began walking, hands clasped behind his back. "One of the females told me something rather worrisome last night."

Luc trailed along beside him, curious. "What was that?"

"That I was not the first god to grace her bed," he murmured. "I know there are others like me, have met a few through the last few centuries, but the way she described him was unlike anyone I've encountered." His emerald eyes lifted to his son. "The god who pleased her before me did not require blood."

"Like me," Luc inferred. "Interesting. Did you birth another son without knowing?"

Aidan shrugged. "Possibly, but he would be of this region. Her description of him, however, suggested otherwise."

"Not blond?"

"Nor light eyed." He stopped at the cliff's edge to admire the icy waves crashing against the rocks below. "She described him as a mind reader with a penchant for enhancing emotion."

"Neither of which is one of your abilities." Unlike Luc, who had inherited Aidan's gift of intelligence and strategy. "Assuming we're right about our genetic traits, he could not belong to you or me."

"Indeed."

"His dual gifts—if she's correct—and lack of dietary requirements indicate he's a descendant, like me."

Aidan nodded. "My thought as well."

Luc observed a pair of humans in the distance attempting to catch their next meal with a spear in the frigid water. "I assume the woman gave you a location?"

"An estimate of one, yes." He smirked as one of the mortals lost his balance. "They'll never learn."

"We've watched them evolve together for over two hundred years, Father. They continue to improve with each generation."

"True. Perhaps one day they'll develop a more effective

3

weapon."

"And use it on each other, no doubt," Luc replied dryly. Mortals seemed to be hardwired for conflict. Even now the two males below seemed to be bickering over their failed attempts, blaming each other rather than working as a team. "Do you think they will ever learn?"

"Perhaps," his father murmured. "But strategy is not a common trait."

True. "Speaking of, I assume you have a plan for tracking down the other 'god'?"

"I do." He pulled a stick from a nearby tree and drew a map in the dirt. "The armor she mentioned was reminiscent of our time southwest of here, closer to the larger of oceans. It's possible he's ventured up from Babylon or descends from another of that origin."

"A reasonable suspicion." All the immortals they knew of seemed to come from that region, his father included.

Aidan pointed to a location on his makeshift map. "We'll pick up a crew and transportation there and sail this direction"—his slender branch shifted left—"then land here and continue to the area she described."

"That's a long way for a female to travel alone."

"Her parents traded her to a local tribe in exchange for bronze."

"Which explains why she ended up in your bed," Luc inferred. "A sacrifice."

Aiden smirked. "Yes. Poor girl thought I meant to drink her dry."

"Is that why she mentioned the other god?"

His father nodded. "She thought to seduce me into saving her life, claimed the other taught her several enticing tricks that I would enjoy more than her blood."

"Did she prove herself correct?" Luc didn't particularly enjoy discussing their sex lives, but this provided intellectual value.

"In more ways than one." His emerald eyes glinted. "She's not lying. Another exists."

"Then we'll find him." A vow, not a request. If there was another like Luc in existence, they should meet. "He may provide answers."

"Or introduce additional questions."

"Either way, he's valuable."

"On that, we are of the same opinion." Aidan glanced at the path that led to town. "Shall we indulge in a meal first?"

"That would be advisable," Luc agreed. "We'll need an ox or two, as well as a wagon."

"Don't fancy a long walk, then?"

"I was thinking for the women." His lips curled in amusement. "Or did you intend to go without while we travel?"

His father chuckled. "I'm sure we can pick a few up along the way, but transportation may be prudent. We can trade it for a wooden boat at the water."

Trading was unnecessary, as the people of this region revered them. All they needed to do was ask and the items were given. But they refused to abuse the power.

So they would trade, likely with someone less fortunate, and continue on their way.

"I've been bored," Luc admitted as they started toward their favorite meal spot. "You should thank your female for me."

Aidan grinned. "I shall, once we return. She'll be sleeping for a while yet."

"Then we leave at dusk." Not a guess so much as a confirmation.

"Yes."

"Perfect." Luc added a little hop to his step. "An adventure, then."

"Be careful what you wish for, Son. This could be a new beginning, and not all changes are good."

"I welcome any at this point," he murmured, meaning it. As much as he adored his immortality, it grew tiresome after decades of the same worship and treatment. His talent for remembering everything he read and saw meant there were very few new experiences left for him in his current lifestyle. He craved more knowledge and a challenge, something that would entertain him for a while longer.

Or eternity would become a very long existence, indeed.

Lucian 1547 BC (Estimated)

CHAPTER TWO

"You don't want to do that." The mortal wouldn't listen to Balthazar, but he had to try anyway. "It won't end well for you."

The short male threw his fist upward, barely nicking Balthazar's chin. Everyone around them gasped, shocked that a human would be so brazen. But jealousy did miraculous things, and this man radiated it in waves.

"Look—"

Another swing and a miss.

Right, restraining the insolent bastard it was, then.

Balthazar caught his third attempt at a hit and applied just enough pressure to the man's fist to force him to his knees. "I really don't want to hurt you, Jeremiah," he murmured. "Violence isn't in my repertoire."

"You fucked my woman!"

"Yes, and numerous others before and after her. I offer pleasure to those in need, and your woman, as you call her, required my special brand. If you would learn how to fuck a female with more than your dick, perhaps you would find yourself with a more satisfied mate." Size didn't matter when one knew how to use it, but this man possessed neither girth nor skill. It was no wonder Bania came to Balthazar for assistance. Poor girl.

"You're evil," the human seethed, eliciting gasps from the crowd. "Sinful!"

Well, that last part was true. "I indulge in pleasure, which is hardly a wrongdoing. But I wouldn't expect a being such as you to understand." As one who only thought about his own indulgences, not others', he couldn't be expected to comprehend such a subject. Pity, really. Most men could be taught through verbal coaching, but this one would never learn.

"You'll lead a solitary existence, friend," Balthazar said as he released the mortal and turned toward the crowd.

They parted for him with reverent hushes, all admiring his impressive height and clearly superior looks. He'd used them for the better part of the last fifty years, mostly in the brothel where his mother had raised him. After an unfortunate incident with another angry male—something that happened more than he preferred—he'd died. Then awoke to the gift of immortality, or so it seemed. He hadn't aged a day since, and most wounds healed far too quickly for a mortal.

His reputation as a god was spreading, just as he desired. There had to be others like him, and if word traveled far enough, he would find them.

He stopped in his temporary home to trade robes, craving one of a deep red for this evening's festivities.

Or perhaps, *afternoon* was the more appropriate term. He dropped the sash to his side, no longer needing to tie it. Not with his favorite lover approaching.

Nythos's indecent thoughts heated his blood, her mind always providing the most delicious of desires. She was the reason he remained here for so long. Every evening a new adventure or experiment, all of which intrigued him.

He turned as she entered and welcomed her with a sensual kiss meant to seduce. All tongue, skill, and wanton ease that she eagerly reciprocated. He knotted his fingers through her thick auburn hair and tugged her head back for better access.

Damn, he adored this woman. Well, he adored *all* women, but this one appealed to him in a way few others did. Mostly because she understood his needs and possessed a lust for life that rivaled his own.

"You should have punched him back," she whispered against his lips. "He more than deserved it."

"Mmm, you know how I feel about unnecessary brutality." His palms slid to her ass, holding her against him. "Making love is always my preference."

"On that subject, I have some friends I want you to meet." Her legs wrapped around his waist as he lifted her from the ground. This was a far more enjoyable position for a conversation.

"They sound intriguing," he murmured, listening to her descriptions of the "friends" in her thoughts. Several males and females, all interested in a variety of oral exploits. "When are we meeting them?" he asked as he laid her on his bed, his lower half settling between her very welcoming thighs.

"After we finish here." She sucked his lower lip into her mouth and bit down hard enough to draw blood. Such an adventurous woman. If he could gift her with immortality, he wouldn't hesitate. The woman possessed all the markings of an excellent protégé, with her wicked ebony eyes, creamy skin, and gorgeous curves. Pair that with her kinky thoughts, and, well, she was perfection on legs.

"A woman after my own heart." He slid her robes up

to her hips while teasing her mouth with his tongue.

"Liar." She arched into him, her body and mind commanding his attention. "We both know it's not your heart that I want."

He grinned as he parted his robe. "There's a direct link, sweetheart." He slid into her welcoming heat, eliciting a moan from her chest. "Pleasure is felt everywhere, even in our souls."

Her nails bit into his neck as she raised her hips in a practiced motion meant to provoke a response.

"Impatient little nymph," he teased, nipping her chin in reprimand.

She repeated the action with a growled "Stop delaying. I need you. Now."

Oh, he didn't need words to know that. Her body told him when she soaked his cock. He thrust deep to the spot he knew she craved.

"Yes," she hissed, her nails scoring his shoulders and pulling down his robe in the process. "More."

Her thoughts erupted into an onslaught of orders, all encouraging and confirming his every move. Decades of experience gave him significant leverage, not to mention his other attributes.

His name sounded like heaven on her lips, as did the groan that followed when he pulled out of her. "Flip," he demanded.

She did, her pert ass resembling perfection on his bed as she raised it in the air. He peeled the rest of her robes off, along with his own, and drew his fingers slowly along the curve of her spine. Teasing was an art form meant to elicit the most extreme of sensations, but it had to be done right.

Goose bumps trailed his featherlight touch. Mmm. She usually wanted it rough, but there was a sensitivity to her today that indicated a different need entirely.

He pressed a kiss to her shoulder as he nudged her thighs apart. His lips trailed the path his finger made to the crease of her thigh. Her shuddering breaths were music to his ears as he settled on his back with his hands on her hips.

God, what a view.

Wet and swollen with arousal. Just the way every woman should be in his presence.

Balthazar blew against her clit and was rewarded with a shiver. Nythos loved sex almost as much as he did, making her the ideal playmate. No matter how many times he sated her, it was never enough. And he fucking adored it.

She tried to rotate, her thoughts indicating her desire to reciprocate.

"Later," he murmured, holding her in place. "Let me take care of you."

While her sexual inclinations were the loudest musings in her mind, an argument from earlier lurked beneath the yearnings. Some sort of family dispute regarding her future and a potential trade involving her marital commitment.

Humans and their desires to feign monogamy. Such a boring existence, indeed.

Nythos relaxed above him, her elbows holding her upper body against the pillows as he drew his thumbs in circles against her hip bones. A gesture meant to soothe, tease, and seduce, and one of his favorites.

"Long morning?" he asked softly, his lips brushing her inner thigh. Some women wanted to talk, then play.

"Yes." She blew out a shuddering breath. "I want to forget for a little while."

They would discuss it later, then. Pleasure first. And then again afterward.

His palms traced her shapely thighs to her ass, pulling her closer. "I can help with that."

"Please." Need thickened her voice as her legs quivered around him.

"Relax, sweetheart." He licked her long and deep, evoking a sigh from her. And she said pleasure wasn't tied to the heart.

More, more, more, she demanded mentally.

He grinned against her sensitive skin. "Don't worry, sweets. I'll take care of you."

Balthazar 1547 BC (Estimated)

CHAPTER THREE

Luc

The moon rose earlier here. Most mortals didn't understand direction, let alone the importance of the stars, but over two centuries of existing had taught Luc quite a bit about the seasonal patterns. It helped that he could recall every detail of every day as well.

"This area has changed since our last visit," he noted, surveying the cavern-like homes and sculpted rock stairs. "More people."

"Yes, every time I pass through, the population expands. I suspect in another thousand years or so, this area will be more of a metropolis. Similar to Babylon, but larger and more advanced."

Luc nodded, agreeing. Every generation brought new ideas and intelligence, suggesting the evolution of the human species. Fascinating to observe, if a little heartwarming.

"Shall we?" He gestured through the middle of the quiet cave toward a tree-laden grotto flickering with firelight. Amazing the way roots grew down here, in addition to moss and leaves.

"Might as well," Aidan replied. "If it's not him, perhaps they'll know where to find him."

"Yes," Luc agreed. The last few settlements they had visited all knew of the immortal they sought—a being referred to as Balthazar. His sexual appetites were renowned, as were his general kindness and spirit.

And the last village informed them of his current location. Here.

They wandered silently down the path, their only belongings the clothes on their backs. The mortals thought them to be gods, making it quite easy to procure accommodations.

Moans colored the night air as they moved closer to the flickering flames, followed by an array of murmurs and voices. All of them sensuous in nature.

His father arched a brow, an indication of his intrigue. Luc shared the feeling.

"Mmm, not bad," a deep voice said as they rounded the corner. "But you need to apply more pressure with your tongue. Nythos, sweetheart, care to demonstrate?"

A curvy woman with auburn hair stood from a nearby blanket, leaving her two partners to continue on without her. They didn't seem to mind much, their mouths otherwise engaged.

She kissed the male who spoke her name soundly on the mouth. "You know me so well, love."

"I do," he murmured. "You're almost as talented as me."

"Liar." She nipped his chin before going to her knees beside a lanky, dark-haired male. All of them were without clothes and very aroused.

Luc's kind of party.

"You need to devour her, Abel," the woman said sternly. "She won't break. Here, watch." She dipped her pretty head to the woman's sex and began to demonstrate while the mortal observed with wide eyes. He seemed far too distracted to take notes on the technique, which really was a damn shame because the woman possessed remarkable skill.

"She's a natural," the instructor agreed, his wicked gaze locking on Luc, and started walking toward them. Naked.

Balthazar.

No question.

Mortals weren't built with flawless physiques and perfect proportions. But this being possessed both, and more.

High cheekbones, a masculine jaw, dark brown irises, matching hair, and a face meant to attract others. No wonder the mortals they'd met referred to him as the God of Pleasure. Luc was intrigued just looking at him.

Balthazar returned the brazen appraisal, his gaze heating as he took in Luc's height and facial structure. Playing together would be fun, but they'd need to invite a few females as well to truly indulge. Luc's pleasurable gifts worked on both sexes, but he always preferred women.

"A sensual talent?" Balthazar murmured. "Tell me more."

Ah, so the mind-reading bit was true. "I'd rather show you." He held out his hand. "Lucian."

"Balthazar." The male accepted the welcoming gesture while holding Luc's gaze intently. "Your mind is intoxicating."

"It's the omniscience," his father replied. "Although, that's technically not the appropriate term. We merely remember everything."

Balthazar nodded. "I can hear that." He switched his focus to Luc's father. "Six hundred years? You look fantastic."

Aidan grinned. "Likewise. How long is your existence?"

"Not nearly as long, perhaps six or seven decades?" He shrugged. "It's hard to say for sure." He shifted his attention between them. "Father and son?"

"Yes," Luc confirmed. "Do you know your father?"

Balthazar snorted. "I was born in a brothel. It could have been anyone."

Fair enough. "And your talents are mind reading and emotion manipulation?" Luc asked, confirming what Aidan's bed partner had said.

"Ariana?" Balthazar's lips curled, revealing dimples. "Oh, yes, her tongue is quite memorable." He must have been responding to something Luc's father had thought. "And yes, she's correct."

"A lethal combination if used correctly," Aidan mused.

"Perhaps, but I prefer to use it to enhance pleasure."

That much was very clear by their surroundings. There were well over a dozen mortals spread out on various blankets, all completely oblivious to their quiet conversation. Fascinating, really.

"The best kind of passion is the kind that removes you from reality," Balthazar replied, clearly having caught Luc's thoughts. "I would much rather play with lust than anxiety."

Ah, so Balthazar had preoccupied the mortals by manipulating their emotions and heightening the sexual frenzy. "Brilliant." It served as a demonstration of power—threat or invitation—while also serving as a distraction.

He smiled. "Definitely an invitation."

Luc returned the amusement. "You barely know us."

"Your thoughts reached me when you crossed the river about thirty minutes ago, and I've been listening intently ever since. You're just as curious about me as I am about you, perhaps even more so." He looked to Aidan. "Though, I am very interested in your need for blood. That's different."

"I'm also singularly talented, unlike you and my son."

"Confirming a genetic mutation when combined with a human host," Luc added. "It must not be common, or there would be more of us." Especially with the way they all enjoyed sex.

"Possibly," his father replied. "Unless it requires a specific host."

"And death." Balthazar shrugged. "I pissed off a male a few decades back after dallying with his chosen mate. He bested me with a knife."

"Must have been shocked when you awoke the next morning," Luc said. "I know the female who stabbed me for personal enjoyment was quite surprised when I returned the favor several hours later."

Balthazar raised a brow. "A woman?"

Luc replayed the events of that evening through his mind—including the part where the sadistic bitch took great pleasure in maiming the more impressive parts of his anatomy.

"She thought to sacrifice me to the gods, and instead I became one." Luc didn't exactly enjoy hurting the female, but as he was not her first victim, she more than deserved the punishment.

"I see." He rubbed his jaw. "Normally, I would be opposed to such recourse against a woman, but that seems justified."

"Not all mortals are deserving of life," Aidan said softly. As the one among them with the oldest existence, he would know.

Balthazar tilted his chin downward, acknowledging his agreement. "There is much I can learn from you both."

"And us from you," Luc's father replied.

"So you'll be staying for a while?" Interest lit Balthazar's expression, his gaze darkening to a molten brown. "Then we should become better acquainted."

The beautiful female—Nythos—joined them, her arm sliding around Balthazar's waist. She'd clearly finished her instructional tasks, and by the sound of it, the woman on the ground was benefiting from it. Maybe the mortal learned something useful after all.

Balthazar kissed her temple, his lips curling into a salacious grin. "We can ask, sweets," he murmured. He looked to the eldest among them. "Aidan, yes?"

"Yes." He smiled at Nythos, his green eyes smoldering with interest. "What would you like to do, darling?"

"You." All female confidence without an ounce of hesitation. Gorgeous, curious, and sexually charged. A lovely combination of assets.

"He bites," Balthazar warned with a smile. "Not that I think you'll mind."

"I require blood," Aidan clarified. "But I won't kill you, and I promise you'll enjoy it."

Nythos smiled seductively, her pupils dilating with sinful intent. "I most certainly will." She turned to Balthazar and wrapped her arms around his neck. "Join us?"

His palms slid to her bare ass to pull her flush against his naked form. "Lucian and I intend to get better acquainted."

Her eyes sparkled as she glanced over her shoulder. "Mmm, that sounds delicious."

"Your call, sweetheart," Balthazar murmured. "And yes, you could join us afterward, but something tells me Aidan will keep you well entertained for a while."

Luc smirked. The mind-reading thing was certainly useful.

She bit her lip and returned her focus to her lover. Some sort of sexually charged conversation flowed between them, indicating a deep connection of trust and understanding.

Balthazar nodded after a moment, lust bright in his eyes. His mouth captured Nythos's in a sensual kiss that singed the air around them, then he released her with a pat on the ass. She wiggled her assets in response and grabbed

Aidan's hand.

"I don't feel like sharing you," she said, as if she had the right to command him.

Aidan grinned. "All right, darling."

Nythos led the way, evoking a chuckle from Luc. "Well, that's not something I see often." Usually, his father commanded the women, not the other way around.

"She's quite gifted," Balthazar murmured. "Speaking of…?" He arched a brow, his expectation clear.

A demonstration.

Hmm.

Luc scanned the mortals—all engaged in various acts of hedonism—and focused on a trio near the corner. The two males were pleasuring a woman, as well as themselves, in a rather simplistic manner.

Balthazar folded his arms as he stepped beside Luc to observe, having captured the goal from his thoughts. The threesome had developed a rhythm, their bodies moving in the waves of ecstasy without reaching peak performance.

Luc latched onto their sensual patterns, felt them with his mind, and slowly increased the receptors. Heightening too quickly could result in overstimulation, or worse, pausing of the heart. It took concentration and skill, but the effects, well, they were beautiful.

The brunette's head fell back against the broader man behind her, as the redhead at her front picked up his pace. Their moans increased, their bodies entranced by Luc's spell. This only worked when sensation was already at play, whether it be pain or pleasure, but he could enhance it to the point of infinite euphoria or suffering.

In this case, he chose gratification.

He tipped the woman over first, spiraling her into a pit of rapture. She deserved it more, and Luc adored the sight of a woman in the throes of passion. Her full lips parted on an endless scream as he enhanced her orgasm to something literally not of this world.

After drinking his fill of the gorgeous scene, he allowed

the males to join her, the three of them falling into a pile of limbs and bliss on the ground. They continued to writhe and groan as he prolonged the intensity. Then, ever so gently, he pulled back and refocused on his new friend.

Admiration and respect shone bright in Balthazar's gaze. He clearly approved.

"Oh, the fun we're going to have together," the male mused. "Now tell me who you want to play with, and we'll properly begin."

"Together?" Because Luc, too, wanted to see this sensual being in action.

"Absolutely. With at least five others, though, because I need to experience that talent of yours up close and personal."

"We should probably test it against your ability to control emotion, see what sort of outcome we're dealing with as a result." It would require several rounds, methods, positions, and personalities. Not that Luc minded. They had eternity to perfect their collaboration.

Balthazar smirked. "A lot of trial and error as well, yes?"

"Naturally. All experiments require it."

"And you'll remember every detail?" He almost sounded awed by that fact, or perhaps a tad jealous.

"Yes." Warmth caressed Luc's insides. This would be an experience to live for, again and again. "Which means I'll be able to weigh all the potential scenarios against each other and determine the one that best suits our needs in any given situation."

"I have a feeling this will take us several decades to master."

"More likely, centuries," Luc replied, meaning it. The opportunity between them was too exponential for anything less. Different cultures, women, men… They had the world to explore.

"Then I look forward to getting to know you very well, Luc." He must have picked up the nickname from his or

Aidan's thoughts. "You should probably call me B."

He smiled, content with the exchange. "B it is, then."

The immortal clapped him on the back. "Let's begin."

"Yes."

CHAPTER FOUR

Waves of furious energy rolled over Balthazar, ripping him from his dream state. The intensity of it crippled his ability to move.

Where? his power demanded, searching all the minds around him for the culprit.

Jeremiah.

His thoughts prickled the morning air, tainting everything in its path.

"What is it?" Luc asked from nearby. He was naked beneath a blanket of humans, same as Balthazar, but his emerald eyes were alert. "What do you sense?"

"Fury," he gritted out as he fought to close the connection. He focused on the others around him, their contentment, and let it drown the anger flooding his heart and soul.

Controlling emotion took its toll in these moments, discoloring his view of reality and sometimes altering his own feelings. But he managed it better each day.

…kill that bitch.

Balthazar sat up, abruptly waking the two women using his body as a pillow.

…best revenge… Nythos.

"Fuck." He jumped to his feet, not caring at all whom he disturbed, and took off at a dead run in the direction of the thoughts.

…asleep… one stab…

…blood.

He rounded the corner to find Jeremiah grinning madly at his massacre on the ground.

Balthazar's heart dropped to his stomach at the sight of Nythos's glassy black eyes staring up at him. "NO!" He fell to his knees beside her, his hands helpless as they ran over her slaughtered form.

"Nythos," he breathed, his chest aching. "Nythos…"

She couldn't hear him. He knew this. Yet, he repeated her name over and over, his soul weeping at her unexpected death. He adored this woman, cherished her, hadn't experienced nearly enough with her, and now…

His head fell to her bloody chest as tears pricked his eyes.

Fuck.

Not her. She didn't deserve this fate. Such a beautiful creature, so full of life and energy, so tender. His lungs tightened beneath the weight of her loss.

"Nythos," he whispered, wishing he had made a different choice. If she'd been by his side, he would have sensed the anger in advance and been able to save her. Alas, she lay here, a destroyed angel, her light gone from those gorgeous eyes.

His shoulders hunched as the world darkened around him.

Jealousy was a cruel demon, inspiring horrendous acts of violence, such as this. But nothing compared to anguish.

Balthazar turned his head to find Jeremiah pressed up against a nearby stone wall with a hand locked firmly around his throat. Luc stood beside him, his expression nonchalant as he restrained the human with the ease of a much stronger man.

It was then that Balthazar realized Aidan had been stabbed as well, his naked body lying lifeless beside Nythos. His eyes were closed, suggesting Jeremiah had slaughtered the immortal in his sleep.

Coward.

Red painted Balthazar's vision as he stood and approached the now quivering mortal. "Do you have any idea what you've done?"

"Hurts, doesn't it?" the imbecile sneered.

Luc cocked a brow as if amused. "He clearly wishes to die."

"And he will," Balthazar agreed. "Slowly." He'd give this human to the people, let them seek their own justice against him one by one. And when they finished, only then would Balthazar end his miserable existence.

A handful of the male mortals finally caught up to them, obviously having sensed a threat. They took in the slaughter and then the lunatic being held against the jutting cavern rocks.

"Restrain him" was all Balthazar said. "We'll tend to the victims first." Nythos deserved the best of ceremonies, and she would have one. Aidan, too, if that was his son's wish.

"My father will be up in about eight hours," Luc said as he handed Jeremiah off to three men. "And I want to examine Nythos."

Balthazar waited until their audience was gone to ask, "What do you mean by 'examine'?"

"Something isn't right." Luc knelt beside her and gently

28

lifted her wrist. "No pulse, and yet, her body remains far warmer than it should." He gestured to her still-flushed neck and cheeks with his chin. "That's not normal." He prodded at her wounds next, causing Balthazar's stomach to churn even as he knelt on the other side of her prone form.

"Your father will wake?" he asked quietly.

"Yes." Luc glanced up at him. "You're not aware of our strengths?"

He shook his head. "I know I heal quickly, but I've not had any other lethal incidents since the first one."

A barrage of information trickled through his mind as Luc unleashed a vault of historical data. Balthazar sat on his heels as he absorbed it all.

The two immortals had died in various ways throughout the centuries, always to awake fully restored within a set number of hours. Neither had tried beheading or fire, however, as they suspected through their various trials that those two methods would be permanent. How they came to that conclusion eluded Balthazar. His mind just wasn't capable of keeping up with the scientific and intellectual complexities riddling Luc's psyche.

Omniscient definitely seemed an appropriate term for him, as he truly seemed to know all. Even now, as he examined Nythos, a million scenarios triggered at once, each one reviewed and discarded in seconds as Luc sorted through hundreds of years of knowledge.

Balthazar pulled back, needing a break from the insanity. He scrubbed a hand over his face, belatedly realizing his palm was covered in blood.

A growl lodged in his throat. "Fucking Jeremiah."

"I take it he's pissed over a woman?" Luc guessed as he continued inspecting Nythos.

"I may have slept with his very dissatisfied mate." Twice. "He didn't approve."

"Clearly." Luc closed Nythos's eyes. "Her body isn't shutting down the way a normal mortal does, and her wounds appear to be healing."

Hope threatened to unfurl in Balthazar's chest. "You think she's one of us?"

"I'm not sure." Luc peered into her mouth. "That's why I want to examine her." He moved to her neck, pulling the hair aside and revealing a bite mark. "Fascinating."

"What about it?"

He didn't reply; just refocused on the worst of her injuries—the killing wound to her heart. Balthazar didn't indulge in torture, but he would take pleasure in ending Jeremiah's life.

All this over a wounded ego. Ridiculous.

Poor Nythos.

He knelt beside her again and pressed a kiss to her forehead. She was warm beneath his touch, lending credence to Luc's theory. Could she be one of them? In all Balthazar's years, he hadn't met anyone with her potential or inclinations. She thrived on passion and life.

"I hope you're right," he whispered. Because a beautiful spirit like hers deserved longer in this world, and to have her existence ended so early on account of some idiotic vendetta against him was wrong.

"I am." Luc hadn't stopped observing the knife laceration to her chest. His mind raced with images and words that Balthazar couldn't follow, not in sequence, anyway. It all resembled scientific gibberish based on centuries of experimentation. "She's healing."

Balthazar studied the same spot and blinked. "How can you tell?"

"The skin is stitching itself back together." Bright green eyes flashing with ancient intelligence finally lifted. "I've cataloged her progress, and at this rate, she'll be awake in ten hours, five minutes, and thirty-two seconds."

Well, that was a useful skill. "You're certain?"

"Yes." No hesitation or question. "She's healing at a slightly slower rate than my father, but age seems to factor into our ability to recover."

Right. He would ask more about that later. "So what do we do?"

"We wait," Luc said simply. "And you may want to rinse somewhere."

Balthazar took in his nude and bloody state. "Right." He'd find something to clean up Nythos as well. "Will you stay with them?"

"Yes." His mind confirmed the statement as well. Leaving his father unattended while in a weakened position went against every grain of his being.

Good. Loyalty was a trait Balthazar respected. "Need anything?"

"Some food?" Luc suggested. "I don't really require it, but I did burn a lot of energy last night."

The reminder of their fun thawed some of the ice coating Balthazar's insides, but it wasn't enough to elicit a grin. Not with Nythos's current state.

Jeremiah would pay dearly for this.

"I'll see what I can do about food," Balthazar said. "And I'll grab you a fresh robe." They were about the same size; he'd find him one of his own.

"Thank you." Luc moved to check Aidan's lacerations. "I'll be here."

Balthazar nodded. "I know."

CHAPTER FIVE

Jay

"A point of clarification: Jayson used to be known as Jedrick. To help better understand this translation of events, I've taken the liberty of updating his name. You're welcome. Waffles make the best tips."
—*Luc*

Another headache. This time because his father had stabbed him in the head. And just like every other fucking time this week, Jayson awoke a few hours later, cold, alone, and very pissed off.

"Prick," he growled as he rubbed his temple.

Artemis just needed to give up already. If he wanted to retain control of this kingdom so bad, he should just man up and do it. Jayson had no interest in taking over the bloody empire. He much preferred to spend his nights with willing women and enjoying life.

Instead, his father kept inventing new ways to kill him.

Next time, Jayson would return the favor. He was done with this madness. The first few times, he hadn't realized his father's intentions until it was too late. Then his father struck right as he started to wake up the next two times. Last night, it had taken five warriors to hold him down while a knife went through his skull.

I'm going to kill them all. No question. Artemis will die last. Slowly, painfully, and thoroughly.

Jayson just needed to find the right way to do it.

Waking up after being killed seven nights in a row had fucked with his head. His senses were all out of sorts. He could *feel* things he probably shouldn't, such as the metal surrounding this cell. It grew stronger each day, allowing him to do things he never could before.

Like open the door without touching it.

"That's fun," he said, smiling. "Let's see just how far that goes."

He stretched his limbs across the hard floor before hopping to his feet. The world spun for a moment, but slowly the bare features of an open cell registered before his eyes.

His father could at least experiment in the comfort of Jayson's quarters. Alas, he chose to degrade his son in the prison ward.

Jayson shook the debris from his dark hair and straightened his soiled linens. He needed a visit to the wash areas. *Badly.* And a new robe.

He took the stone steps two at a time and smiled at the two warriors standing guard.

"Good morning." It could have been afternoon or evening for all he cared, but the greeting seemed appropriate. Both turned with wide eyes and advanced on him.

"Where are your manners?" Jayson chastised as he took hold of their metal armor with his mind.

They squeaked as he squeezed—slowly—watching the bits and pieces of their warrior garb bite into their flesh. Their cries turned to screams, forcing Jayson to expedite the process. Torture was his father's playtime preference, not his.

The two humans collapsed onto the ground in a heap of flesh, bone, and contorted copper. *Fascinating.* Jayson felt alive with power, his skin humming with the need to experiment. This was the first morning he'd awoken without his father there to kill him again. Perhaps he thought the knife did the trick? Whatever the reason, Jayson intended to use it to his advantage.

But first, he needed to clean himself up.

He kicked the bodies down the stairs and started toward the nearest watering source.

The sound of his name rolling off a scathing tongue gave him pause. He turned to meet his father's brown eyes.

"If you think I'm going to let you try again, old man, think again." With that, he continued on his way, only to freeze midstep as his legs ceased working. He frowned at his bare feet, struggling to move, and glowered over his shoulder. "What the hell are you up to now?"

Jayson wore no metal, something he learned long ago not to do in the presence of his father. The immortal male possessed an affinity for the substance, something Jayson seemed to have inherited with his death. He couldn't wait to surprise the old man with his newfound ability.

Just need to learn how it works first.

A shorter man with olive-toned skin stepped into the hall with his hands clasped behind his back. Piercing green eyes took in the scene, his stature superior in every sense of the word.

"Osiris," Jayson growled, irritated. The ancient being had a knack for persuasion, hence Jayson's feet being glued to the floor unwillingly. "Of course."

"You were right, Artemis. This truly is fascinating," Osiris murmured. He studied Jayson in an appraising manner, his expression impressed. "How many times have you tried to kill him?"

"Seven." His father spat the word. "He won't fucking die."

Osiris nodded slowly. "What have you tried?"

His father recounted the last week of hell while Jayson fought not to cringe. Hearing the methods reiterated was almost as bad as experiencing them.

"Have you tried beheading him?" Osiris asked conversationally.

A scheming grin lit up his father's face. "Not yet. Shall we do that now?"

Jayson narrowed his gaze as he tapped into his new cognitive ability. He was done with this cruel game. He just needed to figure out how to sharpen his control...

"Perhaps." Osiris sauntered forward and circled Jayson, inspecting him as one would a bug. "There must be more like him in existence."

"He's my only progeny."

Thank fuck for that, Jayson thought sourly.

"Yes, I meant others like us may have created more like him. We need to gather our brethren, find out if any of them have produced beings with similar traits." Osiris's tone held a touch of awe that churned Jayson's stomach.

"You mean to collect them all," his father surmised.

"Indeed. Starting with your son."

"I thought we just agreed to try beheading him?" Such a petulant response from a man who considered himself an emperor.

And the award for "Father of the Year" goes to... Jayson suppressed an eye roll while continuing to sink his mental claws into all the bronze items in the home. His father fancied war, which meant they had a lot of weapons. Metal ones.

Osiris shrugged. "He could be useful. Even now I can sense his gifts." Emerald eyes locked on Jayson. "You're quite powerful."

"Yeah?" His lips curled. "Want a demonstration?" *Because I'm ready when you are, buddy.*

A flicker of amusement dilated those ancient pupils. "Yes."

He ignored the strangled sound coming from his father and harnessed all the metallic energy flowing in the air, sending it directly to the source of his hatred.

Artemis blocked the majority of the blows, his own gift igniting to protect himself, but Jayson had spent two decades watching his father's every move. He knew his style and used it against him. Two lethal shards pierced his father from behind, one lodging deep in his heart and the other in his skull, sending the immortal to the ground in a heap of blood and gore.

"Hurts, doesn't it?" he growled. He sent a third through the man's groin for good measure. His body would push it out as it healed, which was really a shame because Jayson would love to watch the jackass pull it out himself later.

He lifted another metal object and sent it flying toward his father's neck—intent on decapitation—only to have it drop as his control snapped.

Osiris clapped, pleased. "Very useful indeed."

More compulsion.

Jayson opened his mouth to reply but found it fused shut.

Shit.

He should have taken out the more powerful of the two when he had a chance. Now he was mute, feet cemented to the floor, and unable to access his gift. That didn't stop him from glowering at Osiris, though.

"You have spirit. Another trait I deeply admire," the ancient one murmured. "Sethios?"

"Yes?" A familiar immortal stepped out of the shadows with a dark-haired male at his side.

Sethios and Ezekiel. Great.

One was a sadistic fuck with a penchant for hypnosis,

while the other was a lethal assassin who couldn't die.

They were unfortunate acquaintances he'd known for years through his father. Everyone—except Artemis—owned up to their immortality and walked among the people as gods. His father, however, had wanted to maintain his "mortal" identity and continue to lead. The only way to do that was to sacrifice Jayson.

That plan failed.

"Do you mind guarding the young one while Ezekiel and I venture out to find the others?" Even though he phrased it as a question, Osiris clearly meant it as a demand.

And fuck being called "young one." Everyone here resembled a male in his twenties, maybe thirties. Just because they all lived longer did not make Jayson a child.

"Of course," Sethios replied. He stepped over some of the contorted metal pieces and moved to Jayson's side. "We'll have fun together."

Osiris smirked. "I'm sure you will." He held out his hand for the more lethal of the pair. "Let's go."

Ezekiel's gold-flecked gaze flicked to Sethios before he grabbed Osiris's wrist. The two immortals disappeared into a cloud of darkness, and relief temporarily touched Jayson's senses. He fixed his uncomfortable position and spun to face his new enemy.

Metal called to him as he gathered all his energy, ready—

"Please don't make me hurt you, Jay. I'm tired, it's been a long fucking day, and it would be far more pleasant if we just accepted our fate together." He cocked a brown brow. "Yes?"

Well, that wasn't what he expected. He paused his bronze-seeking efforts and took in the man's casual stance. It didn't appear to be a trick. If anything, Sethios looked bored. "What did you have in mind?" he asked slowly.

"For starters? Cleaning you up. Then perhaps we can find a few willing women to spend the evening with."

"Willing?" Jayson repeated. "I thought you preferred yours more compliant?"

Sethios's lips twitched. "Let's start with changing your robes, and then we'll see where the night goes."

Interesting. Sethios could flatten Jayson in a second if he wanted to. The man possessed age, experience, and a superior skill, but he preferred to keep things civil. Why argue? It gave Jayson time to explore his new powers and formulate an escape plan while Sethios was properly distracted.

Game on.

"All right," Jayson said.

Sethios smiled. "There's a smart lad."

Jayson fought the urge to growl at the belittling remark. All the immortals in his acquaintance considered him a boy. What they all failed to realize was he had reached manhood over a decade ago. With a father like Artemis, he never had a choice.

He sent another sheet of metal into the dead man on the floor for good measure. Wouldn't hurt to keep him down for as long as possible, and it helped alleviate some of his frustration.

"Right." Jayson rolled his shoulders and met Sethios's amused gaze. "I'm ready."

"You sure you don't want to sever his head? Might kill him for good."

"Oh, I want him to wake up. So I can kill him again. And again." *And again.*

Sethios chuckled. "You and I will get on just fine." He gestured toward the exit. "Let's go have some fun, Jay."

CHAPTER SIX

"Why isn't she awake?" Balthazar asked, arms folded, legs braced.

Nythos lay in his bed with her pretty head on his pillow while the rest of them stood around her. All of her wounds had healed on their own, but her eyes remained closed.

"She's young," Aidan murmured. "If you and Lucian died by the same means today, my son would wake before you."

"Yes, Aidan always heals faster than me," Luc added. "But he's several centuries older."

Balthazar listened as both immortals recounted several of their experiments. Such complex logic existed in their minds—like a maze without an end. Mortal brains were easy to navigate, even the most intelligent among them, but the knowledge these two possessed was overwhelming.

He pulled away from their thoughts and focused on the delicate woman wrapped up in his favorite linens. Such a beautiful female. Balthazar wasn't one to love singularly. He enjoyed all people, but this one touched him in a way very few ever had.

Aidan bent to check her neck and then her wrist. "It should be any minute now."

Luc crouched beside Nythos and picked up her opposite arm. "Yes." He glanced up at Balthazar. "I suggest you lie with her. It'll help with her transition."

"I agree. She's going to be quite disoriented, perhaps even violent, considering her final memory. I believe you're equipped to handle that?" Aidan phrased it as a question, but it came across as more rhetorical.

Still, Balthazar felt the need to confirm more for himself than anything else. "She'll be fine."

Aidan stood with a nod. "We'll leave you to it."

Luc joined his father and gave Balthazar a nudge on the shoulder as he walked by. "We'll bring back food and other things." He winked, his insinuation clear. "I think she'll be up for it." He followed Aidan outside, leaving Balthazar grinning after him.

Not even a day and already they understood each other.

Of course, they'd discussed the idea earlier when deciding what to do about Jeremiah. They both concluded that the best person to enact revenge on the imbecile would be a very pissed off Nythos. She was more of a lover than a fighter, but the woman could hold her own. And if she chose not to kill him, then they would let the pathetic mortal live. Whatever punishment they doled out would be of her choosing. She earned it most.

Balthazar went to the blanket beside her, wrapping his arm around her bare abdomen and resting his head on their shared pillow. He closed his eyes and listened for her thoughts.

Nothing.

If she weren't warm beneath his touch, he'd assume this all to be a ridiculous hoax. Thankfully, she felt very much alive.

He checked her pulse and sighed as it thrummed beneath his fingertips.

"Wake up," he whispered. "Come back to me, love."

No response.

Aidan hadn't awoken earlier so much as popped up—his gaze wide and perplexed, and then furious as he recalled the incidents that led to his death. Balthazar wasn't all that familiar with the process, only having died once before. He'd been far too alarmed at the time to focus on the details of his rebirth.

…pain… anger… blood…

His eyes opened as the trickle of words pierced his mind.

…excruciating…

Nythos remained utterly still, but her ruminations grew louder with each second as she recalled the events that led to her death. So quick she hadn't even realized what was happening until Jeremiah shoved a bronze blade into her chest. The coward had attacked them while they slept, killing Aidan first before moving on to Nythos.

Jeremiah would suffer for his sins.

Why? Who? Her lids fluttered. *Oh, B.*

His heart fractured on that broken thought. Nythos had mourned the loss of him most of all. Their bond went deeper than most, as they understood each other on a level few others could ever comprehend. It was a mutual respect that emboldened their relationship and allowed it to flourish. He would forever cherish her for such a gift.

"B?" she rasped, her full lips barely parting. She tried again, but no sound escaped. He pressed a cup to her mouth, encouraging her to drink some fresh water. She refused at first, but he gently coaxed her into accepting the much-needed liquid.

I don't… What's happening? she asked, her thoughts tinged with concern.

"Shh, give it a moment." Somehow, he managed to sound stern, yet soft, even while his pulse raced with joy. *She's alive.* While all activity over the last few hours suggested this would happen, he had refused to believe until now. It hurt too much to dream. But she was moving. Her eyelids fluttering. Her chest rising and falling.

Fuck, he had missed her.

"I'm so sorry," he said softly as she finished the water. Jeremiah's actions were technically not Balthazar's fault, but he felt guilty nonetheless. "That coward wouldn't have done this if it wasn't for me."

She made a noise in her throat that sounded an awful lot like a snort. *He's an imbecile*, she projected to him. *Don't ever apologize for* his *actions.*

Balthazar grinned and set the cup aside. "Already chastising me?"

You know it. Her lips curled as her gorgeous eyes met his. *Tell me what happened.*

He snuggled closer to her and kissed her temple and then her cheek. Luc had suggested they clean her up after she finished healing, something he very much appreciated now. She looked refreshed—brand new.

"You're immortal, love." He nuzzled her neck. "We're not sure how, but you've been reborn. Like me."

Her ebony irises narrowed as her pupils widened. "I'm… what?" Already her voice sounded stronger, with only a hint of the hoarseness from before. "Are you sure?"

He nodded. "You were dead, and now you're very much alive." He punctuated the point by brushing his lips against hers.

She responded by threading her fingers through his hair and holding him to her mouth. "I don't feel any different."

"You don't look any different either." She appeared well rested and very healthy. "In fact"—he slid his palm to her stomach and upward to her breasts—"you feel the same as well, if a little hot."

She arched into him on a moan, her hormones swiftly catching up to the game as her mind raced with wicked ideas. He grinned against her lips. "There's my Nythos."

Her tongue slid into his mouth, exploring and coaxing. A sensual energy surrounded her, one that excited all his nerves and lit his soul on fire.

"Fuck," he whispered, needing more of whatever she'd ignited in him. It had never been like this with her. So hot, addicting, and all-encompassing.

Balthazar knew passion—had mastered it well over the years—but *this*…

"Nythos," he breathed, deepening their kiss. Her hands went to his robes, ripping them from him in a practiced move that left him hard and ready for whatever she delivered.

"Closer," she demanded, her nails scoring up his sides and drawing a path in blood.

Whatever immortality had granted her, he approved because, fuck, that was hot.

He joined her beneath the blanket and settled between her thighs. His thick arousal met her damp heat, prodding her gently. She wasn't breakable, but he wanted to cherish—

She flipped him onto his back with a strength that surprised him, and straddled his thighs.

"I'm in charge." Her throaty voice rolled over all his senses, heightening his instincts and intriguing him at the same time.

Submitting to a woman wasn't in his repertoire, but he could play along for her benefit. For a little while, anyway.

"Are you now?" He tucked his hands behind his head. "All right, sweetheart. Have at it."

She dug her nails into his chest, eliciting a slight pain that mingled pleasantly with the action of her hips over his. More of that foreign sensation crawled over his skin, deepening his need and escalating his heartbeat.

Whatever it was, he loved it and wanted more.

"Kiss me," he demanded.

She shook her head and bit her lip. "I want to taste you."

Well, he couldn't argue with that. "Then do it."

Nythos ground her center against his erection, stirring all manner of desires, then bent her pretty head to lick his neck. Her path revealed itself in his mind, suggesting a new experience between them.

"Mmm," he murmured. "Only if I can return the favor, sweets."

She increased the friction between them as she moaned, "Oh, yes, please."

"Then nibble away." He closed his eyes as her tongue trailed across his skin.

"I want to do more than nibble," she whispered darkly.

"I know." He'd heard her intentions quite clearly. "Remind me to thank Aidan later for inspiring these ideas."

She grinned against his throat. "I didn't particularly care for it when I drank from him, but something about you..." She trailed off, but her thoughts continued. *His blood... so sweet... smells amazing. Fuck, I need it.*

A wave of desire caressed his insides, eliciting a groan from him. Fuck if that wasn't the most addicting feeling ever. Almost *too* addicting.

His brain fought to understand, to claw itself out of the thick haze of desire surrounding them. It had something important to say, a notion as to what might be exciting this reaction in him, but his groin overruled it.

Roll with it.

Such an appropriate statement as Nythos moved her hips against his, her slickness taunting his cock in the most delicious of ways.

Giving her control—or the illusion of it—seemed to be working for them both.

He twined his fingers in her hair, encouraging her to continue, while luxuriating in her sinful cravings. She scraped her teeth over his pulse and moaned. "I *need*." Her voice was so low and sultry.

"Whatever you want, love. You know—"

Her sharp incisors pierced his skin on a growl he felt in his heart. It ricocheted around them, raising goose bumps all along his arms.

Something about it didn't feel right.

He'd been bitten before, though not quite as deep as this, and it always resulted in a pleasurable pain.

This, however, didn't.

It soured his insides and churned his stomach.

The sensual cloud they'd fallen under seemed to dissipate as her body went eerily still. Her mind silent.

He frowned. "Nythos?"

She didn't reply—perhaps too mortified by the moment?

"Nythos," he murmured as he rolled them without resistance. "Talk to—"

Her ebony eyes gazed unseeingly up at him, her mouth etched into one of shock and coated in his blood.

"I don't... Nythos?" He went to his knees.

Her naked, lifeless body lay limp on his bed. All the light from her features gone.

"I..." He swallowed. "Nythos?"

She couldn't be...

No.

He just had her energetic body above him, her mind racing with sinful delight.

Why would...?

His throat worked as he tried to come up with something. Anything. A word. A signal.

How?

He checked her pulse, her wrist flimsy beneath his touch. No beat. Her neck, still warm, provided no encouragement.

No breaths inhaled or exhaled. No sign of any life.

Just a gorgeous, very—

He shuffled to the side, grabbing his robe. "No. *Fuck no.*" This was not happening. She'd been alive, God damn it. Only seconds ago. How the hell…? "No."

He jumped to his feet, determined.

This had to be a relapse, some sort of mistake.

Luc and Aidan would know how to fix it.

She'd healed. All the way. Had spoken to him. Had seduced him.

"No," he repeated, heading outside.

The two immortals he needed were standing near another cavern home, chatting with a group of females. Balthazar froze and opened his mouth, but no words escaped him. Not even a groan or a cry. He couldn't… This wasn't happening. Not again. She'd just come back to life!

Luc glanced his way, his brow furrowing and his thoughts shifting from seduction to concern. He nudged Aidan, and the two started toward him. Too slow. Their steps were too. Fucking. Slow.

Didn't they realize? Didn't they understand?

Nythos…

His legs shook.

She had to be fine. Not dead. Not because of him. Again. Not that he knew how or why, or even—

"Talk to me, B," Luc demanded as Aidan passed them outside and entered Balthazar's home.

"She's… she's…" He couldn't say it. The words just refused to dislodge from his heart. Because they weren't true. They couldn't be *true.*

"Lucian," Aidan called from inside as his unspoken words assaulted Balthazar's senses. *Death… Unexpected… Mistake?*

Balthazar collapsed to the ground, his knees scraping against the rocks beneath him. He felt nothing. And everything.

His chest ached with loss, so much worse than this morning. Despite his words and anticipations, he'd allowed himself to hope, to consider an eternity with Nythos. Whether as a lover or a friend, it didn't matter. He adored her—his female protégé with her kinky thoughts and gorgeous smile.

A tear slipped from his eye, rolling down his cheek.

Another followed.

More.

The consensus from the immortals inside pricked his conscious, confirming what he already knew. She wasn't coming back.

Perhaps it had all been a cruel hoax delivered by fate, a way to remind Balthazar he would forever be alone—to watch everyone he ever loved die around him. His mother, his closest friends, the various females in his life, and now Nythos.

His head fell to his palms, his shoulders shaking.

It hurt.

It fucking *hurt*.

He couldn't breathe beneath the assault of images pummeling his memories. All of a gorgeous, dark-haired beauty who lived life to the fullest without regret. Such an alluring spirit, one who deserved so much longer on this earth.

My sweet, sweet Nythos.

Luc placed his palm against Balthazar's back as he joined him on the ground. "I'm here." The words were underlined in comfort and loyalty but did little to dispel the agony ripping Balthazar apart inside.

She's gone.

His forehead hit the ground as he allowed the sobs to take him, his heart shattering for a woman he could have truly loved. A being so unlike anyone else he'd ever met. Someone he would forever miss and never forget.

My Nythos…

CHAPTER SEVEN

Luc

Balthazar sat against the wall with his knees tucked up to his chest, saying nothing. Instead, he stared out at the maze of tree roots lining the grotto around them, his heart evident in his chocolate gaze.

"I'm going to check in with Aidan," Luc said softly. His strategic side desired an explanation because Nythos had displayed all signs of immortality. She shouldn't be dead.

Balthazar nodded but said nothing.

Luc squeezed Balthazar's shoulder to remind him that he wasn't alone, then joined his father inside. His hand was poised over Nythos's thigh, knife in hand. He conveyed his intentions with a glance before drawing the sharp object across her thigh.

Blood oozed from the femoral artery rather than

spurting—an indication of her death. But that wasn't the purpose of this test.

Luc knelt beside her, his gaze cataloging every moment, waiting for some subtle change to occur.

Minutes passed.

No signs of immortal life.

Aidan lifted her lips to reveal two sharpened incisors and a mouthful of red fluid. His nose twitched. "Balthazar's blood."

"How do you know?"

"It's sweet. Like yours." He released her and used a nearby rag to wipe the fluid from his hand. "And I don't see a fatal wound."

"Perhaps her rebirth failed?" Luc suggested.

Aidan shook his head. "Or we misunderstood her recovery." He stood, his emerald eyes flashing with knowledge. "Perhaps there are ways to create an immortal outside of procreation."

Luc joined him, folding his arms. "What are you suggesting?"

"That exchanging blood prior to her initial death caused her resurrection."

"But you've exchanged blood before," Luc murmured.

"True. However, she's the first to be killed so soon after."

"Meaning your essence thrived inside her when death tried to take her under." Luc scratched his jaw. "It's reasonable since your blood is what gives me life."

"But a different kind."

"Indeed." How fascinating. "Do you think she possessed a power as well?"

"Perhaps," Aidan replied. "We would need to ask Balthazar if she exuded any sort of unique energy prior to her death, something I doubt he's in the frame of mind to answer now."

A fair point. "What do you believe killed her?" Because she was most certainly dead. Immortals at least showed signs of healing. Her body did not.

Aidan cocked a brow. "Care for my theory?"

"Always."

"Balthazar's blood," he replied. "You know I've long suspected that your essence is toxic to me, which is why I've never bitten you."

"True." His father always fed from mortals.

"If Nythos was like me—a being with a singular ability who requires blood—it's possible Balthazar's blood, as well as yours, was poison to her." Aidan shrugged. "As I said, it's a theory. We would need—"

"*What?*" Balthazar stood just inside the door, likely having listened to their conversation or thoughts from outside. "I… You mean to say… But I…" He stumbled into the wall beside them, his hand over his heart. "*No.*" He started to shake his head. "*Stop.*"

He covered his head, falling to the ground in a heap of excruciating pain. It pierced Luc's soul to see his new friend in such torment. He had clearly cared for this woman deeply.

Luc joined Balthazar on the floor and wrapped an arm around him. "We don't actually know," he murmured. "*You* couldn't have known."

Aidan met Luc's gaze, his expression thoughtful. They both wanted more information, but now clearly wasn't the time to request it from their mourning friend.

Or maybe it's just the distraction he needs.

If Nythos was like Aidan, it opened a whole realm of possibilities.

They would need to test the concept on a mortal—an exchange of blood, then kill the person to see if he or she woke. Why hadn't they considered this option previously? All their speculations were in regard to procreation, something Luc learned early on was not a potential for himself. But Aidan reproduced just fine.

What happens if I exchange blood?

Balthazar went rigid, his gaze snapping up to Aidan.

"Repeat that," he demanded.

Luc frowned while his father cleared his throat. He didn't reply out loud but seemed to be communicating silently with the mind reader.

He must have come to the same conclusion regarding an intellectual distraction, and it seemed to be working.

"Okay. Now elaborate." The strength in Balthazar's voice seemed to intensify the atmosphere between them. No one commanded Aidan to do anything, but he conceded with a nod.

"It's just an idea." He started to pace while Luc and Balthazar watched. "Well, a theory—"

"That you want to evaluate," Balthazar interjected flatly as he sat up, hands at his sides.

"Again, just an—"

"I get that part already. Explain how you arrived at that notion."

Aidan sighed as he met Balthazar's gaze, then dove into a complex explanation regarding the genetics of immortals. Or rather, the understanding Luc and Aidan had developed throughout the centuries.

Aidan existed for reasons neither of them could prove, but they suspected someone, somehow, had created him. He possessed memories of his mortal childhood, but not of his death, something that troubled him greatly since he could remember everything else in significant detail.

By contrast, Luc recalled his death down to his last breath and every second of his rebirth. His resurrection, coupled with his dual abilities and lack of a need for blood, classified him as "different."

Further, it seemed that Aidan's coupling with a human produced immortal children—or the potential for them. An untimely death at a younger age appeared to be a requirement for rebirth, something they discovered after Aidan had allowed a progeny to die naturally. The male never woke up. Luc, however, had died unexpectedly at nineteen and woke up the next morning.

Now, it seemed, they'd determined a new way to make an immortal. And perhaps, for the first time, may have finally found the way Aidan was created.

"And you want to experiment on Jeremiah," Balthazar concluded, his expression devoid of emotion.

"Seems fitting," Aidan replied. "Though, I suppose it's also slightly cruel."

"Cruel," Balthazar repeated as if tasting the word. "What he did to my Nythos was cruel. She died not once, but *twice*." His hands fisted, his brown eyes smoldering with fury. "Do it."

Luc frowned. "Are you sure?"

From what he'd observed of Balthazar, he seemed to value life and love, not revenge and torment. But as the male stared at him, he could see the warrior who lurked beneath the exterior. The immortal who would do right by those he loved, even if it meant evoking pain.

He said nothing because words between them weren't needed.

From that single exchange, Luc already understood.

"We'll do it now," Luc said with a glance at his father.

"Then I'll retrieve him from the mortal guards."

"One thing," Balthazar said, causing Aidan to pause at the threshold. "I don't know if Nythos had a power or not, but if she did, it was seductive in nature." The words sounded forced, as if being pulled from the depths of his soul. He cleared his throat before adding, "While I adore sex, I felt lost to her when she woke. Rather unnaturally so."

Aidan considered him carefully. "That would be fitting, given her proclivities. Did you feel incapable of rational thought?"

"No, just different. Overwhelmed." He seemed unable to elaborate.

Luc met Aidan's gaze. *He's not ready,* he said through his eyes.

Agreed, his father nodded and left to retrieve the mortal.

Balthazar ran his hands through his hair and shifted away to a corner of the room. He sat with his knees tucked to his chest and his arms wrapped around his shins. Every time he glanced at Nythos, he flinched.

Luc found a loose blanket on the bed and gently tucked it over her, hiding the scene but not the scent. "We'll give her a proper burial," he murmured softly.

Balthazar nodded, his eyes misting. He appeared so young in that moment—a man having his heart broken for the first time. But Luc didn't for a second consider him weak. It took great strength to embrace such emotions, and substantial resolve to maintain a clear head in the process.

"You think my decision regarding Jeremiah is based on logic," Balthazar murmured. "I assure you, it's not."

Luc settled opposite him, crossing his long legs at the ankles while stretched along the floor. "Most assume anything tied to emotion is thereby irrational, when, in fact, some of the best decisions are identified in the most hypersensitive of moments. You may think this is about revenge, but it's also founded in curiosity."

For knowing the truth would help them never make this mistake again. Not that it would ease the pain his friend must be feeling.

Luc was almost jealous. He'd never met a woman or a man who elicited such feeling in him. There were several he enjoyed sexually, but no one ever touched his heart or mind. Perhaps because his intellectual needs far superseded most. Finding an equal, or even one who entertained him for long periods, would be near to impossible.

"You think I loved her," Balthazar said softly.

"Am I wrong?"

Those dark chocolate orbs locked on Luc for a long moment. "It's hard to say. I love so many, but she meant more to me than most. I adored her enthusiasm, her company, and her spirit. Such a gorgeous woman inside and out." He sighed, his eyes falling shut as he rested his head against the wall behind him. "I'll never forget her."

On the surface, Balthazar exuded a sexual appeal that attracted many, but beneath that layer existed a male with strong ties to his inner emotions. Fascinating. It explained both of the immortal's gifts while also offering significant revelations about the man himself.

"Shall I analyze you as well?" Balthazar offered without looking at him.

"I imagine your insight into my mind would make that a simple enough task."

His lips twitched. "Your intellectual maze is exhausting, but it defines you. Complex, regal, seductive, and charming. But most importantly, your assessment of my warrior side brings to light your leadership qualities."

Balthazar shifted away from the wall and captured Luc's gaze.

"Your gift centers around strategy more than omniscience, as does Aidan's," he continued. "His interest in testing theories on Jeremiah isn't a result of craving knowledge so much as requiring it for future decisions. Because you both suspect our lives will one day be in jeopardy."

Luc stared at him. "How far have you gone into my head?"

"Far enough to know why you truly desired to find another like yourself." No hint of concern, merely issuing a fact. "It's more than a need not to spend eternity alone. You want to find others of our caliber—dual powered, immortal, no thirst for blood—to ensure survival."

"Because humankind will not always be so accepting of our existence," Luc finished for him. "Already I see the consequences of jealousy and hatred, those who do not understand why we're gifted and not them, and that will only increase as the population grows."

"Exactly. You're strategizing for centuries and millennia to come, examining every angle and outcome.

It's fascinating, if a little daunting. But it's what marks you as a leader."

"And you choose to hide beneath a veneer of pleasure."

Balthazar grinned at that. "Who says it's a veneer?"

"To have deduced all that implies otherwise," Luc replied.

"A conversation to be debated at another time." Balthazar flicked his gaze to the entrance. "We have a theory to test."

Aidan appeared with a barely conscious Jeremiah and tossed him to the ground. "I've already completed the blood exchange, thanks to his little escape attempt, but I thought you might want to kill him?" He held up a blade, his focus on Balthazar.

The pathetic excuse of a male whimpered on the floor, his mouth dribbling blood. Luc eyed him curiously. "Did he imbibe enough?" he asked. Because it appeared he'd spit most of it up onto his clothes.

"I held my wrist to his mouth for sixty seconds while holding his nose. It's enough." Aidan's disgruntled tone sent Luc's eyebrows upward. His father rarely lost his patience or cool around the mortals.

"He tried to stab him again," Balthazar murmured, responding to Luc's unspoken question. "And here I thought he was a coward."

"He's an imbecile who deserves this fate and that of ten others," Aidan stated irritably. "If you don't stab him, I'll gladly do the honors."

Balthazar stood. "How about I stab him in the heart while you slit his throat?"

Aidan's mouth curved upward while Jeremiah whined something incoherent on the floor.

"Yes. I accept that recourse." His father handed a knife to Balthazar. "It's like you can read my mind, B."

"Fancy that?" the mind reader replied, his tone lacking humor as he focused on the mortal. "Stand him up."

Luc didn't need to be told twice. He hefted the cowardly human up by the neck of his robes and held him steady.

Balthazar stared down at the much shorter man. "Do you know why Bania came to me?" he asked softly. He waited a beat, his expression emotionless. "Hmm, I can hear that you don't. You see, she was dissatisfied with your performance, or lack thereof, in bed, and she blamed herself. She sought me out for a lesson in sensuality, hoping it would improve your relationship."

He paused and twirled the sharp weapon while Jeremiah went eerily still.

"Yes, now you understand. She wasn't cheating so much as learning, which is a shame since she won't be able to demonstrate anything I taught her on you. However, I'll be a gentleman in your absence and help console her after your death. I'm charitable like that." He drove the knife through the man's heart without blinking an eye or showing an ounce of remorse.

Aidan followed it up by slitting the bastard's throat, then wiped the blade against the mortal's robes. "See you in a bit."

CHAPTER EIGHT

Nythos always wore red well. It suited her complexion and hair and showcased her love for life.

Such a sensual spirit.

He laid a bouquet of her favorite flowers beside her in the canoe and bent to kiss her forehead. Spirits and souls weren't something he knew a lot about, but he hoped she existed somewhere feeling cherished and adored.

Fuck, he would miss her for eternity. No one would ever replace her in any way. "My darling Nythos," he murmured, his hand over hers. "May you fly and live again. Someday."

Her family stood off to the side, their thoughts assaulting him in waves of remorse. He blamed himself for her death, as did her brothers, but her mother silently thanked him for giving her daughter a full life. Balthazar held on to that gratitude and wound it around his heart. Because while knowing him may have led to her early demise, Nythos wouldn't have truly lived had it not been for him. He provided her with the gifts of freedom and independence and the ability to thrive without censor.

Her spirit is finally free.

Firelight danced over the water as Balthazar stood once more. "Gone but never forgotten," he whispered, a piece of his heart breaking off to sail with her. He nudged the canoe from the shore. "Until we meet again, my little nymph."

No one spoke as she drifted, but the mental murmurs bespoke sadness and mourning. Luc and Aidan stood near the back, their support a solid presence in his mind. They spent the last three days experimenting on Jeremiah while Balthazar made arrangements with Nythos's family for their future. He intended to leave them everything he owned, an act that seemed to appease her father more than anyone else. The older man appeared to care only about the financial loss of her passing, while the rest of the family grieved.

He rolled his neck and met her mother's gaze.

Thank you, she said again. *She would have loved this.*

He agreed with a nod. Nythos loved the rivers. He frequently found her bathing in the calmer areas, her hair glistening in the moonlight. How many times had they made love near and beneath the falls?

"Siren," he once called her.

"Do you require a song?" she asked, a devilish twinkle in her eyes.

He lifted her into his arms. "Mmm, yes, I think I do."

"It will be about you," she whispered as her legs circled his waist. "And all the ways you've changed me for the better."

"I think you have our roles reversed." He braced her back against a rock. "You are the one who has changed me."

The memory of her laughter caressed his heart. He

swore he heard it even now, carrying on the wind as the last vestiges of her ceremonial canoe disappeared over the water's edge. Her body disappeared beneath the sea, her spirit laid to rest surrounded by nature. A fitting burial for one who adored life.

Balthazar bowed respectfully to Nythos's mother and the rest of her family. Only the maternal one among them returned the gesture before sitting beside the water. They would host a private ritual now, meant for the blood relatives.

Goodbye, my sweet.

He excused himself from their beliefs, needing to handle his grief in a different manner. Because while he acknowledged that his blood killed her, he also knew the real person to blame lay tied up a few hundred yards away. And he intended to return the favor. Tonight.

Luc and Aidan joined him on the path, their thoughts torn between remorse and intrigue. They'd discovered several aspects regarding immortality while playing with Jeremiah. He was indeed like Aidan—requiring mortal blood to survive—and only possessed one gift.

Retrocognition.

It seemed appropriate that the man was doomed to forever access the past. A single touch sent him backward in time to experience it as himself. Aidan had enjoyed exploiting the gift by forcing Jeremiah to mentally relive each of his deaths throughout the years, including the one the new immortal had inflicted on him several days ago.

At least a few positive results came from all of this, as they now possessed confirmation that two immortal types existed. It solved an ancient puzzle for Aidan and how he came to be as well. From Balthazar's dive through the older being's thoughts, he learned that there were other blood drinkers in existence, none of whom knew anything about their origins. Luc, however, was the only other known dually gifted immortal.

Fear assaulted Balthazar's senses as he reached their

captive, leaving a bitter taste in his mouth. He understood why all the tests were needed, including the ones regarding how fast Jeremiah healed, but he wanted this done.

"Have you tried your blood?" Balthazar asked, his gaze on Aidan.

"Not yet." He rolled up the sleeves of his robes while he spoke. "I don't think it'll impact him."

"Good." That was Balthazar's expectation. "It means I can kill him with mine. A suitable death, considering the crime."

Jeremiah's eyes bugged as he tried to speak over the gag in his mouth. *Don't! I'm sorry! I didn't mean—*

"But you're not," Balthazar replied flatly. "Your surface thoughts can't hide the monster lurking within, Jeremiah." The one who happily slaughtered Nythos and rejoiced in his revenge plot. "You're not a good man." And he deserved death.

Rage stirred in the male's gaze, matching the downward spiral of his thoughts.

"That only confirms my judgment," Balthazar murmured with a nod to Aidan. "Do it."

"Gladly." He slit his wrist, pulled down the gag, and forced the blood into the other man's mouth.

Aside from coughing and sputtering, Jeremiah didn't react beyond a few enraged mental barbs aimed at Balthazar. He rose a brow at Luc, who merely shrugged. "It's either because Aidan is his creator, or their kind isn't toxic to each other."

"I suspect it's a defense mechanism," Aidan murmured as he wiped his already healing wrist against Jeremiah's robes. "It provides a means for the dual-gifted to kill their Sires should the need ever arise, something that could be quite useful against those driven by a thirst for blood."

"It could have something to do with the rebirth as well, genetically speaking," Luc added. He dove into a diatribe regarding scientific properties and gibberish. Balthazar tried·to listen but lacked the energy to keep up. The last few days had drained him. All he wanted was to finish with this mess and move on to a new location. This place retained too many intimate memories.

Luc and Aidan continued their debate while Balthazar focused on Jeremiah. The new immortal glowered right back at him, his mind triumphant at having passed this last test. Too bad for him, this next one wouldn't be so easy.

Balthazar retrieved a discarded blade and ran it across his thumb without breaking his stride and placed just the tip at Jeremiah's mouth.

"Goodbye," Balthazar murmured as he pressed the wound to the other man's tongue.

That was all it took.

One drop.

And the immortal's head lolled to the side.

Aidan's and Luc's brains erupted in theories, their strategic talents twisting and turning through all their collective knowledge, which provided Balthazar with a colossal headache. He really needed to master the art of tuning people out.

Just focus on the strands and shut the door...

But too many exist.

He lost himself in their maze of puzzles and felt his knees quiver beneath him.

I just took a life. Two.

It was the right thing to do. He knew that, felt confident in his decision, but it went against his belief to cherish every second of life. To live in a world of passion and love, to enjoy pleasure and embrace friendship.

But Jeremiah wasn't one who adhered to the same principles. He chose hatred and jealousy, pain and hurt, and murder. He earned his fate.

...close by... Ichor...

Sethios was right. His father...

...run, little mortals, run.

Balthazar frowned at the unfamiliar voice. Dark. Lethal. Other.

…last stop… home… Babylon.
Poor sods don't stand a chance against Osiris.

The being's thought about another suggested his nearby presence, but Balthazar heard no other voice. Still, he sensed the dangerous emotions heading their way and the terror of his village mates.

Two gods.
Pray.
Bringers of death.
"Have you seen a blond male? Answers to the name of Aidan?"

Balthazar overheard the question through the thoughts of a terrified human male. His pain traveled down the line seconds later as whoever had requested the information punished the mortal for not responding fast enough.

He just took his own life!
By command!
Run!
Please don't see me.

"We need to maim Jeremiah," Balthazar said quickly, instinct demanding they hide their newfound discovery. "Now."

Aidan and Luc turned wide eyes on him, neither of them aware of what was approaching.

"*Now,*" he repeated, his gaze darting to the entrance. "We have company."

"How much time?" Luc asked as he untied Jeremiah and laid him flat on the ground.

"Long enough to make it look like we tortured and killed a mortal," Balthazar said as he tossed the knife to Luc. "No time to hide him."

Aidan's brow furrowed. "His wounds will be postmortem."

"Then I suggest you two come up with something because the two immortals approaching are not friendly," he replied as he accessed the minds around them again.

"Can you hear their names?" Aidan asked.

"One is Osiris, the other I haven't—"

Aidan waved him off. "Slit his throat and perform chest compressions. Quickly."

Luc began the process before his father even finished speaking, their minds clearly in sync.

A full catalog of details regarding the one called Osiris unfolded through the cerebral pathways, providing Balthazar with ample understanding of who was coming for them. An ancient with the ability to compel, which explained the mortal taking his own life. But more than that, he possessed no humanity, felt no remorse, and was feared by all those who encountered him. Aidan apparently knew him well, even seemed to have maintained a friendship with the immortal at one point, but he did not share the male's proclivity for slaughter.

Jeremiah's corpse appeared thoroughly beaten by the time Luc finished with him, providing a gruesome scene that their newcomers would likely appreciate.

...can't wait to be finished with this; of course, it'll only be the beginning of a bloodbath until they all succumb to Osiris's command. The mental sigh that followed sent a chill down Balthazar's spine. *Such a waste of immortal life.*

"We need to play this carefully," Aidan informed. "Osiris is not a being to take lightly."

"Why is Osiris here?" Luc asked.

"For us," Balthazar said quietly. "And they're outside."

"What do you want to do with the body?" Aiden asked conversationally. "Because I personally don't feel he's earned a proper ceremony."

"Agreed," Luc replied as he cleaned his blade. "I say we burn him."

"Burning flesh reeks," Balthazar pointed out, playing along and ignoring the presence behind him. It took considerable effort not to turn or acknowledge the darkness, but the longer he kept his mind-reading ability a secret, the better.

"True, I suppose..." Aidan lifted his head and an eyebrow. "Osiris. This is a surprise."

Luc glanced up at the same time, while Balthazar turned toward the newcomers. The one with long dark hair and ebony eyes owned the mind he'd overheard. *Ezekiel.* While the other—an olive-toned, bald man with an athletic physique—remained quiet.

Interesting.

Osiris eyed all of them with interest, his heartless gaze confirming the quick character sketch provided by Aidan. The man exuded power and purpose, redefining the meaning of *god.*

Yet, Balthazar couldn't read him at all in emotion or in the mind. The immortal was immune. A secondary gift, or something else?

"Aidan." His smooth voice held a touch of an accent, something ancient and unfamiliar. "It's been a few centuries. Have we interrupted something important?" He flicked his gaze to Jeremiah.

"We just finished handling, shall we call it, a disagreement?" Aidan grinned, his candor shifting to one of nonchalance. "What brings you to the area?"

"A discovery." Osiris took a step forward. "One you appear to be knowledgeable of, if I'm not mistaken."

Here it goes. Ezekiel's mental voice was bored. *Cooperate or die.*

A barrage of graphic details followed, including how they'd dispensed of the last pair of immortals before arriving. Balthazar fought not to react to the news of how to properly kill one of his kind.

Beheading or fire.

"You bear a striking resemblance to Aidan," Osiris continued, his focus on Luc. "Father and son?"

"Yes. I'm Lucian," Luc replied, his posture confident. "And yes, I share his gift for omniscience."

"Fascinating. What else?" he prompted, confirming that he knew about their dual abilities.

"A sensory skill—I can heighten pain." A strategic response to show his worth, suggesting Luc had picked up on the lethal air as well.

Balthazar met his gaze briefly to show he understood.

"Are there others?" Aidan asked, his voice curious while his analytical brain fired with calculated plays. He, too, sensed the danger.

"Yes, I've found several." Osiris turned to Balthazar. "You do not belong to Aidan."

"No, we're recently acquainted. I'm Balthazar." *And as we'll not be friends, you can continue to call me Balthazar. Not B.*

He didn't seem to care one way or the other about his name. "Who is your father?"

Balthazar shrugged. "Your guess is as good as mine. I was born in a brothel."

"Interesting. And tell me your gifts."

A squeezing force contracted his throat, forcing the words from his mouth without preamble. "Mind reading and emotion control."

Osiris's dark eyebrows lifted. "Indeed? Can you read mine?"

The noose tightened as he admitted, "No."

Compulsion, Aidan warned. *He can use it on hundreds at once, including us.*

Yes, Balthazar had already deduced as much. "But my mind reading isn't as strong as my emotional control," he lied. When he had admitted his skill, Ezekiel's eyebrows had shot upward, suggesting his surprise, and he'd immediately labeled Balthazar as a threat. Toning down his ability could only work in his favor. "I can turn a crowd of unhappy humans into a war zone or an orgy." *Preferably the latter.*

"Fascinating," Osiris murmured. "I wonder if Ishmed is your creator. Perhaps I'll introduce you."

Here we go, Ezekiel growled. *I want to go home.*

"We should catch up, Aidan," the bald immortal continued. "Perhaps in Babylon?"

He phrases that as a choice, but it's not, Aidan informed. Out loud he said, "Yes, it's been a while since I've been home. Has much changed?"

"Oh, a great many things." Osiris tapped his chin in a theatrical move meant to stall and heighten tension. His buddy didn't seem all that impressed, while the rest of them merely waited.

We may outnumber them, but we stand no chance in a fight, Aidan informed.

Balthazar didn't need the barrage of statistics and outcomes that followed to agree with him. Surviving these two would require planning and time. Going along with whatever game they were playing was their best option for now.

"Ezekiel here has the most delightful talent." Osiris's smile was the thing of nightmares—charmingly evil. The kind a sovereign wore before sentencing a subject to death. "He traces to familiar blood sources, of which there are many at home. How about we let him go ahead with Balthazar and Lucian while you and I discuss some recent findings over dinner?"

Go with Luc and keep your ear to the ground. The urgency in Aidan's mental voice did not match his calm tones as he replied, "Absolutely. I look forward to it."

Luc met his father's gaze briefly before moving to Balthazar's side. "A tracing ability?" He actually sounded intrigued, but his puzzle of a brain was running through various scenarios, cataloging routes, and assessing the odds of each one. So many ideas and outcomes, over half of them lethal.

Nothing like living life a little dangerously.

"Similar to teleporting." Ezekiel held out his hands. "Shall we?"

Trust no one, Aidan advised. *I'll be along shortly.* He sounded very sure of that and estimated his chances at around ninety percent. Reasonable odds.

Luc came to the same conclusion not a second later as he accepted Ezekiel's palm. "This should be fun."

"Sure," Balthazar agreed. "Fun."

CHAPTER NINE

Luc

Nineteen immortals.

Mostly males.

It made sense when one considered the requirements for rebirth. Females weren't often killed early on in life or in unnatural ways. They lived to a full death, which implied that age diluted the essence of resurrection.

Amazing.

Everything clearly related to bloodlines and souls. Once a person reached a certain life stage, their bodies couldn't handle the change. Or that was Luc's theory, anyway. He would have to test it later with Aidan. Whenever he figured out how to escape this mess.

All of the dual-gifted beings were in an oversized firelit cavern with sentries at the exits. Ezekiel had dropped Luc and B here with a little wave before disappearing.

Judgment appeared to be the theme. Aidan and Luc had always suspected this would happen once the blood-drinking immortals realized their offspring could be reborn with multiple powers. None of their hypotheses for this moment were good.

"What do you hear?" Luc asked.

Balthazar folded his arms beside him, his brown gaze scanning the room. "A lot of confusion and fury, some poor plotting, and the voice of one who is not what he seems."

Luc arched a brow. "One similar to Aidan?"

A nod from the mind reader toward an auburn-haired woman cowering near one of the exits. Her gaze was downcast, her slim shoulders curved into the perfect pose of submission.

A ruse?

Another nod. "She's a pyrokinetic and powerful and does not belong in this room."

"A safeguard," Luc murmured. "In case we misbehave."

Balthazar nodded. "There's a meeting scheduled at sunset to decide our fate. It's her job to make sure we play nice until then."

"I see." That couldn't be too long from now, though it was hard to tell from their place inside the cave. "Can you hear my father?"

"Not yet, but the lethal one who traced us here hasn't returned again."

Thereby suggesting Osiris, Ezekiel, and Aidan were still together. Luc kicked a foot up against the wall behind them and relaxed against it in a falsely casual pose. "Tell me about our choices." *Who can we trust? Who can we use?* he added.

Balthazar remained quiet, his eyes assessing. *Listening*, Luc realized. He waited patiently beside his ally, not wishing to rush the man's judgment. Recruiting a few immortals could aid their escape, but only if they chose wisely.

Several of them wore defeated expressions, others one of immense hatred, and a handful displayed a calm thoughtfulness similar to his own.

"The one brooding in the corner," Balthazar murmured. "He's useful."

Luc followed his gaze to a young male with long brown hair. He had a knee drawn up to his chest and the opposite leg stretched out along the ground. The immortal beside him appeared to be trying to make small talk—unsuccessfully.

"He's telepathic and claimed his other gift to be linguistics," B continued. "But that's not all he can do."

Dark brown eyes lifted to them—sensing their interest—and narrowed.

Balthazar smiled. "Extremely useful."

"He doesn't seem too eager."

"Leave that part to me," B replied, his focus shifting. "We need that one too." He nodded toward another dark-haired man, this one grinning at the nearby sentry. "He's new—only a few weeks into his immortality—but he grew up here. His father apparently tried to kill him a few times and told Osiris. That's the reason we're all here."

"Why is he smiling?" Luc wondered, frowning. The man looked almost happy to be here.

"He's taunting the guard, and it's working. They know each other."

"Could be a good distraction." If the young immortal took on the sentry, others would likely follow while Luc and Balthazar slipped out the side. But B was already shaking his head.

"We need him alive and helpful. He can manipulate metal—for miles."

Luc's eyes widened. "That's impressive. What else?"

"Not what, but who. There's one not amongst us." He faced the exit farthest from them. "Someone is being kept beyond those walls—he was too lethal to trust in the room. He kills by touch."

"That would indeed be useful."

"Assuming we can free him, which we'll need the woman lying on her back over there to do. She's petite, but her telekinesis is on point. And she can read minds, too, but only one at a time." The female in question lifted her blonde head and winked at them. "She's definitely with us."

Luc grinned at her. "Fine by me. Anyone else?"

"Not yet." He popped his shoulder against the wall, arms still folded. "The power outside of this room is vast."

"Tell me about it."

Balthazar detailed the various gifts hitting his senses—most of them replicated in the immortals among them, as they were offspring of those beyond the walls—and the various opinions of the immortals outside the cavern. "Some want us dead; others think we could be useful" was his conclusion.

"Meaning our independence is off the table," Luc translated.

"That's what it sounds like—either we cooperate or die."

Are any of them aware of our blood's impact on them?

The blonde on the floor rolled her gaze their way again, her expression curious.

"No," Balthazar replied. "Which reminds me, I've recently learned that both of our kinds can die by fire or beheading."

Luc considered the biological attributes of each and nodded. "That makes sense. Flames would destroy the chemical properties in our blood, and a beheading removes the flow to our brains." That confirmed his theory that souls were connected to the electrical connectivity of the cerebrum.

"So why...?" Balthazar trailed off as he conveyed the rest of that question with his eyes.

Why does our blood impact them? A nod from the mind reader. *Probably because our immortality is a mutated version. They rely on human essence for survival, and our souls are tainted. So rather than provide them with the life they need to maintain their immortal selves, we do the opposite.*

"An interesting supposition." Balthazar scratched his chin as the petite blonde rolled to her feet. Rather than approach them, she sauntered over to the young immortal. "Patreena chose the newbie. Let's go meet the telepath."

Luc pushed off the wall to follow B. The male in the corner glowered at them as they approached.

Fuck. Off. The growl entered his mind, the voice unfamiliar but clearly belonging to their target.

"He's friendly," Luc murmured.

"I love him already," B agreed as they stopped before him. "Hello, Alik."

Two dark eyes slit up at them. "How do you know my name?"

"I'm Balthazar," he continued as if the other man hadn't spoken. "This is Lucian. I think we…" He trailed off as his attention shifted to the entry. "They're back."

"Aidan?" Luc asked.

B nodded, his lips flattening as he went eerily still.

The telepath stood, his head coming up to Luc's chin. "What's wrong with him?"

"He's listening," Luc whispered.

Patreena seemed oblivious, her focus on the young one who seemed more than happy to flirt with her. She ran her nails up and down his arm, her lips curled in amusement. Whatever they were discussing did not appear related to a potential escape, which was likely the entire point. His suspicions were confirmed as she rose up onto her tiptoes to whisper in the male's ear, causing his friendly gaze to shift to Luc. Understanding rimmed those dark brown irises while he listened to whatever she told him.

"We can't make a move yet," Balthazar said, breaking Luc's focus. "Aidan says to tell you there is much we don't understand, that if we try to escape, we won't make it to the gates. Our best chances are to remain agreeable while he works behind the scenes."

"Who the fuck is Aidan?" Alik asked, his arms crossed.

"My father." Luc held Balthazar's gaze. "What else has he said?"

"He's in strategy mode, it's…" Balthazar shook his head. "I can't navigate."

"Then he's concerned." Luc's mind worked similarly when in danger. He constantly analyzed every tiny detail.

"Yeah, like that," Balthazar muttered, massaging his temples. "Our odds increase if we cooperate. They expect us to fight and are more than ready to handle us all." His focus went to Alik. "Not even you. There's over a hundred of them, and while I admire and respect what you can do, it's not the smart play."

Alik scoffed. "Then you clearly underestimate my skill."

"No, I've heard all about it loud and clear in my head, and while admirable, we need to be smart about it."

"We? There is no *we*." He gestured between the three of them. "I work alone."

"Then you'll die alone," Balthazar replied calmly. "To survive what's coming, we need to work together. They're better trained and prepared for our retaliation, and on top of that, they've developed trust in each other over the centuries. We're all new to one another, putting us at an extreme disadvantage. But hey, if you want to go reveal your gift preemptively, have at it."

Luc snorted. *And you call me the leader.* He couldn't have said it better himself.

Distrust and annoyance radiated from the telepath as he folded his arms. "And I assume you're in charge of this little arrangement?"

Balthazar chuckled. "No, that would be Lucian. He's over several hundred years old, is a master of strategy, and has an ally on the inside."

"When did I volunteer for that position?" Luc asked, serious.

"You didn't, which is why you're the leader." Balthazar cocked a brow at Alik. "Whether we continue this conversation or not is entirely up to you, but I'd suggest it. Especially since I can hear what Cyprus has planned for you."

The telepath scowled. "I'm going to rip that bastard apart limb by limb when I get out of here."

"Can't say I blame you. Your father is a real dick." B crossed his arms. "What's it going to be? A team effort, or a solo mission?"

Alik looked them up and down. "You're clearly a mind reader of some sort, but what else can you do?"

Balthazar smiled. "How pissed off are you at your current situation?"

"What?"

"On a scale of one to ten, how angry are you?"

"Are you serious?" The telepath's brow crumpled. "I'm fucking furious. You?" Sarcasm dripped from his voice, causing Luc to hide a grin behind his hand. He knew exactly what his mind-reading friend had planned.

Balthazar nodded and rubbed his jaw, saying nothing for several seconds. Luc knew his play even before he saw the light flicker in Alik's otherwise dark gaze. That it took so little effort to manipulate such a furious individual spoke highly of B's true power. Definitely an asset, not that Luc ever doubted him.

"How do you feel now?" B asked softly.

"Hmm, what?" Alik blinked dazedly at him. "What do you mean?"

"Are you still angry?"

"Angry? Nah, I'm good." Alik leaned against the wall, his body relaxing. "So yeah, I'm in."

"Can we hold him to that?" Luc smiled with his eyes, amused. "Or is that cheating?"

"I don't think it'll matter in a few seconds," B mused as

he took a step backward.

Alik blinked again, his expression clouding, then his eyebrows lifting. "That…" He ran his fingers through his hair. "Can you do that to multiple people at once?"

"Easily," B replied. "And to answer your unspoken question, Lucian is essentially omniscient, as he remembers everything, and he can enhance physical pain or pleasure. So sort of like you, except the pain has to be real."

Alik's eyes flashed as he reappraised them both. "All right, and if I decide to join this insanity, who else do you have in mind?"

"You've already decided," Balthazar replied, his gaze knowing. "And we've tapped those two over there." He motioned with his head subtly. "They're staying put for now so as not to make things obvious."

"And what's the plan?"

"For now?" Balthazar shrugged. "To play along. That's really all we can do until we have a better understanding of the situation."

"Acting on impulse is never the desired ploy," Luc added. "We observe, we learn, and we act when the opportunity presents itself. It might not happen immediately, but one of the perks of immortality is unlimited time. We'll act when we're ready, and in the interim, we'll determine how best to pair our gifts."

"What about the others?" Alik asked, glancing around the room.

"I'm still assessing," Balthazar said softly. "Recruiting them all would be ideal, but likely improbable. Not everyone shares our will to survive."

Luc nodded. "Let's discuss our choices and go from there." He arched a brow at the telepath. "Assuming you're officially in?" He hadn't actually agreed yet.

"It's not like I have a better option." Alik tucked his hands into his pockets. "Just be advised, I'm not a team player."

"I can work with that." Luc palmed the back of his

neck and rolled his shoulders. "All right, I need to know more about everyone's gifts in the room, B. Detail them for me."

CHAPTER TEN

B

Balthazar needed a break. Luc's mental web of ideas and solutions, coupled with all the other thoughts of this place, were killing him. All the lethal notions, fear, and general hatred weighed heavily on his conscious. Was it really just last night that he said farewell to Nythos? Because it felt like years or decades ago.

He sat with his head in his hands while Luc and Alik spoke above him. After cracking the male's exterior, he'd opened up and taken a liking to Luc's analytical side. The telepath was smart, hence his flair for languages and lying to Osiris on the fly about his true gifts.

The moment Balthazar had heard the man's mind, he knew he would be an asset. The one called Jayson, too. Despite his easy candor and grins, he possessed a warrior's spirit. His affinity for metal would be useful, in addition to his need for vengeance.

Balthazar. It's starting. Aidan's voice trickled through his head, causing him to focus on the myriad of beings outside the doors. Several hundred minds, not all of them belonging to immortals, came to life at once. He picked through them one at a time, sorting them into piles. Most weren't useful, but a select few fell to the important pile. Osiris remained mute to him, his presence not found.

"Osiris is immune," he said, interrupting whatever Luc had been saying to Alik. "Their leader, the one who can compel, I can't read him."

Luc frowned. "Can you feel his emotions?"

Balthazar shook his head. "He's not accessible."

"I can't reach him either," Alik added. "I tried. You know, when he showed up yesterday."

His memory trickled down the mental pathways. Alik had attempted to incapacitate Osiris to escape, and when his attempt had failed, he'd lied about his abilities. "Smart play," Balthazar said, impressed.

"If he's not susceptible to our gifts, there could be others." Luc folded his arms, concern etched into his brow. "Anything from Aidan?"

"The debate regarding our futures has begun." Balthazar leaned against the wall for balance as he dove back into the voices. Organizing them all took patience and skill. It wasn't as simple as just ignoring one over the other; it had more to do with volume and finding that one amongst the crowd he desired to hear most.

…smell sweet…

…kill them all…

…I wouldn't mind using a few of them for my own personal means. That feminine tone was one he saved for later. It might be useful.

…don't know about the blood, Aidan thought at him while he formulated a speech in his head. *Their blood possesses no value to us, just as ours is of no value to each other. We feed on the*

human essence to stay alive. While it may be enjoyable to experiment with the dual-powered ones, I feel it's a degradation to both us and them. Why bother with something that truly yields no value?

"Your father is trying to convince them not to use us for blood," Balthazar murmured, his brain still focused on the conversation.

...it's a valid point.

...like eating our own children.

... still might be fun, especially during sex. And it's not like any of them are mine.

...why are we even discussing this?

I'm more interested in their abilities and what they can do, Aidan continued. *Their gifts are unique, with some being far stronger than others.*

... a threat.

... potential ally.

... friend.

... how boring. Would anyone notice if Ezekiel traced us out of here? Surely he would prefer a break from all of my father's madness. I certainly desire one.

Balthazar frowned as the voice abruptly cut off, as if the being had flipped a switch and shoved him out. *Did he sense me?* No one else seemed aware of him when he intruded in someone's mind.

He shook it off and continued his mental perusal, locking on Aidan again. *It's working. They're considering your worth, though some still see you all as a potential threat. Osiris has suggested the notion of regulations for your kind, rules that will keep you in line. It's a temporary solution until they can learn more and provides us with time to plan. Tell Lucian.*

Balthazar passed on the message.

Luc scratched his chin. "They wish to experiment and test our limits, which is a way to weaken us while learning more."

That wasn't exactly what Aidan said; however, it sounded right. "Will they separate us?"

"That, or they'll keep us together in an attempt to use

us against one another. The latter carries a stronger probability—most react irrationally when under stress or in pain, which leads to poor decisions and actions. Why bother wasting energy on killing us when we can murder ourselves?" Luc shrugged as if that future outcome meant little to him.

"And what do you suggest?" Alik prompted.

"Hmm." A variety of maps and designs unfolded in Luc's mind, adding to Balthazar's headache. He attempted to tune out the strategic master and focus on Aidan, but his brain showcased a similar vortex of ideas.

He rubbed his temples and slid down the wall to the floor, his brain overloaded with all the emotions and thoughts within a several-mile radius. So much hurt, hunger, and hubris. Death. Torment. Desire.

How many days had it been since Balthazar slept? Three? Four? He couldn't remember. It all seemed like a distant memory, even his Nythos. This new nightmare had taken over, forcing him to consider the future and a necessary escape. But when?

Balthazar, Aidan called. *They've reached a verdict. All of you are to be tested and kept here for evaluation. Osiris has assigned me the task of cataloging all the findings, which will be used in a future discussion to decide your fates. He's labeled you all the Children of Ichor—an essence of the gods. And you are to be kept together, likely because he wants to encourage fighting. You and Luc must rally everyone together. Be smart. Strategize. Survive. We're coming.*

Balthazar relayed the details to Alik and Luc, his voice tired. "This is not going to be easy."

"Nothing worth having ever is," Luc replied, his emerald gaze shining. "But we have something they'll never be able to take from us. And, in fact, it will only strengthen over time."

"And what's that?" Alik asked flatly.

"The will to survive." Luc took in the room, his expression that of a leader blossoming into his true purpose. "This is our beginning. Let them underestimate us. Let them think we're meek and compliant. And when they've grown comfortable and complacent, we attack."

"What about those who don't want to fight?" Balthazar asked, sensing at least six in the room who were either too weak or too depressed to try.

"We motivate them." Luc leaned against the wall. "But for now, we see what tests they have planned. The strongest among us will remain alive, and those will be our allies. The others were never meant to survive."

Balthazar looked up at him. "That's a bit harsh."

"Yet practical," Alik said. "We can't afford any weak links."

"Agreed." Luc rolled his neck, his arms tensing and loosening with the move. "So we wait, we observe, and we learn. They may outnumber us, but we have the talent among us to put up one hell of a fight. And with my father feeding us information, we stand a reasonable chance."

"How long will it take?" Alik stood with his hands in his pockets, his shoulders hunched. "How many days?"

Luc grinned, but it was sad. "Not days, friend, but months. Perhaps even years. We'll very likely only have one chance, and if we rush it, we'll all suffer. Trust and planning require time. Fortunately, we have forever."

"The gift of immortality," Balthazar muttered. "We're going to be here a while."

Yes. This is just the beginning, my friend.

"Calling this 'The End' would be wrong. It's more accurately 'The Beginning.' Hopefully, my translations were adequate enough. I need a drink after all that. Talk about a trip down memory lane."
—Luc

THE ELDERS READER DISCUSSION

"So, what did you all think?"

—B

Lizzie: *Hmm, yeah, I have a question. Is Patreena still alive? You know, the female mind reader who chose Jay?*

Jay: *No. And it was a long time ago, Red.*

Lizzie: *A long time ago, meaning…?*

Alik: *Am I excused yet?*

B & Luc: *No.*

Alik: *Fine.*

Lizzie: *Just because he interrupted me doesn't mean you're off the hook.*

Jay: *I already fucking hate this book, and we haven't even gotten to Brazil yet.*

Lizzie: *What happened in Brazil?*

B: *Keep reading, sweetheart.*

Stas: *No, hold on. Before we go on, you're telling me this whole thing started before 1500 BC, but your war with the Ichorians didn't* *start until the 13th century, right?*

Luc: *Essentially, yes. It wasn't until the Ichorians finally realized our blood is toxic to them that they decided to start killing us. Before then, we were just seen as the weaker race and treated as such.*

B: *Writing all that would turn this novella into an epic, something we should totally do.*

Luc: *Another time, B. In summary, Stas, after a hundred or so years of experimenting, they rounded us up and dropped us off on an island with various sentries. We were given menial tasks, no means to survive, and essentially used as needed.*

Alik: *It sucked.*

Luc: *Yeah, but it only brought us closer. And as more of our kind were created, they were shipped off to the island—thanks to an edict issued by Osiris. Since we were not considered a threat after all the trials, just "lesser" beings, the "higher" immortals were allowed to make us. As a result, our numbers continued to increase, as did our power. It wasn't until seven or eight centuries ago that someone discovered the truth about our blood.*

B: *One of our best-kept secrets, and Osiris's strongly worded suggestion that his brethren not drink from us only aided our attempts.*

Luc: *He means it was a law punishable by death—literally. It was my brilliant father who convinced him of it during the trials.*

Alik: *Yeah, yeah. Can we move on? I'm bored.*

B: *Someone's eager to get back to Brazil.*

Alik: *"Someone" is eager to finish this fucking book.*

Issac: *I agree with Alik.*

B: *We'll get to you soon, Wakefield. Don't worry your pretty little head.*

Issac: *Can I write a short story where Balthazar dies? I think it would be quite entertaining, if a little tragic. And bloody.*

B: *If he gets to create that story, then I want to write one about Wakefield being Hydraian so I can introduce him to what he's missing. Oh wait, I can do that with a few graphic visuals.*

Stas: *You two have fun with that. I want to know more about what happened after the Ichorians realized Hydraian blood could kill them.*

Alik: *War. People died. The end.*

Luc: *It's a little more complicated than that.*

B: *Story time?*

Luc: *Story time.*

B: *Let's go.*

TREATY OF 1747

"Spoiler alert: I killed a lot of Ichorians. Can we move on?"

—*Alik*

CHAPTER ONE

Alik

Hello, gorgeous. Alik sent the telepathic message to the curvy blonde dancing in the waves a few yards away. She flung out her arms and spun in a circle as fire flickered across her fingertips.

His lips curled in amusement. Jenika always did this after battle. It was the adrenaline rush from engaging her pyrokinesis that left her exuberant and smiling. Even covered in blood, she looked radiant and full of life.

He admired her exposed legs as she pulled her white shift over her head, tossing it into the ocean. All that long, silky hair flowed down her naked back as she whirled an intoxicating mix of water and flames.

Alik had never seen someone so beautiful. He lounged on the black sand—legs stretched out and crossed at the ankles—and supported his upper body on his elbows.

Dance for me, he whispered seductively into her mind.

Her hazel eyes glimmered with arousal as she moved in a way that drove him wild. The water only reached her thighs, leaving everything on display for his open perusal. So fucking sexy.

Do not come anywhere near the beach, he told everyone within a mile radius. *Or you'll regret it.*

His ability to torture mentally, coupled with Jenika's affinity for water and fire, made them quite the formidable pair.

She continued to gyrate her hips enticingly while he observed beneath hooded eyes. This was their sport of choice—a silent pastime meant to entice and seduce—and it drove him wild.

Do that again, he murmured to her.

With a laugh, she tossed her head back, arching her body in a way that beckoned sex.

Mmm, yes.

Fire engulfed her being, followed by water, as she responded in kind.

Being with her was a risk. Flames could kill an immortal if they burned hot enough, for their gift of life existed in the blood. That was a trick they'd discovered a few centuries back when Alik first met Jenika. She'd glowed so hot as she burned her enemy to the ground.

He licked his lips. Thinking of that day aroused him even now. It'd been lust at first sight, which blossomed into love soon after.

She curled a finger toward him, inviting him to come play.

You're ready for me already? he taunted, tilting his head to the side.

Jenika responded with a sultry pout as a twirl of embers danced within an inch of his hands on each side.

Threatening me, love?

The heat increased as she set the sand ablaze all around him, leaving a path to the ocean as his only option.

He smiled. *Demanding little thing, aren't you?*

She returned his amusement with a saucy grin, then the fibers of his clothes sizzled while she expertly undressed him with her mind.

It took a great deal of trust, especially when she reached his groin. Yet, he remained utterly still for her and waited until the last vestiges of his outfit turned to ash before climbing to his bare feet.

You realize that was my last pair of viable breeches, yes?

She shrugged.

Of course she didn't care. Jenika preferred him nude.

He sauntered toward her, his skin warming for an entirely different reason as he reached the water. *How long can you hold your breath?* he asked darkly. With her ability to control water, it gave them a unique way to play with one another.

She blew him a kiss as she danced backward into the waves, encouraging him to follow.

God, this woman. Would he ever tire of her? Several hundred years and he wanted her as badly now as he did the day they met. That kind of love…

He paused in his pursuit.

Something… wasn't right.

Jenika's expression confirmed the inkling of unease trickling down his spine.

Danger, he sent to all the minds he knew on Hydria. *Something is coming.*

He swam to Jenika's side, his gaze flicking between the darkening horizon and the beach.

"They were all dead," she whispered.

Alik didn't doubt that. What concerned him was the very real possibility that the most recent battle had been a ruse. The Ichorians were getting desperate. They'd expected his kind to die easily.

They'd thought wrong.

After several centuries at war, Alik's brethren had proven themselves not only resilient but also powerful. All those years of being treated as second-class citizens no longer applied. The Hydraians—as they called themselves—were lethal, were strong, and knew how to function as a unit. They understood the importance of family and love.

Jenika touched his hand beneath the water. "Beach."

He spotted the approaching trio, latched onto their minds, and sent them to their knees with ease. Their cries should have caused his lips to curl, but the unease skirting along his skin didn't relent.

Where are you? The message was meant for his brothers—Lucian, Jayson, Eli, and Balthazar. They should have arrived by now.

"Alik," Jenika's gargled voice startled his concentration. Water spilled from her mouth as she tried to speak.

He caught her hip, pulling her to him. "What…?"

An inferno burst from her eyes, her body going rigid while an agonized sound escaped through her water-logged throat.

"Jen!" he shouted as her entire body went up in blue flames. His hand sizzled and burned so hot he let go on instinct. "Fuck!"

Garbled screams rent the air as the fire turned an ungodly shade of purple.

"Jenika!" he yelled, his heart beating a mile a minute. "JENIKA!"

Glowing embers flickered into the night, confusing him more. Until he realized it was pieces of *her* being carried off in the wind.

He grabbed her again, his own skin melting from the contact. But he didn't care.

"Jenika!" This had never happened before. She knew how to control it. Why was it hurting her now?

He tried to pull her under the water, but his grip slid

from their decayed flesh.

Oh God…

The salt water burned like a son of a bitch.

No.

He couldn't… This… No!

His nerves disintegrated, his hands—or what was left of them—fell limply to his sides.

"Jenika!" he screamed her name, his anguish and confusion coloring the night for all to hear. And yet still she burned.

A giant ball of purplish blue blazed along the waves, then erupted in a cloud of ash. He stared unseeingly at the spot where Jenika had stood. Her long blonde hair no longer billowing in the breeze. Her seductive form no longer dancing hypnotically. Her heart-shaped face no longer smiling.

Just. Gone.

His legs gave out beneath him.

The water continued to abrade his wounds, sending daggers of pain to his brain, yet he sat lost in the waves. His mind shattered. His heart… nowhere to be found.

"Jenika?" he whispered brokenly.

This had to be a dream. A nightmare. A hellish mind trick. She couldn't just… disappear. Not his Jenika. It was impossible. She controlled fire, not the other way around. This—

A cruel, chilling laugh carried to his ears. Feminine, high-pitched cackling. Like a witch in the night.

He hardly registered his head turning toward the sound—his body still semi-drowning beneath him. If he'd been in deeper water, he would have gone under. And would he care? He wasn't sure. He felt… empty. Alone. Dead inside.

"Oh, I may just have to let you live for fun," a woman trilled. "You look positively distraught." Another chortle.

Alik blinked as fire flickered from the beach.

"Jenika?" he whispered, finding his footing and

stumbling toward her. "Oh, thank…" He trailed off as he realized the woman possessing the flames had red hair. The strands glowed in the light, a dark auburn shade that was all too wrong. As was the svelte figure and wicked smile.

"I guess we know who the stronger pyrokinetic is, hmm?" The bitch smiled, her eyes twinkling with mirth. "Not even her gift for water could save her." She tapped her lip. "Now, if only you'd realized what was happening, she might still be alive. Or not."

Heat scorched his insides, knocking him off balance against a wave.

"Hmm, it is really too bad I have to kill you. Watching you suffer would be oh-so fun. But I suppose you can consider it a gift. Maybe your souls will find each other." Her confident, calm tone triggered something inside him. Something hotter than the inferno engulfing his body.

Power rippled out of him, directed at the redheaded bitch. He put everything he had into that mental punch, all his pain and agony, and tripled it inside her mind.

The air around him cooled immediately. Third-degree burns lined every inch of his being, the salt water around him only worsening the condition, and yet, he felt nothing.

No pain.

No torment.

He'd pushed it all out and into the redheaded Ichorian writhing on the ground.

I'm empty.

Others came spilling onto the sand beyond her, all of them wielding various powers he knew nothing about. He didn't care who they were or where they came from. Just touched all their minds. Every. Single. One. And spread the torture rampant.

Everyone fell to their knees.

Agonized yells littered the beach.

Alik stepped out of the ocean, his legs shaking with the effort. And yet, his mind felt fine. He searched out all the intruders on the island, over a hundred of them, and sent shock waves of his dangerous gift through all of them.

Die...

He wanted them all to fucking die.

Starting with the redhead crying a few feet away from him.

Alik stood over her without pity as he crushed her trachea with his bloody foot. She gargled—just like Jenika had—and sputtered. Life dimmed in her eyes. He observed from the outside of his body, or so it seemed. Killing her wasn't enough. Good thing her immortal genes would wake her again in a few hours so he could do it all over again.

As for the rest, he'd rip their heads from their bodies with his own bare hands. One by one. After he healed. Until then, they'd continue to ride his waves of pain, over and over and over again.

He collapsed in the sand to wait for his body to heal while the terrorized screeches around him soothed his broken soul. "Burn," he managed through his dry throat. "Fucking. Burn."

CHAPTER TWO

Luc

Two Days Later…

Luc paced the room, his mind whirring with a thousand different outcomes at once. Alik's display of power the other night had turned the tide, quite literally, in their favor. And yet, to consider an armistice felt *wrong*.

Aidan stood to the side, his shoulder against the wall, emerald gaze pensive. "While I understand your desire to allow emotions to win, we both know that will only lead to more lives lost in the end."

Of course Luc knew that; it was why he hadn't voiced an opinion yet. His logical side always won, but that didn't mean he lacked a heart. He had to think about Alik—his brother of three millennia—and how he would want this handled. This went far beyond a simple game of logic. Their biggest asset and best friend was walking death. If it hadn't been for Balthazar's ability to subtly curb the man's emotional state, they'd have lost him to insanity.

When they found him on the beach severing heads… with his bare hands…

Luc shuddered.

It'd been a gory sight, a bloodbath of epic proportions. To kill in such a state did something to a man, as they all witnessed firsthand.

He rubbed a hand over his face, his own emotions rioting inside. This whole damn war had taken its toll. They'd lost countless allies and friends, all because the Ichorians saw the Hydraians as threats. Well, now they knew just how threatening, thanks to Alik's display. He had disabled hundreds of their enemies with a single thought and never broke a sweat despite being covered in burns.

That magnitude of his power was terrifying. He would become a target, not that Alik seemed to be in a caring state. With his broken heart and soul, he'd more likely court death than fight it.

"Shit," Luc muttered, not for the first time. He stopped at the door and rested his forearm against the wall overhead. "We have to accept."

"Yes," Aidan agreed. "That was never a question."

True. They all knew this armistice was the goal. "It'll be temporary."

"Of course." Issac spoke for the first time, his presence an enigma in the room. Many on the island weren't sure what to think of the Ichorian, but his loyalty had been proven through the decades. It helped that Luc's father had raised Issac as his own son after the male's birth father had died.

Such a complicated history, and not something Luc had

time to consider now.

"But that's where Aidan and I come in," Issac added. "We'll be your eyes and ears, attending every Conclave to report back."

Luc straightened and nodded once, agreeing with the plan. Osiris, and many of the others, trusted Aidan. They considered him the eldest of all the Ichorians—an honor never proven but widely accepted. His status carried weight, hence the reason the Ichorians were even considering an armistice. Aidan had been the one to suggest it, and they all knew better than to ignore the master strategist.

Balthazar and Eli entered, followed by Jayson, all of their expressions tired. Luc moved out of their way, going to the corner and leaning against the wall for much-needed support.

Alik? Luc asked the mind reader, guessing their friend's emotionless state was the cause for the flood of sadness and despair swimming around the room.

"Everyone," Balthazar replied, his gaze shadowed in sorrow. "We may have won the other night, but the emotions on the island are dim at best. Too many losses. Too much pain." He collapsed in a chair, his head falling to his hands. "There's only so much energy left."

Luc understood what he meant—Balthazar was powerful, but not even he could fix an army of exhausted soldiers.

Eli's broad frame towered over Issac as he moved to the Ichorian's side. Their friendship was a unique one, considering Eli was essentially mated to Issac's only sister. Amelia also happened to be Luc's half sister, thanks to Aidan being her father, but he didn't share the same kinship with her. She and Issac grew up together—shared the same mother—and possessed a stronger bond.

"How's Amelia?" Issac murmured now.

"Resting," Eli replied. "She's worried about Alik."

"We all are," Jayson put in as he settled beside

Balthazar. "Luc, we can't go on like this. It's killing morale. And Alik… Fuck, man, I think he's broken."

"He just lost the love of his life." Eli ran his fingers through his black hair. "If I lost Amelia…" He just shook his head, as if he couldn't even fathom such a loss.

"That's actually a point I want to address," Aidan said, grabbing everyone's attention. "While you're all incredibly powerful and clearly a formidable foe, your biggest strength is also your biggest weakness."

Luc nodded, already understanding. "We love each other, which makes us undeniably strong, but also takes its toll in times such as this."

"Exactly. If Osiris were to strike now—"

"He'd destroy us," Eli grumbled, cutting off the eldest in the room. "We'd be too caught up in trying to protect our wounded loved ones to actually fight."

"Precisely." Aidan clasped his hands before him as he pushed off the wall. "It's why I suggested an armistice. The Ichorians think you're living in victory at having defeated them."

"Because you told them we were celebrating." Luc almost grinned, but his face refused. "A nice way to buy us some time, but not much."

"No," Aidan murmured. "The offer expires at sundown."

"Giving us less than two hours to decide," Luc translated.

"Is it valid?" Jayson asked. "I mean, he sent Aidan here to deliver it. How do we know Osiris hasn't realized Aidan's on our side and this is all just a fancy diversion?"

"He knows my relationship with Luc was once a strong one, and he chose to take a gamble." Luc's father shrugged. "It's a practical play, one I suggested."

"Aidan also encouraged Osiris to send me with the entourage as protection," Issac added.

Balthazar snorted. "He clearly thinks highly of your ability."

Sapphire eyes narrowed at the mind reader, then smiled as Balthazar flinched. "And you do not?" Issac asked, his English accent flat.

Luc ignored their bickering and met his father's expectant gaze. "Osiris is in Athens and expects me to return with you, correct?"

Aidan gave a subtle nod.

"Then we should go." Because there was no other choice. If they didn't agree to the armistice, this war would continue. "A future battle is inevitable, but it doesn't have to be tomorrow or even next year. If we accept, we'll have time to heal and rebuild, and when the peace ends, we'll be ready."

He looked to Balthazar first and arched a brow. *Do you accept?*

"It's our only play," the mind reader murmured. "To do otherwise will only jeopardize more lives."

Luc nodded and met Eli's gaze next. "And you?"

"I'd rather kill them all, but not everyone has a magical touch." He waggled his lethal fingers. "I agree this is our best option."

Another nod before focusing on Jayson. He would be the hardest to convince, except for maybe Alik. "If we agree to the terms, Artemis will remain off-limits unless he steps out of bounds. You good with that?"

Jayson cleared his throat. "Not really, but if it means all my friends will remain among the living, I can't exactly complain about an ancient vendetta, can I? Family—this family—first. Always. I'm in."

Then there was only one person left to ask.

"You don't need to," Balthazar murmured as Luc took a step. He'd clearly read his mind while also hearing the thoughts of the newcomer—Alik—who stood in the doorway with dead eyes.

Luc cleared his throat uncomfortably. He hadn't actually expected Alik to join them, let alone listen to the conversation. How long had he been standing just outside the door in the hall, listening to them all?

"Al—"

"Yes," Alik said flatly, interrupting Luc. "I agree." He left without another word.

"He's not pleased, but he understands it's the best play." Balthazar sounded almost sad. "But he will forever hunt the one who hurt…" He trailed off, as if he couldn't say Jenika's name.

None of them appeared able to speak of her, too raw and hurt by her unexpected and sudden loss. Her murderer had escaped in the chaos that followed Alik's descent into the darkness. Not many survived, but somehow, she'd managed it.

Lucinda, Aidan had informed them. One of Osiris's favorite pets.

And if they signed this treaty, she, too, would be off-limits.

"He won't care," Balthazar whispered. "He'll hunt her, even if it means crossing boundaries."

"He may see reason," Aidan informed. "In time."

Balthazar shook his head. "I'm not certain of that."

"He will if it's part of the long-term plan," Luc suggested. "If we play the long game, there's a chance for all of us to win. But we have to play it right." Strategies flashed through his mind, several outcomes, different paths, all leading to potential victory in the end. So many avenues and turns and twists, so many options available, all of them tied to their agreement now. They'd already survived two millennia. What were a few hundred more years if it meant finally beating their makers at their own game?

"That… was a lot to take in," Balthazar said, massaging his temples.

"Sorry," Luc murmured, returning to the task at hand. Thousands of years of data had unloaded at once as his brain sought the perfect design. "There are several options."

Aidan was already bobbing his head in agreement. "All of which require us to arrive in Athens as soon as possible."

"Indeed." That came from Issac, who wasn't a master strategist but a male with the ability to manipulate visions. Which meant he'd seen the strategy unfolding in Aidan's and Luc's minds. "We should go."

"Yes," Luc replied, concurring. "We have a unanimous vote amongst the Elders. It's decided."

The Treaty of 1747 would be signed.

Ichorians would remain immune from violence if they stayed in New York City.

Hydraians would remain immune from violence if they stayed in Hydria.

Anyone caught outside those boundaries did so at their own risk.

Anyone caught inside an opposite boundary also did so at their own risk.

And so it was settled.

A temporary peace.

"The Treaty of 1747 allowed us a semblance of peace for nearly three hundred years. Alas, with the uprising of a new power, the armistice is crumbling at the seams, and I happily welcome the destruction it will bring. Vengeance will be mine."
—Alik

TREATY OF 1747 READER DISCUSSION

"Uh, maybe we should just move on to the next story…?"

—B

Luc: *Yes, I think that would be wise.*

Jay: *This isn't nearly as fun as I thought it would be. I think we should skip forward.*

B: *To Brazil?*

Jay: *Or we could skip that altogether.*

Amelia: *But I want to know what happened in Brazil.*

Jay: *I thought we were friends, Amelia.*

Amelia: *What? I just want to know the outcome of the bet.*

Tom: *Me too.*

Jay: *You're only saying that to agree with Amelia.*

B: *Because he's a smart man. But we're moving in chronological order here. Brazil is later.*

Amelia: *What's next?*

Luc: *A story you're not going to like, but one that should be told.*

AND THEN
THERE WERE
FOUR

"This is the worst story ever written."

—*Eli*

CHAPTER ONE

Eli

Blueberry muffins. Eli could smell them from the master bedroom, where he stood in a pair of jeans and shoes. Amelia had laid out a shirt for him on the bed, but he wasn't in the mood for light blue. He preferred black, like his hair.

Eli stalked over to their walk-in closet to find something more suitable. Amelia disliked the dark colors because they gave him an intimidating appearance that frightened their guests.

He snorted. Everyone who visited them feared for their survival within a few feet of him not because of his clothes but because of his power. He could kill by touch. That tended to quiet a conversation real fast.

Alas, his little flower tried to make him more

approachable by dressing him in softer colors. Darling woman, how he adored her. But he would be wearing black tonight.

The front bell sounded as he finished buttoning his long-sleeved shirt.

"Got it!" The yell was necessary for Amelia to hear him from all the way upstairs in their room. A downside to a huge estate.

Eli preferred their home in Hydria, but this oversized manor in the Hamptons was a gift to Amelia from her billionaire brother. A way for her to be close by without being in danger. It made her happy, so Eli didn't complain when she wanted to visit.

He finger-combed his hair as he skipped down the master staircase toward the three-story foyer. The French doors stood open at the bottom, their two visitors standing just outside.

One he recognized. The other he did not. Amelia mentioned Jonathan might bring a friend or a date, and it seemed he'd opted for a colleague instead. Or perhaps the male was a bodyguard? He certainly had the right build for it.

"Jonathan," Eli greeted the shorter of the two men. Jonathan wore a tailored suit and held a bottle of red wine. It was likely laced with blood, the Ichorian's personal favorite.

"Eli," Jonathan returned without an ounce of fear. Their friendship dated back over a century. If Eli wanted to kill the immortal, he would have acted ages ago.

"Come in, come in." Eli waved them inside as he bounced back to allow them both entry. Amelia had left the door open for a reason, yet Jonathan—formal as always—had chosen to ring the bell anyway. Perhaps he felt it was needed with the unknown male at his side. "And introduce your friend," Eli added, more curious than irritated.

Jonathan chuckled. "This is Stark. I recently promoted

him to the head of my Sentinel unit with the CRF. He's also serving as my bodyguard for the evening."

"And you felt he was needed here?" Amelia asked with a slight admonishment as she entered the foyer. Her heels clicked over the marble as her royal blue dress swished against her long legs.

"Only on the way here. I also thought it would be a nice opportunity to introduce him to some of my close Hydraian friends." He grinned charismatically at the end, causing Amelia's lips to twitch. "And you did say I could bring a date."

The Sentinel didn't flinch or react, merely eyed the interior of their home with bored interest. Something about him struck Eli as different from the usual men Jonathan hired. His blond hair was a tad too long to be recent military, and while his posture radiated protective detail, a quiet confidence lurked beneath his exterior that suggested not much fazed him.

"I expected one of the female variety, but I forget sometimes how married you are to your job." She went onto her toes to kiss Jonathan on the cheek. "Don't fret, love; I made extra."

What she wouldn't admit was how frustrated she'd been only hours ago by the last-minute dinner request. It was one of the many traits Eli adored about her—she always commanded the home and played the part of perfect hostess. It was a skill he lacked. He preferred bluntness to polite formality, while Amelia exuded generosity and goodness. And she was always taking care of everyone.

The perfect woman.

His perfect woman.

"Darling, can you close the gate?" Amelia asked, her sapphire gaze on Eli. "I left it open after giving Robert the night off."

"Yep." He wandered into their living area to fuss with the buttons on the wall panel that controlled several

107

aspects of their home.

"Robert and Cherie are out for the night?" Jonathan asked from the foyer. "I was rather hoping to see them."

"They have something at the school for their daughter." Eli could hear the smile in her voice, even from the other room. "I cooked a little extra for them as well, including some muffins."

My muffins? Eli thought as he watched the gate close on their wall screen.

"If you're still here later, I'm sure they'll want to see you as well," Amelia added.

"They knew we were coming?" Jonathan asked, sounding disappointed.

Amelia giggled, eliciting a grin from Eli. That sound always warmed his heart. "No, I knew if I mentioned it, they would cancel their plans," she said softly. "I figure we'll surprise them later. And Cherie will be thrilled not to cook."

"Always thinking of others," Jonathan murmured. That tone used to irritate Eli, but he learned over time that the Ichorian enjoyed charming all women, not just Amelia. Besides, everyone had a soft spot for her. She was gorgeous, kind, and essentially royalty as a widowed duchess's daughter.

"Flirt." Humor lightened her tone. "I'm sorry. I'm being rude by ignoring our new friend. Stark, right? That's unique."

"It's a nickname," the male replied, his tone flat. It reminded Eli of a boring professor about to lead a stoic lecture.

He rejoined them in the foyer as Amelia asked, "What's your real name?"

"Gabriel." No elaboration or a hint of feeling. Very strange, as was the intelligent gleam in his light green gaze as he took in their surroundings again. He seemed quite alert for being in the comfort of a friend's home.

"I'm Eli, by the way," Eli said, holding out his hand.

Jonathan had failed to do introductions earlier, likely because he already gave the Sentinel a heads-up on who was whom.

The broad-shouldered male accepted the gesture with a firm shake and gazed impassively at him. "I know" was all he said before letting go of Eli's palm.

"You didn't warn him of what I can do?" Eli guessed, his focus flickering to Jonathan in surprise. "Most of your men refuse to touch me."

Jonathan shrugged. "There's a reason Stark has risen so quickly in my ranks."

"If you wanted to kill me, you wouldn't need my cooperation," Stark added. "I was also told this would be a friendly dinner."

And yet, you seem cautious. Why?

"It certainly is; Jonathan is family," Amelia replied. She moved to Eli's side to wrap her arm around his lower back. It was her way of trying to soften him, and as always, it worked. He kissed her forehead and draped his arm over her slender shoulders.

"You're not giving Robert and Cherie all the muffins, are you?" he asked softly.

Her vivid blue eyes lifted to his with a smile. "There's a plate waiting for you at the table."

He kissed her tenderly, not caring at all about their audience. "Have I told you today that I love you?"

"Only twice."

"I love you, little flower." He nuzzled her nose. "Very much."

"You love my muffins," she taunted, pinching his side. "Now stop mauling me. We have company."

"Yes, ma'am." He kissed her on the cheek before returning to their guests. "Shall we?"

"After you." Jonathan gestured in the direction of the main dining area.

Amelia linked her fingers through Eli's and tugged him toward the scent of blueberries. His stomach rumbled at the thought of how many of those delicious pastries he could devour in one sitting. At over six and a half feet tall, he could eat two trays easily. Sometimes it paid to be an immortal. His body always returned to the shape he'd originally died in—a fantastic perk in addition to all the others.

"You all can take your seats. I just need to get our main course from the kitchen," Amelia said as she left Eli to entertain.

Jonathan took the chair at the head of the table while Stark flanked his left. Eli sat across from Jonathan, thereby leaving several empty spaces between them all. The large dining set was required when his Hydraian brothers came to visit, but tonight it just felt vapid and too big.

He idly considered calling Balthazar, or even Issac, just to fill the void, but decided against it. Jonathan had requested the dinner after saying he had some sort of news to share, and it sounded as though he wanted to run it by them before alerting the others. Hence the reason they kept this engagement small.

"So, how's the CRF?" Eli asked as he plucked a muffin from the tray in front of him. He didn't particularly care how the renowned humanitarian organization was doing, but this seemed appropriate polite conversation. Amelia would approve.

"Excellent. We're in the process of expanding our research wing, actually." Jonathan smiled. "Perhaps I'll give you or Amelia a tour sometime."

Yeah, that wasn't likely to happen. Eli enjoyed a good armory, but a science lab? Unless they were developing unique military weapons and testing their accuracy—which was unlikely, given the organization's purpose—no, thanks.

Still, he nodded because that was the kind thing to do. "Sounds enlightening." *And boring as fuck.*

"Oh, you have no idea," Jonathan replied. "There's so much to learn."

Eli supposed that might be true for an Ichorian of only a few centuries, but as someone who had lived several millennia, he disagreed. Rather than say that out loud, he changed the subject to something of value. "How's your son? Tom's attending university, right?" By Eli's estimation, the kid was around twenty or twenty-one human years old now.

"Yes, in New York City so he's close to me." Jonathan uncorked his wine bottle and poured himself a healthy amount. When he didn't offer it to anyone else, it confirmed Eli's suspicions that he'd laced the liquid with blood. "He's completing a program with the Special Forces, however, to better ready himself for a job at the CRF. So he's actually overseas at the moment."

Military training. Nice. "That'll be helpful when he becomes a Hydraian as well," Eli remarked as Amelia entered with their main course. He admired the fit of her dress as she bent to place the food on the table. Taking that off her later would be very enjoyable.

"When who becomes a Hydraian?" she asked.

"Jonathan's son." Eli started unwrapping the muffin now that Amelia had joined them. "He's undergoing some military training, which I said would be helpful when he joins us in Hydria."

"*If* he joins you," Jonathan corrected. "He might choose to stay with me and run the CRF."

Eli chuckled. "I'm sure Luc will be thrilled by the idea of having a Hydraian in renowned Ichorian territory."

"It's not exactly his decision, is it?" A hard edge lined Jonathan's tone, indicating this to be a sore subject. Which, yeah, Eli imagined having his only child fated to live in a world where his father wasn't welcome wouldn't be all that appealing.

Still... "It's a conversation for you and the Hydraian King." Which Eli knew would not go in Jonathan's favor. Fledglings were hard to come by, thanks to the notorious Blood Laws, and they needed all the Hydraians they could

111

find for future wars.

Amelia sat beside him and cleared her throat. "Yes, I agree. Let's discuss something else." *Always the mediator.*

God, how he adored this woman. He found her hand beneath the table and gave it a squeeze. "Jonathan has invited us to see his new research facility," he said, knowing full well Amelia would have no interest.

"Oh?" She unfolded her napkin over her lap with her free hand. "That sounds lovely." Her words lacked heart, but she delivered them with a smile so sweet that no one would think otherwise. Except Eli. He knew her too well.

He took a bite of the muffin and groaned at the delicious flavor. *Definitely returning the favor after the guests are gone*, he thought with a wink at the now-blushing Amelia.

"Eli said the same, though I think he used the term *enlightening*." Jonathan sipped his wine thoughtfully and set it down with a sigh. "It's just too bad, really."

"What is?" Amelia asked, her head cocked slightly to the side. Eli would have smiled at her adorable look if he wasn't also wondering what Jonathan meant. He set the muffin aside as he waited for the Ichorian to elaborate.

"Well…" Jonathan dabbed his mouth with a napkin and set it on his plate. An odd gesture, considering he hadn't eaten anything yet. Unless he considered the wine a meal? "I did mention I needed to discuss something with you both."

"Yes, I have to admit I worried something was wrong," Amelia said. "But you look quite fine."

Jonathan's lips quirked up. "I'm more than fine. Actually, I've never been better."

Instincts prickled Eli's insides. Something about that tone didn't *feel* right. He sat up a little straighter, while Amelia sagged in relief beside him.

"Good," she sighed. "It's just been so quiet lately, causing me to wonder when the other shoe might fall. Or is it drop?"

Eli kissed her on the cheek. "Drop, love. Waiting for

the inevitable."

"Yes, that." She waved her delicate hand. "Such an odd phrase, really. Anyway, you were saying, Jonathan?"

There was a beat of silence that scattered goose bumps down Eli's arms. Was it the Sentinel stirring such distrust? Or that gleam in Jonathan's dark eyes?

Something is very wrong.

"Well, as I said, it's a shame, really, because while I'd love to show you both the new facility, I can only take one of you." Jonathan shrugged as if to ask, *What can you do?*

Amelia frowned. "I don't understand."

Neither do I.

"To put it bluntly, your gift for humanoid shifting is worth more to me than Eli's ability to kill by touch." A touch of insanity lurked in Jonathan's dark eyes as he met Eli's gaze. "I can't really risk you killing everyone. You understand."

He opened his mouth to say he didn't, when a flash of silver appeared before him.

A gun.

The chair scraped the floor as he stood, his hands out in front of him. "Jonathan—"

"Sorry, old friend. But it's the only way."

What?

The muzzle flashed before Eli could even think to react.

Amelia!

Oh, shit. Oh, holy shit. No...This...What the fuck just happened?!

His heart ached, his breath leaving on a sharp gasp. No. This couldn't be real. A nightmare. How many millennia had he lived? How many centuries with his Amelia? Protecting her, loving her, cherishing her...

To go down like this? To fail her?

Amelia...

His head dropped, his vision blackening.

Not like this.

113

A dark hole whirled around him, different from all the other times he'd died. He usually fell into a state of unconsciousness and awoke later as if from a dream. But this wasn't right.

Her fingers clutched his as the last vestiges of reality left him on a whoosh of air.

My final breath.

Whatever was in those bullets—oh, it didn't matter.

All that mattered was the icy hand in his, or the memory of it.

His Amelia.

I'll always love…

Chapter Two

Luc

"How many?" Luc asked as he swirled the contents of his glass.

"Five," Balthazar replied. He stood beside Luc's stool with his back and elbows resting on the counter.

Normally, Luc spied their future conquests while Balthazar read their minds without looking, but tonight they'd opted to switch roles. Just for fun.

"Thoughts?" Luc prompted.

"Mostly kinky, though one is a bit shy due to inexperience. There's also a sixth across the room who seems to favor pain."

"If only Alik had joined us." Luc sipped his bourbon slowly. "And their interest levels?"

"Extremely high. They seem to be debating how to

approach us."

"Then perhaps we should go to them?"

"Maybe." Balthazar turned to pick up his drink. "They're currently daring the redhead to approach us."

"Curvy?"

"Totally Jay's type, yup."

Luc sighed. "I'd send Jacque to retrieve him, but we both know the teleporter won't leave my side."

"Said teleporter can hear you too, and you're right." The floppy-haired Hydraian spun on his stool as though to add to his proclamation of attendance. "I'll take the redhead, though."

"I think the little brunette is more your speed," Balthazar murmured. "She thinks you're cute."

Jacque stopped spinning, his silver-gray eyes widening. "She does?"

"Why is he shocked?" Luc asked conversationally. "It's not like he's bad-looking. He's lean, but athletic. Women like that."

"It's a confidence thing with us here," Balthazar replied. "He feels overwhelmed by our presence."

"I can still hear you," the teleporter pointed out. "And stop reading my mind."

"He's not sure his sexual 'prowess'—his term—is up to par either," Balthazar continued as if Jacque hadn't spoken. "Which is why I recommended the brunette. She doesn't need a night of fun, just an hour or two."

Luc nodded. "Good thinking."

"I hate both of you," Jacque muttered.

Balthazar took another sip before setting his drink down. "But what he really wants to do is observe one of us in action to learn, which I'm happy to take on so long as he promises not to write notes like he's thinking of doing."

"I'm not—"

"That would be a buzzkill," Luc agreed, cutting off the teleporter. "But also explains why he requires a lesson."

Balthazar smirked. "Oh, there are many more reasons

for that, including his young age and shy demeanor. Even now, he's uncertain about the brunette despite my confirming her mutual attraction. We'll have to work on him."

"I'm going to teleport you both to the ocean and watch you drown," Jacque growled, causing Luc to chuckle.

"I think you've upset him, B," he murmured, understanding the game.

"Have I?" B finally looked at the teleporter. "I'm sorry. I merely meant to explain the situation fully. Unless you'd like to prove me wrong?"

"Oh, he can't do that. He's too intimidated, right? We might outshine him." Luc gazed pityingly at his favorite Guardian. "Do you want me to demonstrate while you take notes? Mentally, of course. I can't have you scribbling things down. It's distracting."

Fury and annoyance glared back at him. "I do not require a *lesson*. I know how to seduce and fuck a woman."

Luc feigned surprise. "Do you?"

"Oh my God." He hopped off the stool. "Brunette, right?"

"With the glasses," Balthazar added helpfully. "Her name is Rosie, and she enjoys intellectual conversation. Turns her on."

Jacque rolled his eyes. "I can do this without the tips."

"Sure," Luc replied, rotating to face the crowd so he could better observe. "Show us."

"Fine." Jacque stalked off with a confident stride toward the group of women.

"How long until he realizes we set him up as bait?" Luc asked.

Balthazar leaned against the bar with one elbow, his body partially angled toward Jacque, but mostly facing Luc. "With how riled up he is? Probably not until after he's taken Rosie to bed, and even then, he might not get it."

Luc chuckled. "Clever. He deserves the female company."

"Yes. He does." Balthazar fell silent, an indication that he was busy reading minds. Luc didn't need to be able to hear the females to see their interest. It was written all over their bodies with the way they angled themselves toward Jacque while he spoke.

"Should we leave him to all five?" Luc wondered. There were several other women in the bar whom they could pick up.

"I don't know if he can handle them all." Balthazar folded his arms, his chocolate gaze thoughtful. "Perhaps one of us should join while the other takes the trio at the back?"

Luc glanced at the three women in question. They were eyeing them with obvious interest. "That looks promising."

"Oh, the blonde is thinking all sorts of kinky thoughts about what you can do with your mouth."

"Is she now?" Luc grinned at the woman in question and winked.

"And…" He trailed off. "It's Tristan."

Luc looked back at him, confused until he spied the phone in his hand. "Ah."

It was quiet enough in the bar for Balthazar to answer. "How's my favorite Ichorian?" he asked.

Luc smirked. Balthazar favored the Ichorian because of his proclivity for mischief. He gave Issac—his maker—absolute hell sometimes, despite being the man's best friend.

Luc's focus returned to the trio, his mind analyzing all the ways he could pleasure them at the same time. His gift would be helpful, if he chose to use it. Sometimes he preferred the skill of his hands and mouth, which the blonde seemed to be studying intently.

What an easy game. Almost boring, really. The pleasure was nice—enjoyable, even—but sometimes it just felt empty. "Don't comment," Luc said, knowing full well Balthazar could hear him. He grinned over his shoulder at the mind reader, and the amusement froze on his face.

Balthazar had gone pale.

His best friend *never* paled.

Luc stood. "What is it?" he asked.

The phone was still to Balthazar's ear, and he seemed to be growing paler by the second. "We're on our way, Tristan," he said, his voice thick with emotion. He slid the device into his pocket with shaking hands. "We need to go to the Hamptons. Now." He started toward Jacque, who met them halfway having already sensed the tension.

"What's wrong?" the teleporter asked.

"I…" Balthazar visibly trembled. "Take us to Wakefield Manor."

Jacque met Luc's stare and cocked a brow. "Now? Here?"

Luc didn't hesitate. "Yes." Something had happened that was horrible enough to render Balthazar, of all people, speechless. And were those tears in his eyes? "Right now."

"Okay." Jacque grabbed them both by the wrist, and the world whirled around them. Luc had experienced teleportation a thousand times, yet he always felt dizzy afterward—a side effect of the tunnel sensation. He ran his fingers through his windswept hair while catching his balance in the foyer of Amelia and Eli's home.

Mateo stood waiting for them, his dark blond head bent over an electronic device. When he glanced upward, his blue irises radiated pain.

"What's happened?" Luc demanded.

The technologically savvy Ichorian cleared his throat. "I thought Tristan—"

"Ballroom," Balthazar choked out. "They're in the ballroom." He fell to his knees, his hand to his chest.

Luc fell beside him. "Talk to me, B."

"Can't," he whispered, his face ashen as he lowered his head to the ground.

Fuck. He couldn't leave Balthazar like this. *What the fuck is happening?*

Then it hit him square in the heart as his own gift registered. Not his intelligence, but the one that allowed him to increase sensations—both good and bad.

Unspeakable pain, Luc realized. It had overwhelmed his oldest friend, so much so that he seemed to be having trouble breathing. He tried to identify the source of it and realized that *everyone* in the manor was experiencing it.

Eli, his instincts whispered.

No. The Hydraian was too powerful, too old, and there would be signs of *something*, right? A fight? Blood splatter?

He searched the room and found both Mateo and Jacque staring at him with concerned expressions.

A leader never shows weakness or fear. He cleared his throat. *For Eli...*

Luc blinked away his thoughts as he stood and focused on Jacque. "I need you to go grab Alik and Jayson." Because if what he suspected was true, he needed his Elders.

"Y-yes, sir." The teleporter vanished.

And Balthazar...Leaving him like this... He swallowed. His mind reader needed a moment to collect his thoughts. Luc could grant him that while he determined what happened here.

Eli, his instincts whispered again. *Which can only mean...*

No. Not yet. He didn't know anything yet.

"I'll be right back, B," he promised.

Balthazar gave no sign of hearing him.

Luc hadn't seen him this upset in centuries—no, millennia.

It has to be Eli...and Amelia. It was the only explanation. "*They're in the ballroom,*" Balthazar had said.

With a forced swallow, Luc headed toward the dreaded room. The moon lit his path through the oversized windows. No other lights were on, something that was distinctly ominous.

Tristan stood just outside the double doors at the end of the long hallway, his green irises thinned around dilated pupils. If the Ichorian looked like this, then—

"It's bad, Luc," he whispered, his expression paler than Luc had ever seen it. "They left his head on the floor and her ashes in a vase on his lap."

Luc's heart stopped beating.

It's true.

He hadn't wanted to believe his instincts, had refused to acknowledge them until he had proof, and now it sat staring him in the face. Literally. From the center of the room beyond Tristan.

He grabbed the wall beside him for support, his lungs forgetting how to function.

Eli and Amelia.

Dead.

Irrevocably.

The world spun around him even as his mind began running through scenarios. Eli was a warrior who lived several thousand years. To get through his defenses should have been impossible.

And yet the evidence spoke for itself. In the form of a headless body sitting in a chair. Issac knelt beside it, his head bowed over what Luc assumed were Amelia's remains.

Our sister.

My brother.

This can't be happening.

"What can I do?" Tristan asked, his voice shaking.

Luc met the Ichorian's tortured gaze. He appeared so young in that moment, so helpless.

And he was asking Luc for direction, as everyone always did.

A leader bears the impossible and carries the burdens of his people. He is the one others look to for guidance, the rock under which his people hide, and the glue that holds a society together.

He wasn't allowed to feel. Not openly. Not when his people relied on *him* to provide direction. These were the moments that mattered most. His leadership was never more important than it was right now.

Luc swallowed the emotion threatening to overcome him. He could break after he took care of those who relied on him. In the comfort of his home, where no one would know.

He needed to think. To catalog every detail. To focus.

"Alik and Jayson are coming. I may need your help when they arrive," Luc said. "Can I rely on you for that?" In his experience, assigning tasks helped in these situations. Everyone craved a distraction, a purpose, something to help them feel better even if it was moot or temporary.

"Yes. Of course."

"Thank you," Luc replied, meaning it. "I need a moment to study the scene."

Tristan nodded.

Luc gathered his resolve and forced his feet to move him into the room. His chest ached as he took in the dark hair and bloody mess on the floor beside Eli's body. Whoever had killed him wanted to make sure the method stuck, hence the beheading. His old friend would never wake again.

His hands fisted at his sides, his blood heating and cooling at the same time.

How had someone bested Eli? Especially in the presence of Amelia—Luc had never known a more protective male over his female.

It didn't make any sense.

Focus, his mind demanded. *See the big picture.*

But he couldn't. There were too many emotions…too many memories…and Issac. Oh, fuck, Issac. He hadn't moved or even acknowledged Luc; he just sat there with his hands covered in ash.

Their sister's remains, or so he assumed. A step closer confirmed it, for resting in Issac's palm was Amelia's ring. The Ichorian seemed entranced by it. His gaze unflinching as he stared at the massive diamond everyone would recognize.

A permanent death. An unnecessary cruelty. To burn to death was a fate Luc refused to imagine.

My darling sister…

Don't.

Not now.

He shut his eyes, just for a moment. One single second. And breathed slowly through his nose.

Everyone is counting on you. Figure this out. Analyze. Redirect your focus.

He could do this.

He had to do this. The others would be here soon, and they would require direction from him, a plan, information, something.

There was no other choice.

"I'm here," Luc whispered to Issac. "We're going to get through this."

"Are we?" Issac asked, his tone lacking life and emotion.

He's shutting himself off.

A practical response to the pain. A necessary one.

"Yes," Luc assured him as he cataloged the rest of the room—the exposed floor-to-ceiling windows allowing the moon to cast an eerie glow over the crimson scene and the two mortals cowering in a corner.

The house staff, he recognized as he returned his gaze to Eli's body in what appeared to be a patio chair. *They must have found him.*

Keep going, his strategic gift urged. Assessing the scene, while gruesome, helped alleviate the pain. Helped him focus.

The Conclave did this. It had their handiwork written all over it, especially the incineration of Amelia's body. They meant to send a message. After centuries of perceived peace, the Ichorians wished to inspire another war. That was the only logical reason for going after an Elder—one they knew mattered to the Hydraians—in the comfort of his own home. Yes, they were close to the Ichorian boundary here, but they weren't inside of it.

And yet, it technically broke no laws. Only Hydria and New York City were considered safe zones. There was also an unspoken rule about touching high-ranking officers on either side. It was the primary reason Alik had yet to go after· Lucinda—Osiris valued her immensely. They all knew if she died, it would stir resentment and provoke a violent response. Just as everyone recognized that touching an Elder would do the same.

Issac gazed up at him then, his midnight-blue eyes vacant. "She's gone, Lucian. Amelia—"

"What the fuck is going on?" Jayson demanded as he jogged into the room. One look at the massacre before him froze him midstep, causing Alik to bump into him from behind. "Oh, fuck." He fell to his knees in the same way Balthazar had. "Eli?"

Alik stepped around him, his dark eyes brewing with malice. "Who? How?"

Luc wished he could answer that, but right now he only had one guess and he knew it wasn't good enough. "The Conclave's motives are written all over this, but I'm not certain yet." He looked at the humans. *Robert and Cherie*, his memory provided. "I need every detail of what happened today."

Cherie shook against Robert's chest while the male cleared his throat. "I, we"—he coughed to cover his choked-up voice—"our daughter had a recital. Amelia gave us the night off but left us a note saying to stop by the main house when we returned. Something about preparing extra food. And…and…Cherie went to pick it up, but…" He visibly shuddered as his wife clutched him harder.

Issac stood, distracting Luc from further questioning. The ornate vase filled with Amelia's ashes rested on the floor at their feet.

"I need to check something" was all the Ichorian said

as he left with a vacant expression. The only sign of his emotion lay in the palm of his hand where he still clutched Amelia's ring.

"Shit," Jayson whispered brokenly. "Eli? I don't understand."

"We need to review his surveillance system," Alik growled. "See which of those fuckers managed to break in."

"It wasn't on." Mateo's voice drifted in from the hallway. He must have followed everyone—including Jacque—toward the ballroom. The only one missing was Balthazar, and now Issac.

I'll be back soon, B. I promise. Luc hoped his oldest friend heard him. Leaving him in the foyer…Fuck. Luc hated all of this.

Fuck!

"What do you mean, 'it wasn't on'?" Alik faced the Ichorian with his hands fisted. "Eli *always* uses his security system. It's why he doesn't need Guardians."

"I checked it when we arrived, and everything was off, all the data erased." Mateo sounded just as disgruntled as Alik. "I tried to fix it, but there's nothing there."

Meaning whoever had done this, had done their homework. Could the Conclave know about the security system?

Luc rubbed a hand over his face.

Something wasn't right. *I'm missing a piece of the puzzle.* But what?

He frowned. "If the Conclave did this, then why were you all not involved in the decision? Has Osiris discovered your true allegiance?" The questions were directed at the two Ichorians in the room.

Tristan snorted. "If that were true, we would be dead."

"He's right. Osiris would have made an example of Issac and Aidan, but he's called no such meeting or trial. The last Conclave meeting was nearly a decade ago." Mateo stuffed his hands into the pockets of his tailored pants. "Osiris has known about Issac's relationship with Amelia for centuries and has done nothing. Why would he act now?"

That's precisely what Luc wanted to know. It was no secret Issac and Aidan both had ties to Hydria and that neither seemed all that keen on harming their family members. Several of the Ichorians had family ties to the Hydraians, which complicated matters. It was part of the reason Aidan had been able to convince them all to form a treaty in 1747.

The armistice, in essence, allowed everyone to coexist without conflict so long as certain guidelines were followed.

Why act now?

Luc studied Eli's remains.

Too quick.

Osiris preferred decadence and grandiose affairs, not covert missions. Unless his goal was to provoke a war, but to what end?

No. This wasn't right at all. If he wanted to inspire conflict, he'd attack Hydria. Which could only mean someone else wanted to stir up trouble.

But who?

CHAPTER THREE

Stark

This was not going to plan at all. When Jonathan invited Stark to attend dinner with Amelia and Eli, he failed to mention his true intentions.

That said, Stark should have known the moment Jonathan started talking about the research lab that he intended to harm them.

Of course the bloody Ichorian wanted Amelia for her shifting abilities. If he could find a way to cultivate her genetics and distribute them to the Sentinel unit, he'd create quite the army. Especially considering all the other testing going on around here.

Stark shook his head as he stalked out the exit of the CRF headquarters. He'd left under the guise of needing a late-night dinner since they'd not eaten at Wakefield

Manor. Jonathan trusted him now, especially after his lack of a reaction to the requests made of him this evening. He'd even patted Stark on the back with a "*Good job, kid.*"

It had taken serious control not to correct the phrasing. He wasn't as old as Jonathan, or really many other immortals, but he wasn't a child either. Seraphim reached full adult status at twenty-five years of existence, which occurred several decades ago for Stark. While young he might be, a kid he was not.

He fixed his leather jacket as he walked toward a bar he knew well. Thank humanity for technology. It made reaching out to Ezekiel far easier these days.

Owen met him at the door with a grimace. "They're both inside."

He raised a brow. *Both of them?* He'd only invited Ezekiel to this meeting. Owen's presence he expected since he owned the bar—a property Ezekiel had gifted the Hydraian years ago in exchange for this arrangement. Not that the poor Hydraian had much choice but to accept.

Stark said nothing as he moved into the dimly lit room. A few patrons sat at the bar, all minding their own business except for the two at the far end who watched him with matching grins.

He sighed. "I never should have introduced Ezekiel to Leela."

Owen grunted in reply on his way back to the bar. Why he'd felt the need to greet Stark at the door was beyond him. The Hydraian possessed some abnormal quirks. Ezekiel's recruitment of him served a grander purpose, one that hadn't come to fruition yet. Once Astasiya moved to New York, however, Owen's role would become vital to the success of their plans.

And now, Stark needed to elaborate on his part and potential failure to the duo laughing together across the room.

He walked toward them and picked up the shot glass Owen passed over along the way. Top-shelf scotch. Stark's favorite. He downed it in one gulp before sitting beside Leela. "Aren't you on guard duty in Havre?" he asked flatly.

She flipped her long brown hair over a shoulder. "Stas is asleep, and I was bored."

He turned to face her and slid one elbow onto the counter. "Meaning, you left her unguarded." Not a question, but a statement.

"Is this the part where you try to act all superior despite my several thousand years of experience over you?" She tsked. "I've gotta say, Gabe, it's rather dull."

"You have one job—"

She pressed a finger to his lips. "That I'm doing as a favor to you and Caro while putting my status with the High Council at risk. Besides, I need more of your blood, something you would know if you bothered to mist by once in a while."

He knocked her hand away from his mouth. "I left you with a six-month supply," he replied flatly. "And you could have called to let me know you needed more of my blood."

"It's really cute how you two fight like siblings," Ezekiel drawled. "But I'd like to know why my evening plans were rearranged for this little chat. Lest you forget, I, too, have a role to play in this game of fate."

Right. Time was always a factor when they met, especially in the heart of Ichorian territory. Fortunately, all three of them could disappear in a flash. Literally. Only Owen would be left to fend for himself, but the protection rune Stark had gifted him a decade ago would help.

On to the more important conversation at hand. "Jonathan assassinated Eli tonight."

The notorious amusement radiating from Ezekiel faded with a blink. "What?"

"As in the Elder?" Leela asked. "For good?"

"Yes." Stark tapped his glass on the counter to attract Owen's attention. He needed another drink. "Jonathan invited me over for a friendly dinner, saying he wanted to introduce me to Eli and Amelia. I suspected it was a test of trust but had no idea he'd lose his fucking mind. He shot the Elder with an incendiary bullet and staged the scene as a Conclave assassination. He even included a vase filled with ashes and put Amelia's jewelry inside of it."

Owen appeared then with the bottle of scotch, his hand frozen in midair. Stark removed the item from his grip and poured himself a healthy portion.

"Thank you," he said before shooting the liquid into the back of his throat and pouring a third. The alcohol would do absolutely nothing to him, but that wasn't the point.

"Amelia and Eli are dead?" Owen whispered, his face ashen as he wobbled a little.

"Only Eli." Stark swallowed the liquor again, enjoying the burn as it went down. "Amelia, however, will wish she's dead by the time Jonathan finishes with her." Poor female. It wasn't in Stark's nature to care, exactly, but he wasn't completely without a heart.

Ezekiel whistled. "He's going to start a war."

"I believe that's his goal," Stark muttered. Which was a problem. They couldn't afford the Hydraians and Ichorians going to battle now, not while Astasiya was still a youth. "We need at least another decade, or a minimum of six or seven years." She was enrolled at Columbia University and destined to start in the fall. If violence erupted between the immortals now, it would destroy all of their plans.

Leela gazed at him thoughtfully. "What hint did you leave?"

"How did you know?" His subtle tampering was why he called this meeting; he just hadn't gotten to that point yet.

"You're the son of Adriel. As a warrior, you always strategize." She smiled. "And I know *you*, Gabe. Tell us what hint you left behind."

"I'm not certain it'll work." He rubbed the back of his neck. Everything had happened so quickly that he didn't have time to really think through his idea. "Jonathan staged the murder scene in the ballroom and sent me off to deal with the surveillance equipment. On my way there, I sort of tinkered with the kitchen."

Leela's brow furrowed. "Sort of?"

"Yeah." He needed to explain this better. "All right, Jonathan gave Amelia a choice to comply or die. When she chose to live, he ordered her to scrub the remains off the table with a cloth—after he severed Eli's head." An exercise the lunatic had taken great pride in because, apparently, lighting the immortal on fire from within wasn't satisfying enough for him.

Stark swallowed, pushing the memory of Amelia's broken expression from his thoughts. Fretting over the past and her tormented future had no practical function. If the opportunity to help her presented itself in a way that he couldn't be implicated, then he'd act on it. Until then, his fated role was to remain calm, stoic, and focused.

Astasiya mattered the most.

"Anyway, when Amelia finished the task, Jonathan knocked her out and tied her up in the trunk of the car. Then he staged the body in the ballroom"—after Stark carried it there—"and left me to handle the cameras and such. On my way there, I put the wine in the fridge."

Ezekiel blinked at him. "Wine?"

Stark nodded. "Jonathan had brought the bottle and opened it before dinner. It's laced with blood. I put it in the fridge." Something someone should pick up on since it was a red wine.

Ezekiel's dark gaze gleamed. "And he didn't notice?"

"I told him I threw it in the trash with all the rags Amelia had used to clean up the massacre in the dining area." Which Jonathan refused to touch because of the potentially lethal substance.

The incendiary bullets turned the blood into a charred

liquid, which supposedly destroyed the essence of immortality. Whether or not that also made a Hydraian's bloodline nontoxic to Ichorians had yet to be tested, and Jonathan didn't seem too keen on being the first to experiment.

Stark blew out a breath. "He wasn't happy, but I reminded him that he told me to remove all evidence, including the bottle."

"And he didn't think to check the fridge for it because why would he?" Ezekiel surmised. "Brilliant. Someone will notice and realize he visited recently, and may even assume Amelia put the bottle there as a sign."

"That's my hope," Stark agreed. "But if they allow emotions to dictate their actions, my subtle hint might not be enough."

"You could always go guardian angel on one of them," Leela murmured. "That is what you messenger Seraphim are supposed to do."

Stark blinked at her. "I completed my task by leaving that bottle. It sends a message."

"And if it doesn't work, you should consider sending another," she replied.

"There isn't another to send." Not without giving up his identity, which he couldn't afford to do yet.

"Then we should discuss a backup plan because Stas isn't ready," Ezekiel cut in with a tap against the counter. "We're going to need more drinks, Owen."

The dark-skinned male had remained still throughout the conversation, his brown eyes glittering with unshed tears. He seemed to shake himself, blinking, then nodded. "Yeah, of course."

"And, Owen." Ezekiel stopped the Hydraian with a hand on his arm. "You realize you can't breathe a word of this to anyone, yes?"

His shoulders sagged in defeat. "They're all going to assume Amelia's dead."

"It's the burden of our fate," Ezekiel murmured.

"A fate I never asked for," he whispered.

Silence thickened the air between them.

The entire plan hinged on their cooperation and teamwork, including Owen's willingness to help. They needed him to befriend Stas, to help protect her in the city by guiding her social life. And very few others were as charismatic or as young as Owen. His lowly abilities helped as well because he served no real purpose on Hydria, which meant no one minded his frequent absence. To find a replacement this late in the game would be impossible, not after all their preparations.

"Jonathan trusts me now," Stark informed. "I'll see what I can do about helping Amelia until the time comes where her liberation can be facilitated, but you need to understand that it could take years before such an occurrence arises." It would require the perfect storm of circumstances to make it unnoticeable. Stark couldn't afford to jeopardize his position for Amelia; he needed the in with the CRF to monitor Astasiya.

"I won't let Jonathan kill her, so long as I can help it," Stark vowed. That was the best he could offer.

Leela wrapped her fingers around Owen's wrist. "Stas will need you more than you realize. We can't do this without you." Her warm tone was very un-Seraphim-like, a consequence of her lust-driven abilities. She felt more than most, himself included. It was partly why he'd recruited her for help with Astasiya, all the way back to the day Caro gave birth.

"I get it, I get it," Owen said, sighing. "I won't say anything."

"This is bigger than all of us," Leela reminded softly.

Owen stared at her, and a hint of adoration touched his gaze. "I know, Lee. Ezekiel has told me the prophecies a hundred times. I understand what's at stake."

Leela released his arm. "Good, because Caro and Sethios are counting on all of us." She focused on Ezekiel. "Speaking of, how is Sethios?"

The Ichorian's face clouded over, his expression dark. "Still alive."

"That sounds promising," Leela deadpanned.

Ezekiel glanced at her. "Osiris allowed him to remember yesterday, just long enough to relay the date and watch his son's reaction. Then he stole it from him. Again. He's in hell. We all are."

"Seven years," Stark said. "That's how long we need. Once Astasiya is twenty-five, everything will change." Or that's what they all hoped, anyway.

And there was much to be done in the interim.

"It seemed appropriate to add my version of events for readers' eyes only. Do not share this section with the other immortals, or I will send Ezekiel after you."
—Stark

CHAPTER FOUR

Luc

"Jacque, I need Aidan," Luc declared after walking around the ballroom for the third time. It wasn't adding up. While the scene screamed "Conclave," it wasn't exciting enough to suit Osiris's preferences. "Take him to the foyer and I'll meet you there. Let me tell him about Amelia."

It was Luc's burden to bear, no one else's. He would be the one to break his father's heart, then mend it with intelligence. He hoped.

"Yes, sir," Jacque replied, disappearing.

"I want to see the surveillance equipment," Alik said, already walking out the door. He'd obviously decided a task was the best way to handle his grief. Alik was never one to admit his feelings, but Luc knew better than anyone that the telepath felt them stronger than most.

"There's nothing there," Mateo assured him as he followed Alik out the door. "It's like the entire system underwent a refresh and…" His voice trailed off as they moved swiftly down the hall.

Two down, Luc thought with a mental sigh. They would help keep each other sane, at least temporarily. And maybe they would find something in the process.

That missing puzzle piece.

"I don't understand how this could happen," Jayson said, still on his knees beside Eli. "It doesn't make any sense."

Luc agreed. Eli would not have gone down without a fight, and yet, his clothes remained mostly unsoiled apart from his own blood. No signs of a struggle, not even a tear in his clothes or a scuff on his shoes. His hands were clean as well.

What am I not seeing? His mind raced with ideas, none of them quite right.

Jayson lifted the vase. "Amelia…" The pain in his voice ceased Luc's thoughts and fractured another piece of his heart.

I need to get out of this room. Everyone needs out.

Then he could think, could figure this out, could determine what to do and how to properly handle the situation.

"Amelia," Jayson repeated. "Why? Why would they target her?"

"Because they knew it would hurt." As Luc said the words, he realized a vital piece of the puzzle. *They knew it would hurt.* Osiris fancied mind games, so much so that he would have required an audience to hammer that nail into the hearts of his victims. A quiet show weakened the impact.

Yet, whoever did this *knew* Amelia's death would result in impractical behavior driven by emotion and a desire for revenge.

To provoke a war on false pretenses.

"But Amelia," Jayson whispered, his body trembling.

Luc flinched at the realization that his strongest warrior was breaking before his eyes and he'd done nothing to help him. *I'm failing them all.*

He needed to keep his head on straight, his brain focused. Even an ounce of emotion slipping in could derail everything. If he fell apart, they all would.

Tasks. They all need tasks.

"Jay, can you escort Cherie and Robert back to their home at the front of the property and check the grounds for anyone or anything that might not belong?" He knelt beside his friend and placed a hand on his shoulder. "I'm sorry to ask, but your gift for metal is our best advantage out there." Luc added a hint of apology to his tone so as to hide the true purpose of his request. He meant to provide his warrior with a distraction—something to help him feel strong in this time of despair.

If only I could provide myself with a similar mission.

Jayson's brown eyes gazed up at him. "Yeah." He cleared his throat. "Yes, right. Yeah. Of course." He nodded and stood on shaky legs. "I can do that."

"I'll go with you," Tristan said. He hadn't spoken much while quietly observing from the wall. Luc met his forest-green gaze. Understanding passed between them as Tristan confirmed with a nod that he recalled Luc's words from earlier. He would help take care of Jayson, keep him strong and focused.

Thank you, he said with his eyes.

Another nod from the Ichorian.

Cherie and Robert huddled close together as Jayson and Tristan guided them outside via the back patio doors of the ballroom.

That's six, all accounted for. And finally he had the room to himself.

A moment alone with no one to see him crumble.

He gazed at the vase beside his old friend. "Oh, Amelia…" How anyone could be so cruel as to harm her, he would never understand. "And Eli."

His face fell as memories assaulted his mind and heart. Omniscience was both a gift and a curse, because he would remember everything. Including this moment and the pain associated with the loss. The heartache of all his friends. The violence of this scene.

His legs threatened to buckle, but his spirit kept him upright. He couldn't afford to falter. Not yet.

But he did allow a tear to fall for his beloved sister, and another for Eli, his old friend, fellow Elder, and brother unrelated by blood.

His family.

Shattered by some senseless act of horror.

"I'll fix this," he vowed. "I'll find whoever did this to you, and I will make them pay." It was all he could say.

I need to solve this, he decided. *For them. For everyone.*

Luc rolled his neck, wiped the damp evidence from his cheeks, and forced his legs to move. He'd given Jacque more than enough time to locate Aidan.

However, when he reached the foyer and found his father hugging Balthazar, he realized he'd given the teleporter too much time. Emerald eyes—so similar to his own—froze him on the spot. A maelstrom of emotion swirled in those ancient depths.

Luc would never have children, and suddenly, he was thankful for that small mercy. Because pain unlike any he understood radiated from his father in that moment.

His heart broke for him, for everyone.

He opened his mouth, but no words came out. He had nothing. No solution. No real information. It was as if his gift had stalled when he needed it most.

Why can't I figure this out?

Again he tried to say something. Anything. And the look in his father's eyes said he understood all too well, which only made it worse.

"Aidan, I need you to make a phone call," Issac announced from the second floor. He stood with his hands on the railing, his stance far too calm.

Balthazar pulled away from Aidan, his brown gaze sharp as he focused on Issac. "Are you certain?" he asked, his voice riddled with shock.

A wave of calm settled over Luc at seeing his number one lieutenant alert and alive. *It's going to be okay*, he realized. *We're going to get through this.* Saying it to the others was one thing; believing it was entirely another.

"Yes," Issac replied as he started down the steps. "For those of you unable to read my mind, I have a theory. Cherie and Robert clued me in to it with their mention of extra food. Amelia was entertaining. So where are the guests?"

He stopped in the foyer and tucked his hands into the pockets of his tailored pants.

"Did you find them?" Aidan asked, his voice low and laden with emotion. Luc hadn't heard that tone from him since Amelia's mother passed several centuries ago. She'd been the love of Aidan's life, not that he spoke of it often.

"No," Issac replied. "But I did find a bottle of red wine in the fridge while searching for evidence of her dinner party."

Luc frowned. "What?"

"Yes, that was my initial reaction. Amelia would never refrigerate red wine. I think she placed it there as a hint." His pupils flared. "It contained blood—O negative—and was from a popular vineyard in the South of France."

"No…" Aidan shook his head. "Jonathan?"

Issac didn't react to the name. "Call him. Ask him when he last saw Amelia and Eli. Say you're trying to get in touch and no one is responding. Something. See how he responds."

"You think Jonathan did this?" Luc asked even as his mind started cataloging the possibility. It would explain how someone entered the home undisturbed, why Eli showed no signs of a fight, and how they knew to destroy the surveillance evidence. Jonathan possessed enough knowledge of the Conclave to fabricate a scene as well. "But what does he gain from this?" *And why hadn't I realized something so obvious?*

"Power," Aidan whispered. "He's always craved it. Isn't that why he created the CRF? He wanted to be in charge of something. But what is he hoping to gain by sparking an Immortal war?"

"I may be able to answer that," Mateo replied as he joined them with a device in his hand.

Issac didn't seem surprised by the declaration, indicating he'd already spoken to his progeny about his theory. "Did you track his phone?" he asked.

Apparently, they'd been busy while Luc was wandering aimlessly around the ballroom. He hadn't even considered Jonathan as a culprit, hadn't really considered anyone other than the Conclave. That wasn't like him at all. For the first time in his existence, his gift had truly failed him. Because of his grief? The weight of having to carry an entire nation on his shoulders? His age? Nearly four thousand years of living took a toll on one such as him.

I need to analyze this later. I can't afford for it to happen again.

"Jonathan was here tonight," Mateo informed, his focus on the screen in his hand. "Just returned to the city about an hour ago."

"Timing is right," Issac replied. "What else?"

"He's building a paramilitary unit that specializes in hunting and killing rogue immortals. There's also something about a new research wing that I haven't been able to hack into yet. His technology is crazy advanced; I'd be envious if I wasn't so fucking irritated by it." Mateo tapped something on his device and sat on the stairs. "I'll keep digging."

"He's mentioned the Sentinel unit to me," Aidan said. "Their primary purpose is to save mortals in dangerous situations. However, he did say he wanted to prepare them to go against immortals should the need arise."

"It seems he's trying to create one." Balthazar crossed

his arms, all signs of sadness gone and replaced by anger. "We need sufficient proof before we act on this."

"Working on it," Mateo mumbled, his mind fully engaged in the task. Issac had chosen well in turning this one into an Ichorian. His affinity for technology was very helpful.

"Why would Osiris allow him to create a military unit in the middle of Ichorian territory?" Luc asked, confused. He could see no logical reason for it to be allowed. Granted, he didn't quite trust his gifts at the moment, given his obvious mishap. Even so…"It seems contrary to his goals."

"Perhaps they have a deal where Jonathan tracks rogues and returns them for punishment?" Aidan suggested. "I'm more interested in knowing where Jonathan procured his funding for the CRF to begin with, because it wasn't from me."

"I've wondered that myself," Issac said. "He was never one for investing or saving."

"Did he approach you for financing?" Aidan wondered.

"No, but he is interested in partnering with Wakefield Pharmaceuticals on a business level, an idea I've not yet entertained."

"Perhaps you should," Aidan replied.

"Or perhaps I should kill him." The nonchalance in Issac's voice did not match the furious gleam in his gaze. "If we find sufficient proof of his guilt, I will slit his throat, allow him to recover, and do it again and again until I'm satisfied with his death. Then I will light him on fire and force him to watch as his body slowly crumbles into ash."

Luc didn't bother to point out the unfeasibility of the latter part of his plan or that he would require an incinerator of high heat to turn the body to ash. *Wait, how did Jonathan turn Amelia to ash?* Another misstep in his intelligence-gathering earlier. "Mateo, is there a crematorium nearby?"

"Ahead of you, and no, there's not. But I suspect he didn't need one." Mateo's brow furrowed. "He's been experimenting with bullets that can incinerate the blood from within, as well as mobile incineration units. Which explains the swift cremation, but, hmm." He stood. "I need to see Eli's body again." He didn't elaborate, just left.

"The blood doesn't look right," Balthazar explained, letting the rest of the room in on Mateo's thought process. "And he's almost certain Jonathan is behind this, based on his research."

The puzzle pieces began to move into place, his gift finally registering the task at hand. It settled over him in a flourish of details, all coming together at once. His mind spun, weaving a scenario that fit. How he didn't see it earlier was beyond him because everything seemed perfectly clear now.

Luc ran his fingers through his hair, relieved to feel somewhat grounded again. "His motive is clear; he'd profit from an Immortal war, especially if it went public. Think of the government funding he'd receive if he could produce an army of super soldiers already equipped to handle Ichorians and Hydraians. It's a risky endeavor, but certainly feeds his power complex."

"Would Osiris ever allow it to succeed to that point?" Aidan asked, his focus on Luc.

"It wouldn't matter," Luc pointed out. "We all know he could care less about humanity and considers himself a superior being. What I don't understand is how Jonathan thinks he could be an even match against Osiris and the Conclave. They would destroy him with ease."

Aidan was already nodding. "He must have some other play, some weapon we're unaware of."

"Likely tied to the financial backer?" Luc suggested.

"Very possible." Aidan's brow furrowed. "Even if we find Jonathan guilty, we need additional information to proceed. Someone is pulling strings. He's not intelligent enough to pull this off on his own."

"Not to interrupt, but Mateo just confirmed his suspicions," Balthazar said, his face pale. "The blood covering Eli doesn't belong to him. It was planted to hide the true cause of death—incineration from within."

A new type of weapon.

One that could incinerate the blood on impact?

"That confirms Jonathan's involvement," he whispered more to himself than to the room. "The Conclave would never develop such technology. They'd prefer mental and physical power over a gun with fancy bullets."

Issac, who had been calm and quiet the entire time, began to pace. "I agree with Aidan. Jonathan is not intelligent enough to orchestrate this on his own. We need to gather more information."

Luc nodded, agreeing. The emotional side of him craved revenge, but the rational side confirmed the need to think this through carefully. They needed a plan. "What do you suggest, Issac?"

His sapphire gaze smoldered. "He wants a partnership. I'll give him one. Then we play the long game, determine whom he's working for, what he is trying to achieve, and take everything from him. Including his life."

"The evidence will be needed to justify the execution with the Conclave as well," Aidan added. "Osiris will not be pleased to lose an Ichorian—even one as weak as Jonathan—without due cause. And unfortunately, assassinating two Hydraians won't qualify even if he did it with the intention of provoking a war."

Hmm, and if they killed Jonathan without proper evidence, that itself could prompt retribution from the Ichorians. Yes, they needed to play this strategically, not emotionally.

"We need to keep this knowledge between us for now. The fewer who know, the better." It would be hard enough for those in this room to remain natural and calm around Jonathan; Luc could not imagine an entire island of pissed-off Hydraians around the culprit of their pain.

Amelia was well loved, as was Eli.

"I concur." Issac stopped pacing. "Where did Tristan go?"

"He went with Jayson and the mortals to the guest house on the property. We'll apprise them both—Alik and Jacque too—of our findings. No one else."

"Not necessary." Balthazar gestured up with his chin. Alik and Jacque both sat on the second-floor landing, their backs against the railing. "They've heard everything, and Alik sent messages to Jayson and Tristan."

Luc nodded. "Good. Then all that's left is to make appropriate arrangements. We need to grieve."

His heart ached with the words, but he knew them to be true. Amelia and Eli required a proper ceremony—a goodbye filled with tears, memories, and, most importantly, love. It's what they both would have wanted and what his people needed.

After he finished holding everyone together and cherishing them all to the best of his ability, Luc would retreat to the serenity of his home. And only then would he allow himself to truly break.

A leader is the strength his people seek when they need reminding of the light. It's in the darkness that he mourns. Alone. Always alone.

Luc cleared his throat and straightened his spine. "All right. Let's bring Eli and Amelia home."

AND THEN THERE WERE FOUR READER DISCUSSION

"Yeah, that was depressing. Not sure why we told that story."

—B

Issac: *To remind us all why Jonathan is going to die?*

Tom: *Yes. Painfully.*

Jayson: *Good to see you two agreeing on something finally.*

Stas: *I have a question.*

Luc: *Shoot.*

Stas: *Why did you skip chapter three?*

Luc: *Chapter three? There were only three chapters.*

Stas: *It goes from two to four.*

B: *Huh. Weird. Seems to be a glitch in the formatting.*

Alik: *Or maybe fate is wishing this book would fucking end already?*

B: *So negative. I think we need a sexy story, Luc, to improve the mood.*

Stas: *Hold on. Before we go there, I have another question. Eli mentioned Amelia being the daughter of a duchess. Does that make Issac a duke?*

Issac: *Yes, I inherited the title when my birth father died.*

Stas: *Seriously?*

Issac: *Does that increase the romance for you, love?*

Stas: *No, but it explains your wealth and, uh, personality.*

Issac: *Meaning?*

B: *Your priggish nature?*

Tom: *Don't forget the arrogance.*

Issac: *Are we going to finish this book or continue to assassinate my character?*

Stas: *I just meant it explained his formality. You should probably start the next story now.*

Amelia: *Can you try for something more uplifting, please? I'm rather tired of living in the past.*

Luc: *Brazil?*

B: *Brazil.*

Leela: *Real version or fake one?*

B: *Well, hello, sweetheart. And just who might you be?*

Leela: *Yeah, I thought the real version too. I'll take over after your introduction, boys.*

146

B: *I like her.*

Luc: *Me too. Who is she?*

B: *No idea. Let's find out.*

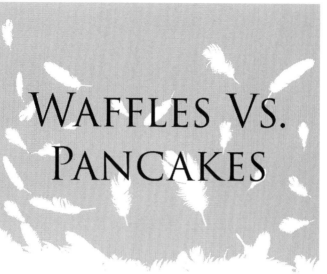

WAFFLES VS. PANCAKES

"Welcome to Brazil."

—B

QUICK REMINDER

"Before we begin, let's make sure you're properly up to speed. Remember this scene from Forbidden Bonds?"

—B

The sadness in his expression answered her thought. He brushed his thumb against her neck in a soothing gesture that made it hard to refuse him. "All right," she murmured and stood.

"Don't go too far, A." The emotion in her brother's voice tugged at her heart. Her relationship with him differed from what she had with Issac, mostly because she didn't grow up with Luc, but she loved him. Even when she disagreed with a decision, such as keeping Tom locked up. He stood as she walked over to him and engulfed her in a hug.

"I'm not going anywhere," she whispered.

"I know." He kissed her hair and held her a little longer than he used to, as if he feared she might disappear on him again. "Let's talk in the morning. I'll make waffles."

Balthazar snorted beside them. "Rubbish."

"Ignore him," Luc replied as he let her go. "Pancakes are flat and shapeless, while waffles are geometrically delicious."

Amelia smiled at the familiar debate. "Good to know not everything has changed around here."

"Pancakes can hold a variety of shapes," Balthazar

argued.

"But do they form pockets for the maple syrup?"

"Not all of us are obsessed with even servings."

Luc arched a haughty brow. "That's not an answer."

"Jesus Christ," Alik muttered. "Make it stop."

Jayson chuckled and shook his head. "B, I thought you were going on a walk, man."

"Right." Balthazar extended his arm to her. "Walk with me, and I'll explain why pancakes are the superior breakfast food along the way."

She slid her arm through his and grinned. "You realize I've heard this debate a thousand times, yes?"

He looked at Luc and addressed him instead of her. "I've proven you wrong a dozen times on that front." His gaze narrowed. "You're on. Next weekend. I choose Brazil. Fine. Yes, maple syrup is allowed. Whipped cream as well. All the toppings, Luc. That, too, and yes, I pick Jay. Deal."

"What kinky challenge did I just agree to?" Jayson asked.

"Luc will fill you in while Amelia and I take a walk."

She snorted. "You act as though I'm a blushing bride." She knew Balthazar and Luc were constantly engaged in a battle of wits, and it usually involved sexual escapades of some sort. Seemed this one involved breakfast, Brazilian women, and teams. *I don't want to know.*

"One day I'll corrupt you, love." Balthazar grinned. "Don't you worry."

———

B: Perfect. Now you're ready. Flip the page to find out why pancakes are superior to waffles.

Luc: He meant why waffles are superior to pancakes.

Alik: *If you two keep this up, we'll never finish this fucking book.*

B: *You say that like it would be a bad thing.*

Alik & Issac: *It would!*

Luc: *No respect for maple syrup. So disappointing.*

B: *We'll show them why it's important.*

Luc: *Yes. I'm ready.*

Leela: *Are you sure? Because I'm about to blow your minds.*

B, Luc, Jay: *Who is Leela?*

Leela: *Nothing to see here. Or, perhaps, everything…*

CHAPTER ONE

Leela

Balthazar.

Lucian.

Alik.

Jayson.

Fuck. This was supposed to be Leela's weekend away from babysitting, but of course, the Elders chose Rio de Janeiro for their latest challenge.

She closed her book and tossed it onto the sand. She could just mist to another beach, but that required new hotel arrangements, a potential check-in with the council, an update to Gabe, and yeah, she really just couldn't be bothered. Might as well make the best of it by staying. None of them would recognize her anyway; it wasn't like they were aware of her existence.

Leela picked up her phone and texted Ezekiel. *Prick.*

He'd been the one to suggest this location for the weekend, and clearly, *this* was why.

His reply came instantly. *I see you received my present.*

I wanted a break, asshole. Away from the wannabe immortals.

Your insults hurt, Lee.

She rolled her eyes. *I hope Stas runs off somewhere romantic with that Ichorian this weekend, just so you have to follow.*

The fledgling can take care of herself, was the reply. *Besides, Stark has it sorted.*

Leela snorted as she typed her reply. *He really should just tell her already.*

On that, we agree. Even through text she could hear his surprise. Working with Ezekiel hadn't been at the top of her happy list, but the Ichorian had grown on her. She could see why Gabe trusted him.

"May the best man win," a sensual voice said nearby.

"Or breakfast, as it were," the oldest among them replied.

This was her punishment for not sticking around in Hydria the other night when they were all celebrating Amelia's return. With Stas safe, Leela had popped over to Athens for a little clubbing and some much-needed wine. Apparently, she'd missed the part where the Elders had decided to venture to Brazil.

Oh well. She'd make do on her own and ignore them.

Leela tossed her phone into her bag and sighed. The sunlight felt amazing against her fair skin. If she were human, she'd burn. Alas, her genetics healed her too quickly for any color to appear. She would forever be a pale blonde with light blue-green eyes. Just like her mother, whom she needed to pay a visit to soon.

Leela's family and friends were used to her frequent disappearances. It was no secret that she preferred life among the mortals—they experienced emotion and pleasure in ways her kind didn't.

Okay, okay, not all of them were stoic. Just the majority. The poor sods didn't understand life and actually considered themselves superior for their ability to disassociate themselves from feelings. They didn't shun those like Leela who chose to embrace humanity, but rather, they pitied the Seraphim "in her situation." Meaning they thought she didn't have a choice because of her gifts. It showed how little they understood.

As if I could ever prefer their lifestyle.

Leela loved sex. Men. Women. Multiple partners or solo, she didn't mind. Her brethren, however, preferred to procreate only when necessary. If they could figure out how to inseminate females without the actual deed, they probably would. If they could figure out how to inseminate females without the actual deed, they probably would. Alas, technology interventions and fertility treatments were for humans alone, while the fate of her kind worked in mysterious ways.

The atmosphere changed, giving her less than a second's warning before an all-too-familiar male took the lounge chair beside hers. His gaze seared her skin as he brazenly admired every inch of her body on display.

Hello, handsome. She was well acquainted with Balthazar's seductive ways and had often considered what it would be like to indulge in him a little. Nevertheless, Stas's guardianship was far more important than Leela's libido. Still, she could have a little fun. He would never know of her true purpose or existence beyond this— assuming she played her part right.

She pulled her sunglasses down to stare at him over the rim. "Like what you see?"

His full lips curled into a deliciously wicked smile. "Do you?"

Leela admired his broad shoulders, defined chest and abdomen, and the fine line of hair leading to the impressive package he kept hidden beneath his dark red swim trunks. She'd seen him nude in Hydria once when misting about and waiting for Stas to return to New York. And, well, Balthazar deserved to be confident.

"Hmm, I'll admit, I think you'd look better naked." She reset her glasses and relaxed in the sun again.

"The feeling is mutual." He waved a hand, calling a waiter over to them, and ordered two fruity concoctions. Leela was a rum punch kind of girl, so that worked for her, not that she acknowledged his little game. If he wanted to play with her, he'd need to work harder.

Balthazar crossed his legs at the ankles and tucked his hands behind his head. A clearly practiced pose intended to entice, and he pulled it off rather nicely. The man had lovely abs and strong thighs. Leela would enjoy tracing all that sinewy muscle with her tongue.

"How did you know I could speak English?" he asked.

If this was his idea of a pickup line, it sucked. "You looked American."

"American?" He chuckled. "One night with me and you'll know that's not at all the case."

She glanced sideways at him. "Who said anything about spending a night together?"

"I may not be able to read your mind, but your body is speaking to me plenty."

The tiny rune on her hip flared with his words, sparking a kindle of unease deep inside. He could hear thoughts, but not hers. No wonder he chose the chair beside her—the silence had piqued his interest. Couple that with his inability to control her emotions, and he had to be completely taken by the challenge.

Well, shit. What now?

Vera. Obviously. Her best friend was going to stop answering the phone whenever Leela called because she always requested the same favor—a memory alteration.

"Don't stop playing with me now," Balthazar murmured. "We were just getting started."

"I don't believe we were doing anything."

"And that's a shame, isn't it? Two beautiful people, lounging on a romantic beach, just chatting?" He held out his hand. "Balthazar. You can call me B."

She eyed his strong fingers, attached to a leanly muscled arm.

What could it hurt? She had to wipe his memory anyway. Might as well enjoy the moment.

Electricity hummed between them as she pressed her palm to his. "Leela. You can call me Lee."

"Lee," he repeated, as if tasting the word. "And if I prefer Leela?"

She shrugged. "Then I'll call you Balthazar."

Sexy dimples appeared. "You can call me whatever you like." He lifted her hand to his lips and pressed a chaste kiss against her knuckles—a tease meant to inspire. And very well executed, in her experienced opinion. Especially the little nibble he added to her wrist before releasing her. It actually tingled.

Easily a ten on the seductive scale. For a normal woman, anyway. Unfortunately for him, Leela wasn't anywhere near common when it came to the sexual arts.

"Not bad," she praised. "But keep trying."

"Oh, I haven't even begun yet."

That she believed. "Good."

Their drinks arrived, and Balthazar handled the tab before raising his glass to hers. "To experimentation and new experiences."

Her lips twitched. Of course he considered her a "new experience." Her immunity to his gifts probably enthralled him.

She tapped her glass to his. "That sounds promising, if a little dangerous."

"I prefer to consider it living life to the fullest." He winked and tasted his drink. Somehow he managed to make the act of sipping through a straw appear masculine, even with the fruit hanging off the edge of his glass. His tongue swept over the bottom of his lip, drawing her gaze. Such a kissable mouth—sensual, strong, seductive.

"How long are you here?" she asked. Maybe she could call Vera tomorrow about the mind alteration. She wouldn't be happy with the longer timetable, but Leela would find a way to pay her back.

"Until I win," he replied.

She arched a brow. "Win?"

Amusement touched his handsome face. "Take a walk with me and I'll show you."

This had to be related to that challenge she overheard whispers of in Hydria. She hadn't stuck around long enough to catch the details. "A sexy stranger asks me to follow him on a Brazilian beach," she mused, tapping her finger against her lips. "To accept or not to accept."

He placed his drink in the sand and leaned into her personal space. Her nipples hardened at the welcome heat bathing her exposed skin. *Oh, yes, closer, please.*

"You strike me as the kind of woman who can more than handle herself, Leela. Take a chance and live a little. This life is all about passion, and sometimes the best experiences occur between two people who hardly know one another."

She shivered as he boldly brushed his mouth over hers.

Such a tease, and yet sexy as fuck. And his chocolate gaze said he knew it too.

Balthazar thought himself the master of sex, but what he failed to realize was he'd just met the mistress of sexual arts. One crook of her finger would have him on his knees begging for more, and yet, he wanted to play.

All right. She'd indulge him for the afternoon and see where it went. Because if anyone understood this game, it was Leela. She invented it, after all. Over five hundred years before his birth.

She slid the straw between their mouths and took hold of it with her teeth. His gaze fell to her lips as she sucked the liquid slowly, her throat working with each swallow. Yes, her oral skills were well perfected and trained, and she demonstrated her knowledge thoroughly before finally setting the glass down beside his.

"Show me what you intend to win, B."

His dark brown eyes glimmered with promise as he stood and held out his hand again. "Come with me."

Energy sizzled between them once more as she accepted his help up from the chair. "Is that an invitation or a promise?" she asked, her opposite palm going to his chest.

"Such a talented mouth," he murmured.

If only he knew. "And I haven't even begun yet." She purposely used his words from earlier, which provoked a smile from him.

"I know." He picked up her book and read the sexy romance title with a grin. "Nice educational material."

Leela laughed. "Hardly. My imagination and experience far surpass the pages of that novel."

Balthazar's pupils dilated as he admired her black bikini top and thong bottom. "I'm keen on learning more."

"Play your cards right and you might."

"I've never dealt a bad hand in my life."

"There's a first time for everything." She trailed her fingers down his chest to the fine line of hair decorating his lower abdomen. What a fun path that would be to follow with her tongue, all the way to his impressive groin.

He caught her wrist and flattened her palm against the defined ridges of his stomach. "All of my firsts are well and truly done." His words served as a clever way of communicating his experience level while also giving her the opportunity to proclaim her own. As if she would make it that easy for him.

"Don't be so sure about that," she murmured, moving closer. "I might just surprise you."

"That's hardly a challenge I can refuse." He dropped the book into her bag and gently slipped the strap over her shoulder. "Can't have you losing that."

"A gentleman too?" She batted her eyes at him playfully. "This is almost too much."

Those dimples flashed again. "I look forward to hearing you say that in earnest later, love."

Oh, I think you might be the one saying that later, love…
"Careful or I'll hold you to that promise."

"I hope you do," he murmured, leading the way.
"Where are you from, Leela?"

She arched a brow. "Small talk?" After all that flirting?
"How disappointing."

Amusement touched his features. "Maybe I want to get
to know you better."

"Is that your typical approach? Warm up the female
with a few innocent questions, show some interest, maybe
even use the information later in conversation, and then
turn up the charm?"

He stopped walking and hooked an arm around her
waist to pull her to him. "No, sweetheart." His lips
whispered over hers. "I don't have an approach." Her
heart skipped a beat at the confidence in his tone.

Now *this?* This she liked.

"Yeah?" She grabbed his bare shoulders and gazed
directly into his sinful eyes. "And why is that?"

His palm moved to the back of her neck while the
other slid to her ass. "Because I don't require one." He
captured her mouth with a boldness that called to her
angelic soul. Oh, how Leela adored a man in control. An
experienced one was even better.

Her blood heated as he slowly parted her lips with his
tongue. So very, very sensual. She more than approved.

Too many males wanted to rush the experience and
display their dominance by fucking a woman's mouth, but
not Balthazar. He took his time exploring, caressing, and
learning with each stroke of his tongue against hers. She
returned the kiss in kind, offering him a hint of her skill—
just enough to entice and tease.

He applied the right amount of pressure against her
neck to assert his control while also offering a tenderness
very few men understood. She didn't question his
preferred position in the bedroom; however, his touch
implied he would yield to a woman's lead, to an extent. A

man like Balthazar would never be able to submit.

A sharp nip to her lip grounded her in the moment, forcing her to focus on the skilled mouth against hers. He was introducing her to a new level of seduction, one that stole the breath from her lungs and lit her insides on fire. His slow method melted into a hot invitation that she happily accepted.

He smiled against her mouth. "Now tell me where you're from, Leela."

A laugh escaped her as she shook her head. It'd been too long since a man had properly played with her that she couldn't help but indulge in the game. "Guess."

Balthazar's lips curled at the challenge. "Hmm." His palms ventured to her hips as his chocolate gaze intimately stroked her pale skin. "Your porcelain complexion, light eyes, and light hair suggest Irish or Nordic descent, but your accent doesn't match either. In fact, your accent is very *other*." His grip tightened. "Which is why I asked about your origin."

Ah, the truth, then. He knew she was something different, just not quite what, and he wanted a hint. All right. She could give him that. "The South Pacific." *On a cluster of islands hidden from the world by runes. Good luck finding it.*

"You must avoid the elements," he replied, clearly skeptical.

"Hardly." She tilted her head back and grinned up at the sun through her sunglasses. "I just never tan. Or burn. Always pale."

His thumbs traced the band of her thong that ran across her hips. "I bet I can redden your skin rather nicely, Leela." He continued his exploration downward by following the triangle of fabric along the crease of her thighs. "In fact, I think you'll blush beautifully."

His words lit a fire in her lower belly, igniting all sorts of sparks within. *Oh, he's good. Very, very good.*

Leela brushed her lips over his. "Or maybe it'll be you

162

blushing, B." She winked as she stepped back and fixed the strap of her bag on her shoulder. "Weren't you going to show me something?"

"Indeed I was," he murmured, his eyes twinkling. "Which is your favorite—waffles or pancakes?"

Oh, that silly debate. She knew just how to answer him. "Waffles. No contest."

Balthazar smiled. "Excellent. This way, please."

CHAPTER TWO

The beauty beside Balthazar was an enigma. He couldn't read her mind or her emotions, and she returned his flirtations with the skill of a woman who knew her opponent well.

So who was she, really? He intended to find out. She thought to toy with him, which he happily allowed. She was a gorgeous woman, after all. But he would uncover her secrets, even if it meant losing this weekend's challenge.

He led her down the path toward the hotel pool where the festivities were taking place. His mission had been to scout the beach and find new players. Her alluring form had captured his attention, then he'd caught her quiet mind.

Definitely not human.

But she wasn't an Ichorian either; otherwise, she never would have allowed him to kiss her as he had on the beach moments ago.

So what are you, sweetheart?

A being from the South Pacific. Right. As if he believed that. She could be a fledgling, in which case Luc would want to recruit her. Or maybe she possessed a rune like Stas's, except Stas's mark blocked Ichorian gifts, not Hydraian talents.

Did that mean Leela could block both?

Mmm, maybe. Regardless, Balthazar would enjoy searching for physical evidence of a rune on her later—with his tongue.

"You're still thinking about where I'm from," she murmured. "I didn't lie to you."

He grinned. "Actually, I was considering all the ways to explore you later. Orally."

She didn't blush the way most women would. Instead, she glanced at him with approval bright in her gaze. "Perhaps I'll be the one exploring you."

He squeezed her hand. "We both know there's no 'perhaps' about it, sweetheart." Her mouth would be on him again very soon, and he showed her that with his eyes.

A squeal pierced the air as they rounded the corner, capturing Leela's attention. Jay had just tossed two women into the pool and followed them in with a splash that soaked a few of the dancers nearby. They jumped on him in the water in a flirtatious manner while two more joined from the stairs.

"B!" Jacque waved from his position near the bar. Several of the Guardians had followed them to Brazil, all with the purpose of protecting their respective Elders. And Jacque had provided their transportation via teleportation.

Balthazar winked at the man and searched for Luc.

"You wanted to show me a party?" Leela asked, her bluish-green eyes on the crowd.

"Not exactly." He pressed his lips to her ear. "How do

165

you feel about maple-flavored liquor?"

"Depends." She turned so her mouth brushed his. "Will I be licking it off of you or someone else?"

"What's your preference?" he wondered, curious. She'd responded openly to him on the beach, but how far would she go?

"Both." No hesitation on her part.

His blood heated at the prospect of watching her with someone else. "I think that could be arranged."

She licked his bottom lip and pulled away with a wicked smile. "No arrangement needed, sweetheart. Watch and learn." She handed him her bag and sauntered across the deck toward the bar.

Balthazar didn't exactly have a type—he merely enjoyed sex—but Leela was undeniably stunning. Her shapely ass looked amazing in that thong bikini bottom, as did her long, athletic legs. Pair that with her ample breasts, thick, blonde hair, and beautiful face, and it was no wonder everyone in her path looked twice.

Thoughts of delight and desire mingled in the air in her wake, as even a few of the waitstaff turned to admire her.

"*Olá, B*," a curvy brunette murmured. Her mind reminded him of her name. *Yasmin*. He'd met her in the lobby shortly after checking in at the reception desk and had recommended she meet him by the pool with her friends.

All four of the Brazilian women surrounded him in a variety of colorful bikinis that more than revealed their alluring assets. And yet, he found his gaze straying back to the black swimsuit caressing pale skin by the bar. Leela was bent over, chatting up the bartender, while several onlookers admired her flawless ass. Most women in his experience would be blushing or nervous, but she owned the show without so much as batting an eye.

Yasmin and her flirty companions spoke fluent Portuguese to him while taking turns stroking his abdomen, arms, and back, and he politely returned the conversation. None of them seemed at all concerned by the bag in his hands, or the implications tied to it. Which he took to mean that they all shared his preference to entertain more than one woman or man at a time.

Leela turned toward him, her elbows going up on the bar behind her as she observed his interaction. No hint of jealousy sparked in her gaze, only curiosity, and what he wouldn't have given in that moment to be able to read her mind. Because fuck if she didn't look a little turned on by the scene before her.

Who is this woman? Balthazar couldn't remember the last time a person intrigued him in this manner.

One of the brunettes infiltrated his view by pressing her palm to his cheek and lifting to plant a kiss on his mouth. Tequila infused his senses as she licked his bottom lip. He grinned down at her and responded flirtatiously in Portuguese. She was beautiful, with her long, dark hair, matching eyes, and tan skin. But his interests returned to the bar, where Leela was lifting a tray of drinks.

The conversation around him quieted as she approached. Catty and jealous thoughts filled his mind from the Brazilian entourage, causing him to rethink his earlier assumption that they would be open to sharing. It seemed the four of them had already agreed to entertain him and they were not interested in adding a fifth.

Balthazar always did enjoy a challenge. *Let's see how far this goes.*

"Maple shots," Leela mused, lowering her tray of drinks to a table beside the pool. She explained the contents in fluent Portuguese—much to the shock of their companions—and surveyed each woman from head to toe.

Balthazar introduced them all by plucking the various names from their minds and listened as each of the females evaluated the situation. Two of them were thinking about finding Luc, including Yasmin. But her thoughts shifted as Leela stepped into her personal space and tucked a strand of dark hair behind the woman's ear.

Who is she? Yasmin wondered. *Oh, but she's quite beautiful...* Interest flared in her pupils as Leela stepped closer.

Balthazar cocked his head to the side, intrigued. *What are you planning, little minx?*

Her quiet mind both enthralled and infuriated him. He'd never experienced this before—all mental pathways were open to him. Except hers.

"It's my understanding that these drinks are best enjoyed between two people," she murmured in Portuguese. "Would you be open to a little... experimentation?" Leela continued to fondle Yasmin's hair while she spoke, trailing the strand down to her breast and up again. Yasmin's nipples pebbled in response, her arousal touching his emotive senses.

He couldn't have executed that move any better himself, and that she chose to perform it on a female who clearly had no interest was all the more arousing.

Yasmin swallowed, her ebony eyes clouding with lust. Balthazar couldn't see Leela's expression, but from what he gathered from Yasmin's internal chatter, it was quite the sight.

"No pressure." Leela ran her finger down the woman's side and across her flat stomach. "I just thought it might be fun." Her perfect Brazilian dialect caused him to smile.

This was no ordinary woman, not by a long shot. Discovering her secrets would be even more enjoyable than proving pancakes were superior to waffles.

"Yes," Yasmin breathed, nodding. "Okay."

The two words were in accented English, but the litany of thoughts that followed were all in her native tongue. Through his connection to her mind, he learned that she'd never truly experimented with a woman before, apart from sharing men with her friends. Apparently, she never engaged in more than a kiss with her companions, and those were always meant to seduce, not to please. Yet, she admitted to herself that she found Leela attractive, something Balthazar found quite amusing. He had enjoyed seducing several males with the same limited experiences in the past.

It was amazing what a person did when they dropped societal pretenses and just *lived*. Two millennia ago, no one cared about sexual preferences. They merely experienced whatever they wanted. He truly missed that era.

Leela turned to him. "Ready for a new experience?" she asked in English this time.

His lips twitched. "You sound quite sure that it'll be something I've never seen."

"Oh, I'm certain."

This would be entertaining. "Give it your best shot, sweetheart." *Pun intended.*

Her eyes gleamed with the challenge. "You may want to sit down for this."

"I prefer to be intimately involved."

"Suit yourself." She brushed a kiss against the corner of his mouth. "I'll go easy on you since it's your first time."

He chuckled as he set her bag down beside the tray. "I appreciate that."

Leela was actually sort of cute thinking she could possibly introduce him to something new. Little did she realize the more than three thousand years of experience he carried under his belt.

He caught her hip as she started to turn and threaded his fingers through her hair. "Hold on, sweets." His mouth sealed over hers in a subtle reminder of who mastered whom here. Because while he could appreciate her vast erotic knowledge, his surpassed hers by many, many years.

By the time he finished, her pupils were dilated with arousal and her cheeks were flushed a pretty shade of pink. "I knew you would blush beautifully," he murmured against her lips. His tongue dipped inside for a final dance that she reciprocated in kind.

"I'm so going to enjoy this," she whispered.

"Me too."

"I know." She nipped his chin and smiled at him with her eyes. "Take notes."

A laugh caressed him inside. "Sure, sweetheart."

Yasmin had considerably cooled off during their exchange and appeared less certain of her earlier acquiescence. Yet when Leela caressed the woman's arm, her inky gaze warmed.

A seductive skill, perhaps?

He leaned to the side for a better view as Yasmin lay down along the edge of the pool. Leela picked up two shot glasses and went to her knees gracefully beside the other woman.

Balthazar drew his thumb across his lower lip as the two females conversed in whispers. The other three women seemed intent on the show as well and huddled beside him, their minds racing with curiosity.

Yasmin shivered at whatever Leela said, and nodded.

Intriguing little minx.

"What am I missing?" Luc asked as he joined them at the pool's edge.

"I'm teaching Balthazar a lesson," Leela replied before Balthazar had a chance.

"Oh?" Luc cocked a brow at him. *Where did you find this one?* he asked without speaking out loud.

"At the beach," he replied.

And she's going to teach you a lesson about what? Luc wondered.

Balthazar shrugged. "She seems to think she has me beat in this game."

"Fascinating." Luc folded his arms and eyed the two females with great interest. "Color me intrigued."

Leela placed a shot glass between Yasmin's thighs, right up against her sweet spot, which elicited a slight squirm from the female on the ground.

I love her already, Luc said through the mental pathways.

"Yep," Balthazar replied. If Jayson wasn't busy

entertaining several women in the pool, he would have called his best friend over for the show. Because he had a feeling this was going to be a sight to behold. "Where's Alik?" He searched for the telepath's mind as he asked, and found him wandering the beach. Alone. "Never mind."

He'll come along when he's ready.

Balthazar nodded, agreeing. Alik wouldn't turn down an evening of pleasure, but they all knew he didn't truly enjoy it. Not like he once did.

Leela poured the second maple shot in a line down Yasmin's body, starting from the base of her neck and all the way down to the woman's bikini bottoms. The stickiness of the liquid helped it stay somewhat it place, which was the design of Luc's creation.

Excellent, his oldest friend thought, mentally patting himself on the back for his concoction working as expected.

Balthazar was too intent on Leela's ass to respond. She bent over Yasmin's prone form and took the woman's mouth in a kiss that raised several eyebrows around them, including his own. His cock attempted to persuade him to join, but he was a man of patience. And he desperately wanted to see how far she intended to go.

Yasmin moaned as Leela left her mouth and began a path down the female's neck to the liquid painting her body. That pretty pink tongue darted out to catch the first drop, eliciting a groan from Yasmin that attracted several onlookers.

Waffles or pancakes? Luc wondered.

"Waffles," Balthazar murmured, his throat dryer than it should be.

Damn, Luc replied.

The whole point was to seduce a woman into changing her mind, which meant Leela qualified for his side of the game since Balthazar preferred pancakes. Not that he really cared anymore. He just wanted to fuck the woman until dawn at this point, and then determine her origins.

Yasmin shuddered as Leela trailed the shot between her breasts, her skin erupting in goose bumps. The intense signs of arousal, coupled with the woman's indecent thoughts, indicated she was maybe a minute away from coming. That was an impressive feat, considering Leela had hardly even touched her. But apparently, her tongue felt like *heaven personified*—according to Yasmin— something Balthazar would experience later.

Chants of praise erupted in the mental pathways, surprising him more.

No. She was going to come in a matter of seconds.

Leela dipped her tongue in the woman's belly button and ventured lower. Her chin barely brushed Yasmin's sex on her way to the shot glass. As her plump lips enclosed the rim, Yasmin arched off the ground on an impressive scream while Leela tilted the contents back into her throat to swallow in one go. She sat on her ankles to admire her handiwork before tilting her head back to meet Balthazar's gaze. He stared down at her with a grin he couldn't help display.

"Execution was a nine, but the orgasm bumped you up to a ten." Because to bring Yasmin to the point of climax so quickly without even really touching her? Yeah, that required skill. He was definitely impressed. "But I'm not inexperienced when it comes to female-on-female action, so you haven't introduced me to anything new yet."

"Come here." She beckoned him with a finger.

She thinks to tame you, Luc joked.

Balthazar smirked as he knelt beside her for fun. An alluring woman in a thong bikini wanted him to join her and another woman? He was an intelligent man, not a stupid one.

"Shock me, sweetheart," he encouraged.

She wrapped her palm around his neck and brought him in for a kiss. Electricity hummed through his veins and went straight to his groin, hardening his cock to a painful degree.

Slow down, some logical part of him urged—the one tied to his ample experience.

He ignored it. Couldn't focus. Couldn't even think beyond the surge of arousal thickening his blood and spiraling downward to his balls. He needed her. Right now. Beneath him.

Fuck, he couldn't remember the last time anyone had done this to him. Her touch was addicting, and yet she only caressed his neck.

What is happening to me?

Leela bit his lip and grinned with her eyes as Yasmin climaxed again beside them.

How…?

Balthazar pulled back to find Leela's palm lying on the scrap of fabric between Yasmin's thighs.

Oh… Oh, she's magical. Barely even flicked my…

He blinked out of the woman's thoughts and met Leela's expectant gaze. "Surprised yet?" she taunted.

Yes. And very alarmed. Because she'd clearly used some sort of mental ability to trigger Yasmin's orgasm, as well as ensnare him in an erotic trap. He'd been seconds from losing his steadfast control and taking her on the deck without consideration of anyone around them.

"Who are you?" he demanded, his voice lethally serious. Now that the fog of desire had lifted, he could see her clearly—still alluring and fuckable—but she was also very aware of her unique qualities.

She's not human. So what is she?

Despite his commanding tone, the little minx grinned. "Wouldn't you like to know?" She brushed her lips over his again. "Find me later and maybe I'll tell you. Maybe I won't."

CHAPTER THREE

"There." Balthazar nodded with his chin. "At the bar."

Leela sat on a stool with her long legs crossed elegantly and pointed toward a broad-shouldered male who seemed far too interested in her cleavage. Balthazar wasn't concerned. He would be the one removing that tight little black dress tonight. The three-inch stilettos, however, he'd probably leave on her.

"Nothing," Alik said, confirming all of their suspicions. "I'm throwing a lot of power at her, and she's not even flinching."

Luc rubbed his jaw as he considered the beauty before them. She hadn't noticed them yet because her back was to the entrance.

"Fledgling?" Balthazar guessed. He'd already told them about the passionate kiss on the beach. They all agreed she

174

couldn't be an Ichorian.

"It's the only option," Luc agreed as Leela laughed at whatever the dude beside her had said. "Because she's definitely not a Seraphim either."

Balthazar snorted. "Right." The Seraphim were ancient beings renowned for their stoicism. Not that he'd ever actually met one. Most considered their kind to be extinct, or perhaps in a state of eternal rest. Regardless, there was no way Leela could be one, considering her reactions to him.

Alik folded his arms and leaned against the wall. "The sensible approach would be to torture the details out of her. However, I assume the plan is for B to seduce the information from her instead, yes?"

"My way is more fun," Balthazar pointed out. And after experiencing what her touch could do at the pool, he craved more. "An in-depth analysis of her abilities is considered practical, right, Luc?"

Their leader nodded. "Definitely. In fact, I should probably join you." He tilted his head to the side as Leela uncrossed and recrossed her long legs. "I wonder what we could accomplish together."

Balthazar rubbed his jaw, considering. Luc was an excellent wingman—his favorite maybe, besides Jay. But something about this challenge felt personal. She dared him with her words earlier. *Find me later and maybe I'll tell you. Maybe I won't.*

Oh, she would definitely talk. Right after he finished exploring her seductive talent to the fullest extent.

"I want her to myself," Balthazar admitted.

Surprise filtered through Alik's and Luc's minds while their expressions remained carefully neutral.

"She intrigues me," Balthazar added. "I'm all for sharing after I figure her out. Besides"—he clapped Luc on the shoulder—"she prefers waffles. I intend to change her mind."

Luc's emerald gaze warmed. "She's like the perfect

woman. Seductive, possibly immortal, understands the importance of geometric shapes, and gorgeous."

Alik rolled his eyes. "Right. Am I excused?"

"No," Balthazar replied. "I need you to handle the Brazilian quartet I left by the pool earlier. They're not pleased, and you know how I feel about leaving my conquests unsatisfied."

"That sounds like a job for Luc or Jay more than me, B."

True. Alik preferred quick and dirty, and while he always reciprocated, it lacked heart. That didn't stop the rest of them from trying to convince him to indulge just a little.

"Jay's busy entertaining several others," Luc said. "And I promised two other women a maple bath."

"Here." Balthazar handed Alik the key Yasmin had left for him. "Just tell them I sent you. I'm certain they won't be disappointed. Brooding is sexy right now. They'll love you."

Alik flipped him off but accepted the plastic card. "Fuck you."

"You're welcome," Balthazar replied with a wink.

The telepath shook his head and stalked off after Balthazar gave him the room number. "Do you really have a maple bath planned?" he asked.

Luc chuckled. "No, but I will soon."

"Clever."

"He needs to get laid more."

Balthazar agreed with a nod. "You'd think he grew up in this religious era, not the one prior."

"Right?" Luc blew out a breath. "I so miss the Roman period, and the Greeks before it."

"Me too." The lack of inhibitions—where humans were driven by desire and indulgence, not the false idea of morals—was considered acceptable, not sinful. Alas, those days were ancient history.

Leela tossed her head back on a laugh at that moment,

grabbing the attention of several at the bar. Sexual energy radiated off of her so strongly that it practically beckoned him to approach.

"A succubus," he mused to Luc. "That's what she is."

Amusement touched his oldest friend's features and his voice as he said, "If one existed, maybe. But I suspect she's a fledgling with a power we'll all enjoy."

"I'll go find out and let you know."

"Please do."

Balthazar's lips quirked upward. "We'll touch base in the morning. I suspect this one is going to require my attention throughout the night."

"I'll be well occupied," Luc replied, his focus already shifting to the people in the room. A handful of them were actually Hydraians, all there with the purpose of guarding their Elders, but Luc wouldn't touch them. His status as the leader of their kind created a conflict when it came to personal relationships; hence, Luc avoided them completely and favored one-night stands with humans.

"Enjoy your evening, Luc." Innuendo filled his tone, causing his friend to grin.

"You too, B."

Luc wandered off, leaving B alone to admire his quarry. Her fingertips were lightly tracing the forearm of the man beside her, and those long stems of hers were crossed toward him as well. Both signs of sexual interest, which the dark-haired male reciprocated in kind with his almond-shaped eyes. She'd chosen a handsome one with a nice smile and a strong jawline.

Balthazar favored women; however, men worked too. If Leela wanted to share, he'd be game. Of course, he'd run the show in every way.

He approached her from behind and wrapped his arms around her sexy little waist while meeting the surprised gaze of the male beside her. Aggression gave way to astonishment in his thoughts, followed by a quick summary of all his perceived shortcomings when compared to Balthazar.

Pity. It seemed confidence wasn't one of the man's strengths.

"Hello, sweetheart." Balthazar lowered his chin to her shoulder as he hugged her from behind. "Did you find us a playmate?"

She hummed in approval as she tilted her head to brush a kiss against his cheek. "I hoped you would find me."

"Does that mean I get a prize?" he asked against her neck.

The mortal beside them stirred uncomfortably, his hand rising to grab the bartender's attention. He wanted to settle his bill and flee. Apparently, the idea of joining Balthazar and Leela in bed intimidated him. Perhaps a demonstration on what he would be missing was in order.

Balthazar knotted his fingers in Leela's silky hair, pulled her head back, and took her mouth in a sensual kiss. No hard or fast moves, but smooth and sexual ones designed to rouse an audience. Her tongue reciprocated with several slow, seductive strokes against his own. This was a lesson in patience and skill, where they both existed as masters in the class.

"Mmm," he murmured against her mouth. "How I adore a skilled woman."

She grazed his lower lip with her teeth. "You have no idea what you're up against."

"Likewise, sweetheart."

She grabbed the collar of his black dress shirt to hold him to her. "Oh, lover, trust me when I say I definitely do and that's the only reason I'm still sitting here."

Was that a hint of some kind? A subtle way of saying she already knew of his reputation, or perhaps even more? He'd never met her before; of that he was certain. He might experience a different woman every night, but he remembered their faces and bodies, and this one was new to him.

Leela twisted in her stool to face him as she stood—every inch of her body brushing his—and put her arms around his neck. "There's a party out near the beach."

"You want to dance." Not a question, but a statement.

She nodded. "With you."

In this dress that barely covered her ass? "Let's go."

Leela glanced over her shoulder at the empty seats. "I guess he didn't want to play after all."

"We can find another that better suits you, if you want," Balthazar replied, his hands caressing her hips. "I'm flexible." He meant that figuratively and literally.

"You'll do for now." She grabbed his wrists and guided his palms up her sides to her breasts and then ever so slowly down the middle. It resulted in a slight gap between their bodies, yet it felt as if they were still touching with the way electricity raced between them. Her hand wrapped around one of his as she stepped to the side. Arousal turned her gaze a dark forest green, but rather than lead the way toward an elevator upstairs, she pulled him toward a set of patio doors.

His blood whirred with excitement at her bold maneuvers. This was a woman who knew what she wanted and took it. Her heels clicked against the stone flooring as she led him outside and down a rocky path.

The moon hung overhead, lending a sexy appeal to the already romantic evening air. Smooth beats and rhythmic sounds came from up ahead, followed by an array of people all enjoying the ambience of the night. Soft lights lit up a nearby bar, a few high top tables stood in the sand, and a hotel pool glistened beyond it.

My kind of atmosphere, he mused as hedonistic thoughts prickled his conscious. Dancing served as foreplay to sex, and some of the members out here were taking that notion to a sensuous level. Balthazar approved.

Leela weaved through the dancers to a darker spot near the middle and started to turn. He caught her hip with his free hand, holding her in place as he pressed his chest to her back. It was his turn to lead.

He skimmed her neck with his mouth and flattened their entwined hands against her stomach, with his on top of hers. His other palm remained on her waist as he guided her to the beat playing overhead.

"You imply that you know me," he said against her ear. "But do you know what I am?"

She lifted her free arm and wrapped her slender fingers around the back of his neck while her hips swayed against him. The subtle distraction curved his lips upward.

"I'm not that easy, sweetheart," he warned. "But if you want to play, we'll play."

Her nails bit into the skin of his nape in a sign of encouragement.

Balthazar grinned against her neck. He always assessed his partner's level of skill before unleashing his sensuality. Most situations required him to hold back, but not this one. He sensed Leela could handle anything he threw at her, and that only excited him more.

The song shifted into a heavier beat that thudded through his veins. He increased their tempo to match the rhythm while keeping her hand trapped between his palm and her abdomen. She met him move-for-move, her ass brushing his groin in a tantalizing manner that excited his instincts. It was purposeful and well practiced, and it alluded to the night they had ahead of them.

He took control of their pace by spinning her around without warning and catching her in a dip that brushed her light hair against the floor. Her dilated pupils captured his as he slowly pulled her upright against him. The faint blush decorating her cheeks urged him to twirl her again, but this time she added a sexy little kick to it and wrapped her calf around his thigh.

A few more whirls caused the other dancers to part around them. He ignored everyone, his sight only for the woman in his arms. Leela thought to best him at one of his favorite sports—seduction by dancing. Oh, how much she had to learn.

He threw her upward and caught her hips as her legs spread on either side of his waist. Her lips were a hairsbreadth away from his own, her heart hammering against his chest. "More," she panted.

"Yeah?" He swung her around his body with one arm beneath her knees and the other guiding her shoulders. Applause broke out in the crowd as she landed deftly on her heels. He blocked their thoughts and focused on the beauty grinding up against him. Her gaze dared him to continue.

"Who are you?" he asked, mesmerized.

"Leela." She winked. "Now do it again."

He chuckled and did as she requested, whirling her with the beat, lifting her, dipping her, and pressing his body intimately against hers with each move.

Pure, honest foreplay.

It could only be improved by nudity, though he enjoyed the tantalizing hints of what lay beneath the clothes. Sometimes barriers provided just the right amount of friction to make things interesting.

He slid his thigh between hers during one of her more intricate moves, eliciting a delectable little gasp from her. She dug her nails into his exposed forearms—he'd rolled his sleeves to the elbows earlier—and her calf once again wrapped around his jean-clad leg. He grabbed her thigh and slid his palm upward beneath the fabric of her dress.

Of course she wore nothing underneath. That explained all the passionate vibes around them; his Leela had given the audience quite the show. And her expression said she didn't care at all.

An exhibitionist too? Perfection on heels.

If Balthazar believed in fate, he might think someone created her just for him. Because she was without a doubt his kind of woman.

He pivoted her once more, placing her back at his front again while his hand slid from one hip to the other beneath her dress. She tilted her head back and to the side, her alluring eyes locking with his as he slowed their movements to an intimate pace.

Mmm. That aroused gleam dilating her pupils was quite lovely. How much hotter could he make her burn?

He lowered his mouth to hers and traced the seam of her lips with his tongue. Fire licked through his veins as she opened for him, tempting him to deepen the kiss. He took advantage of the angle and explored her the way he preferred, all the while maintaining a perfect rhythm with the beat.

Her skin burned beneath his fingers as he drew circles against her hip with his thumb. His fingers spanned her upper thigh, close enough to know she kept herself well groomed. Not that he expected otherwise after seeing her in that tiny thong earlier.

Fuck, she had a perfect ass. His hard cock agreed as he pressed against her. The things he *would* do to her tonight…

She caught his bottom lip between her teeth and gave it a sharp tug. A demand for more. He grinned against her mouth and wrapped a hand around her throat while his other ventured to the warm, wet flesh between her legs.

So ready for him and he hadn't truly started yet.

But he would now.

Leela arched against him and moaned as his tongue dipped inside to dance with hers. His intentions were obvious to everyone around them, yet hidden beneath the guise of a dance. Where was his hand? What was he doing? The thoughts were endless, and the fantasies only added fuel to the already simmering fire.

His finger slipped through her damp slit as his thumb found her clit. He caught her gasp with his mouth and tightened his grip around her neck. She responded with a shiver that told him everything he needed to know. While Leela played the part of sensual mistress well, a submissive lurked beneath her confident skin. And oh, how he would exploit that later to meet both their needs.

He pinched her sensitive bud, then massaged it as she trembled against him. His cock ached and pulsed, begged him to take this to the next level, but he needed to see her fall apart. Just for a moment.

His lips went to her ear while he slid two fingers deep into her channel to that spot that made all women weak in the knees. "Can you feel their eyes on you, watching your body quiver against mine? They all know what I'm doing to you, Leela. Everyone wants to watch you come undone."

She practically purred in response, her hips moving as she shamelessly rode his hand. Her pulse quickened beneath his lips as he trailed hot, openmouthed kisses up and down the slender column of her neck.

"Come for me so I can taste you," he murmured. "I want them all to see you shatter, so when I'm licking my fingers afterward, they know it's your essence on my skin."

Her groan vibrated his chest, and he caught her mouth in another searing kiss meant to disable. He'd held back before, slowly learning her tastes and preferences, and now he used them all against her. The pace between her thighs increased as he applied subtle pressure to her pleasure point.

There it is, that subtle squirming. You're mine now, Lee.

The last vestiges of her control unraveled as an orgasm ripped through her body. She caressed Balthazar's lips with his name over and over, her body quivering unabashedly for the audience around them. They all knew, their minds blossoming with varying states of arousal and lust, suggesting a new type of party was about to begin.

All because of the gorgeous woman melting against him.

He removed his hand from her sensitive flesh and lifted it to his mouth, just as he said. His eyes closed as he tasted her, so sweet and fresh, and positively addicting. He would be devouring her in his bed after this. In full. For hours.

She turned and caught his wrist, then went onto her toes to lick his other finger clean. Flames engulfed him from head to toe as he pictured her doing that to his cock. Her mouth was unbelievably wicked and oh-so talented.

Balthazar gazed down at her, inviting her to do her worst, and smiled when she slipped a finger into the belt loop of his jeans. She tugged him forward as she stepped backward toward a bar dusted in shadows. The source of music and drinks came from the opposite end of the dance floor, while this side appeared to only be used during daylight. That meant it was mostly vacant, but with a very public view.

His lips curled. It didn't take a mind reader to know where this was headed.

She nudged him onto a stool and stepped between his spread legs, hands on his thighs. "My turn," she said, her voice husky.

The hushed bass of the song playing nearby matched the rhythm of his heart. "Whatever you want, sweetheart."

Her fingers trailed up to the top of his jeans. "Oh, I know what I want." She deftly unfastened his belt, popped open the button, and slid down the zipper.

He grinned at her heated expression. "You're not the only one who prefers to go without underwear, Leela." It made everything easier, including seduction in public settings.

She licked her lips. "I approve."

He glanced at the delicate hand looming just above his shaft. "That's my line."

Leela wrapped her fingers around him and stroked him from head to base. "Is it?"

"Yes." He lifted his elbows to the counter behind him and relaxed against it. "Keep going." *Because it feels like fucking heaven.*

Much to his chagrin, she released him. And damn if it didn't hurt a little. Balthazar loved a good game of delayed

184

gratification, but Leela possessed a magical touch and he wanted more. So much more.

"I have something else in mind." She stepped out of his legs and pushed them closed while leaving him intimately exposed. "Don't move."

He grinned, intrigued. "All right. Do your best."

Her eyes sparkled as she met his gaze. "I'll need all weekend for that."

"Fine by me, sweets."

She leaned in to brush her lips over his. "I'm about to blow your mind, B."

His dick liked the sound of that. "I'm still waiting, Lee."

CHAPTER FOUR

Leela

So cocky, and yet well deserved. Especially after that demonstration on the dance floor. God, Balthazar had lit her on fire like no one else ever had. Leela had expected it after witnessing the male in action on several occasions, but to experience it was an entirely different entity.

An inferno climaxed inside of her just at the sight of him lounging lazily before her, fully erect. Leela had seen thousands of naked males in her life, but none were quite as exquisite as this one. He truly was perfect in every way.

Not that she would admit it out loud. Balthazar was arrogant enough.

She drew her nails up and down his jean-covered thighs, causing his gaze to smolder.

Sexy. That was the best way to describe him in that moment with those hooded chocolate eyes, slight quirk of his mouth, and obvious interest only inches from her hand.

They could be interrupted at any second, which only further spurred her on. So few partners possessed the confidence and stamina for an act like this, but she knew without a doubt that Balthazar would be up to the task.

Leela grabbed the counter on either side of him to stabilize herself as she stepped onto the wooden struts of his stool and straddled him.

"I like where this is going," he said, not moving as she requested.

She thought he might, because she did too. Very much so.

Her mouth hovered over his as she slowly and expertly lowered herself onto his gorgeous cock. He filled her deliciously, inch by inch, until she seated herself on him completely. All without using her hands. And she'd managed to keep it mostly hidden from their audience by using her dress. Of course, they all *knew* what they were up to. The collective arousal of their audience rolled over her skin, heightening and intensifying everything. She could elicit orgasms from all of them with a switch of her mind, send everyone into a fit of pleasure-filled screams, but she reserved her strength for Balthazar.

Not for their first time, though. She wanted to feel every move without provocation. Very few could please her without a little mental foreplay, marking this a unique experience for her. And she intended to drink her fill of him first.

"You feel amazing," she whispered as she allowed herself a subtle thrust to deepen the physical connection between them.

He merely smiled, waiting.

Leela released the counter and dug her nails into his shoulders instead. He didn't even flinch or shift an inch, still abiding by her request.

Such restraint.

She could feel him pulsing inside of her. So hot and ready, and very, very intimate. Her body responded in kind, sending a flood of heat to her core. This man evoked an almost foreign reaction in her. She was ready to come again without any real foreplay, merely because he sat beneath her.

Her nipples chaffed against her dress, begging to meet his mouth, his hands, anything, and fuck, every other part of her body desired him too.

It had to be because she knew what he could do, that he possessed more talent and experience than everyone else in existence except her.

Oh, how she longed to master the master, to teach him something new when no one else could. And maybe a tiny part of her hoped he might show her a new trick or two as well. Immortality was a long, long time. Boredom threatened them all, insanity too. Leela wanted to live, to feel, to *be*. Could Balthazar aid her in that pursuit? Even if just for the weekend?

Only one way to find out.

She threaded her fingers through his thick hair and pulled him impossibly closer.

"Touch me," she demanded against his mouth. "I want to know what you can do. What you can *really* do."

"I thought you'd never ask." His tongue parted her lips in a domineering way that set her blood on fire just as his arm came around her lower back to force her into a different angle. The head of his cock hit her insides in the most delicious way, causing her to rock back on him with a groan that he promptly swallowed.

Oh God.

He could move.

Really, really, move.

Even seated on a stool, he still managed to pound into her with a force that stoked her inner flames. She gave up trying to analyze it and gave in to the power of *him*. Of Balthazar, and the way he dominated her body with knowing strokes inside her.

And oh, yes, his palm, exploring her breast, pinching her nipple, and squeezing at precisely the right moment. *Yes, yes, just like that*.

The arm around her lower back kept her from falling as he fucked her blind. She was on top, but there was no mistaking who was in charge here. And she allowed it. Accepted it. *Loved* it.

As did the crowd.

Oh Christ, she could feel all their admiring gazes and lust-filled desires. It intoxicated her senses, pushing her closer to the edge of infinite pleasure.

Balthazar had to feel it too, with his gifts, yet control radiated from him. Despite all her expectations, he yet again proved her wrong.

The perfect mate, she thought blindly. He truly would be her ideal, if love existed for someone like her.

Not now. Not with him driving into her so hard, so incredibly... Fuck.

She clung to his biceps, her world splintering as his mouth swallowed her screams. The orgasm had hit her out of nowhere, fracturing her insides and sending her spiraling into the clouds.

Misting, she realized. *Shit*. She stopped, but, holy hell, that had taken her to a new plane of existence. Grounded again, she returned in time to watch Balthazar come undone inside her. He'd still been able to *feel* her, even when she'd gone ethereal. That shouldn't have been possible, though she'd not done that before during sex.

Something new.

Oh, and the man even came beautifully.

This wasn't fair at all.

Ecstasy darkened his eyes to a smolder as his lips parted on her name. His muscles tensed around her, eliciting delicious little spasms down below that sent her spiraling into another haze of arousal.

Intoxicating. That's what this was. Explosive too.

She kissed him to stop herself from saying something she couldn't take back. His ego didn't require stroking. Neither did hers. They both knew this was amazing. She saw it in his eyes right before attacking his mouth.

He returned the kiss while continuing to move inside her, his arm still around her back. They needed to switch locations. Their audience was going to explode in a sexual frenzy if this continued, and Leela knew the local authorities would frown upon that.

Granted, Balthazar could just manipulate their emotions, but alas, no. She wanted him to herself.

At least for the night.

No energy spent anywhere else. Or on anyone else.

Only each other.

She smiled against his lips, an idea forming at the thought. Oh, this would be delicious fun. He introduced her to his prowess, so why not return the favor?

"I like that look, Leela," he murmured. "What are you thinking?"

"It's hard not knowing, isn't it?" She nipped his chin as she found her footing to stand.

His hands went to her hips, holding her to him. "We're not done yet."

"Oh, don't I know it." She slid upward and paused with her hands on his shoulders. "Want to see what I can do now?"

Surprise briefly flitted through his features. How cute. He thought she'd already demonstrated for him.

"That was just my body, lover," she whispered while stepping onto the sand-covered concrete. "Spread." She tapped his thighs and he obliged without question, allowing her to move in between his legs again. "Ready?"

"Always."

Her heart raced at the unhindered boldness in his voice. It was laced with a demand, as were the hands still grasping her hips. He didn't seem ready to let go—a feeling they shared. She wrapped her fingers around his

190

wrists and guided his palms upward.

"Feel free to hold on, lover. You might need it."

Leela didn't wait for him to reply as she bent her head and took his thick head into her mouth. He hissed out a breath, his fingers going to her hair as her tongue licked the salty essence from the tip.

She adored the taste of uninhibited sex, and it coated his member all the way to the base. Leela sucked him clean, luxuriating in the beauty of their coupling. He fit her in every way. Provocative. Shameless. Perfect.

Her core pulsed with the need to feel him again, even as his warm seed trickled down her own thighs. This could so easily become an addiction.

One weekend, she promised herself. *That's all.*

And she had better make it worth her while. Starting with a proper introduction into what she could offer.

Her eyes locked with his as she pulled him deep into her throat. His grip tightened, his body tensing, but she knew he was nowhere near an orgasm, not after just coming inside her. Which was entirely the point.

She flattened her palms on his thighs as she dropped to her knees and held her breath while taking him impossibly deeper.

Then she unleashed her gift.

It hummed from her fingertips, quiet at first, as she pulsed sexual energy into him and infiltrated his very being with so much lust that she knew he wouldn't be able to see straight. His chocolate gaze widened, the only indication that he felt her intrusion, and then his body came to life beneath her touch.

She could rip the orgasm from him, but no, she wanted him to feel every sensation. Her tongue and mouth worked him while her power slithered through his veins, encouraging his climax to build faster and harder than ever before.

"Fuck," he whispered, his grip tightening in her hair. "What are you doing to me?"

She increased the intensity in response, causing his head to fall back on a groan. A countdown started in her thoughts. With each passing second, she upped the power a notch and watched him slowly lose his grasp on reality and succumb to overwhelming desire.

His hot seed hit the back of her throat as she reached the final number. It was a true crime for a man to taste this good, not that Leela was surprised. Everything about Balthazar surpassed expectations.

Most Seraphim referred to Ichorians and Hydraians as abominations. While Leela might agree to an extent, there was nothing disgraceful about this particular Hydraian. He resembled a god even when lost to the thrills of ecstasy, and he was staring down at her in complete awe now.

She let him go with a pop of her mouth and slowly stood. His hands went to her hips again, his grip stronger now.

"Worried I might disappear?" she asked coyly while carefully zipping up his pants. "We agreed to a weekend, lover. I've only just begun with you. Unless you think that was my best?"

His heated gaze ran over her slowly, thoroughly, cataloging every detail. "My suite has a kitchen."

"Are you suggesting we might be there a few days?"

"Yes." No hesitation.

"What about your challenge?"

"I have a new one." He smiled. "Want to play?"

She returned the amusement. "You know I do."

"Then let's go."

She stepped backward and held out her hand to help him up. He smirked even as he accepted the gesture, and then he used the link to tug her against his hard body. His lips met her ear. "You may have impressed me with your oral skills, sweetheart, but I'm far from exhausted. I want to see what else you can do."

"Likewise," she returned. "Now stop stalling and take me upstairs."

CHAPTER FIVE

B

Leela was a Seraphim.

No, not just a Seraphim, but an *emotional* Seraphim.

Balthazar almost didn't believe it, but the minds of those around them at the bar confirmed everything. Leela had gone ethereal mid-orgasm. He could feel her the entire time, even as her body flickered in and out of sight.

A Seraphim.

What an unreal experience. All of it. Including the mind-numbing orgasm she'd gifted him, using her very talented mouth. He required more of that, as well as a taste of his own.

He linked his fingers with hers as they walked with purpose through the lobby toward the elevators. Energy and heat simmered between them, neither of their needs near sated despite the interlude outside.

Balthazar desired a thorough introduction to her abilities and intended to repay the favor. All night. And along the way, he'd learn everything he could about her, while having a little fun in the process.

As soon as the doors closed, he pushed her up against the wall and took her mouth with a ferocity he rarely exuded. She responded in kind, threading her fingers through his hair and holding him as if he belonged to her.

This woman... *Fuck.* She'd undone him in a way he didn't know was possible. He had so many questions.

Who are you?

What else can you do?

Where are you really from?

Are there more of you?

He asked her with his tongue, and he swore she answered with, *Keep going and maybe I'll tell you.*

The ding of their arrival on his floor barely registered as he lifted her into the air, her legs wrapping around his waist, and he walked them in the general direction of his room.

Balthazar needed her naked. Now.

Her lips traveled to his neck, nibbling as she went, while he opened the door on his first try.

God, yes. Flames caressed his lower abdomen where she rubbed herself shamelessly against him. So wet. So fucking hot.

"Kitchen or wall, Lee?" He kicked the door closed with his foot.

"Both," she panted. "Definitely both."

"My kind of woman."

"My kind of man."

He grinned and set her on the marble counter. "I love this dress." He found the zipper at her back. "Let's not ruin it."

Leela drew her thumb down his buttons, her eyes radiating wicked intent. "You have more of these, right?" She hooked her fingers into his shirt and tugged it open, sending buttons flying. "Oops."

"Hmm." Someone was impatient. While he felt the same, he opted to ever so gently glide the zipper down, one divot at a time.

Her palms flattened against his undershirt and traveled lower to his jeans. Such deftly skilled hands. She had his belt undone and jeans unfastened before he hit the base of her spine.

He followed the loose fabric up to her shoulder blades and down again. "So soft," he murmured.

She grasped his still-hard cock. "Yes. It is." Her now-bare feet crept up his thighs, then pushed the fabric downward to reveal him completely. "And nicely proportioned as well."

His lips twitched. "You should see how I use it."

"Oh, I've already had my test-drive. I'm ready for another round whenever you are, lover."

He kicked off his shoes and pants and placed his palms on the counter on either side of her hips. "You need to experience the whole package, sweetheart. Not just my cock."

She raised a brow, her hand slowing its exploration of his shaft. "I'm listening."

His thumbs slid to her thighs, tracing the trim of her short dress. "My tongue is well exercised." He pushed the fabric higher, exposing her intimately. "Care for a demonstration?"

"I'm tempted."

He drew his finger through her damp folds while keeping his other hand on the marble surface beside her. "Are you?" He stopped at her entrance and leaned in as if to kiss her. "Remove your dress and lie back on your elbows," he said against her lips.

Her pupils flared. "Yes, sir." She released him to obey, pulling the black satin up over her head as he requested, before falling back—naked—onto the counter for his review. "Like what you see?" she asked, repeating the first words she spoke to him this morning.

He removed his ruined button-down and undershirt while she watched. "Do you?"

Her eyes raked over him slowly and thoroughly. "I was right. You do look better naked."

Balthazar smiled, enjoying this little game. "Likewise, sweetheart." Using his hands, he widened her legs and took a step back to take in every detail. *Utter perfection.* "Mmm, actually, you look amazing like this."

Her thighs tensed beneath his palms, and her tongue darted out to lick her lips. *So beautifully aroused.* Would she disappear again for him? Scream his name while in her ethereal state?

Only one way to find out.

He lightly skimmed his fingers upward to her hips and then higher to her breasts, tracing, memorizing every glorious inch of her soft skin. His stomach clenched at the sight, his own needs stirring deeply and readily inside of him.

Soon. Balthazar wanted her so turned on that she couldn't see straight. Leela seemed to think she knew him, and maybe she did, but he was known for surpassing expectations. And she leveled a challenge at him unlike any other.

He couldn't hear her thoughts, couldn't play with her emotions, and she clearly had her own seductive talents. This relied on pure sexual strength alone, which he had in spades.

Goose bumps pebbled beneath his featherlight touch, her body radiating approval. He explored her curves, her stomach, the center of her chest, all the while cataloging each of her tells. The hitch of her breath, the way her nipples tightened when he brushed the sides of her breasts, and the subtle clenching of her fists.

She wanted him to do more.

He wanted her desperate for it.

Fire danced in her gaze as he bent to nibble on her hip

bone—in that perfect spot most women didn't even know existed. Just a tiny bit of pressure… She arched into him, and he pressed her back down with a palm against her abdomen.

"Balthazar…"

"I do enjoy hearing my name spoken in such a manner," he murmured against her skin. He traced a path with his tongue along her lower belly and paused when he reached her other side. A tiny heart-shaped rune lingered beneath his mouth. He grinned against the familiar design—Stas had one on her lower back that repelled Ichorian gifts. Apparently, Leela's version protected her from Hydraian talents, and likely from Ichorian abilities as well.

It seemed his little Seraphim was filled with secrets, and maybe some answers too.

He nipped her again, this time holding her in place when she reacted.

"Fuck," she whispered, her head moving from side to side.

He hadn't even touched her intimately yet, and already he could sense the stirrings inside of her. It seemed her sexual energy was twofold, something she could unleash on her partner, but also a constant burning flame within. Fascinating.

Heat radiated from her core like a beacon, daring him to taste, but he moved upward instead to take one stiff peak into his mouth. He sucked. Hard. Her head fell back, her eyes closing, her lips parting, and damn if that wasn't a lovely picture. His cock readily agreed, eager to move this along, but this was about Leela. He wanted to give her an orgasm so intense that she lost control. Again.

Balthazar switched breasts, his teeth gently biting her along the way. A not-so-gentle pinch to her other nipple had her legs coming around his waist in an effort to force him closer.

He chuckled. "Need something, love?"

She growled low in her throat. "Tease."

He grabbed her hips and pulled her to the edge of the counter. His lips hovered over hers. "Tease," he repeated, pressing his aching dick against her wet and ready heat. "This is teasing," he corrected as his head expertly located her clit.

Leela grabbed his shoulders, her nails digging into his skin. "Now."

"Not yet." He kissed her softly, rocking his erection against her at just the right angle to please without allowing her to tip over into ecstasy. Her heels dug into his ass, encouraging him to move, but he maintained control. His tongue dipped inside to duel with hers, and oh, did she know how to indulge a man. Even in her half-blissed state, she still managed to seduce him with her clever mouth. He rewarded her by finding her entrance and thrusting inside once, twice, then pulled out of her again.

"Balthazar!" Her nails scraped down his back, drawing blood. "Fuck me."

"I intend to," he murmured, his mouth already traveling downward. "With my tongue."

She moaned, her hips flexing upward against his hands as he caught her and forced her back down. "Harder," she demanded.

He tightened his grip on her hip bones, enough to bruise, yet his little minx sighed contentedly.

Pain. Most immortals required it in some variation, and he definitely knew how to provide it. But first... His tongue met her slick folds, licking her deep and savoring the taste of her. So. Fucking. Good. He devoured her in his next pass, already addicted to the feel of her against his mouth and the little sounds of approval she made in response.

Shit, who is seducing whom here? His balls tightened in excitement, his cock throbbing for release.

Delicious.

Addicting.

Mine.

He stopped thinking and consumed her, allowing all his experience and knowledge to drive his instincts, and bathed in her resulting moans. His fingers joined the fun, his teeth nibbling her clit, as her body unraveled beneath his expert touch.

She screamed his name, but it wasn't good enough. He didn't stop, simply continued his assault, while her body trembled and vibrated beneath his mouth. Electricity sizzled between them, her hands on his head, urging him never to stop, her body beading with sweat—fuck, he'd never seen anything like it.

A goddess.

Such perfection.

Her lips parted on another moan, her eyes closing, her very essence flickering in and out of existence before him, but he could still *taste* her, could still *feel* her.

A Seraphim in the throes of passion was a sight to behold. He swore there were wings. Purple and black feathers, visible and then gone in an instant. Actual fire—blue fire—surrounding her, but not burning him. And onward she fell, his name a benediction in the air as she completely shattered.

Two orgasms? Three? He lost count, didn't care, not with the magnificent sight of her casting a permanent spell over him. His jaw actually ached, something that had not happened to him in several thousand years, and he welcomed the change. The new experience. Her.

He'd been living all these centuries thinking pleasure and sex were all that mattered. But this moment changed him irrevocably. Balthazar couldn't identify the source, or how he knew, yet he felt sure of it. His soul had finally found peace, and it existed in this female.

He released her, startled. But she pulled him back to her, only upward to her mouth, where she licked her pleasure from his lips and mouth, and wrapped her legs around his hips again. This time he didn't fight her and slid into her weeping entrance, his cock thrusting deep without consideration of what this all meant. No hesitation. Just feeling. Sensation. Indulgence.

"Amazing," he whispered in between her demanding kisses. "Fucking amazing."

He let go. Stopped worrying. Just enjoyed and yielded to his needs. It was intoxicating, dangerous, and so damn good. They came together, her moans mingling with his, their bodies slick with sweat. His forehead met hers, his breathing rapid, her chest heaving, and still he craved more.

"Again," she demanded. "It shouldn't be possible, but again."

"Yes." He lifted her, his direction the bedroom. "All night."

"And morning."

"All weekend."

Leela nodded, her lips brushing his as she gulped in air. "Take me, B."

He lowered her onto his bed, their bodies still joined. "With pleasure, love."

CHAPTER SIX

Leela

Sunlight streamed through the windows, stirring Leela to consciousness. She stretched her legs and flinched at the ache between her thighs.

I'm sore. She blinked. *I'm never sore.*

A glance at the clock displayed the late afternoon hour, and another look around the room confirmed she was alone. Her brow furrowed. Balthazar didn't seem the type to leave his lovers unattended in bed.

She slipped out of the sheets, found one of his button-down shirts, and slid it on without bothering with the buttons. It hit her mid-thigh and carried a woodsy scent that was all Balthazar. Her sex pulsed at the thought, craving him again already.

How many times had they fucked through the night? She'd lost count after five, or was it six? *Who cares?* The male possessed inhuman stamina, and his skill… wow. Leela didn't have words to describe it. She'd never experienced anyone in her long existence who could evoke such pleasure from her. And he never stopped.

Her body tingled as she walked, her hard nipples chaffing against the fabric of Balthazar's shirt, her body humming with need. She was the one who descended from the sexual line, not him. Yet, it felt a hell of a lot like he'd woven a spell over her and not the other way around.

Leela found her lover in the kitchen—naked—flipping a pancake.

She popped her hip against the entryway, folded an arm across her stomach, and raised her opposite hand to her mouth, where she gently bit her finger to keep from speaking. No sense in disturbing the chef, especially with him so focused on the task.

Such a fine ass. Perfectly sculpted, athletic, and oh-so touchable. It flexed as he moved, his strong thighs moving too, and all that sinewy muscle danced along his back. Oh, yes. She approved of this male specimen.

He grabbed a plate, granting her a nice side view of his impressive package. Heavy, hot, and fucking irresistible. Paintings had been created in honor of his physique, murals to the gods, statues erected in his memory. None of them did him an ounce of justice.

"Enjoying the show, Lee?" he asked softly without looking at her.

"Yes."

He chuckled and continued assembling the dish. Fresh fruit, some sort of cream, syrup, and fluffy pancakes. She smiled. "That looks amazing."

"Sit." He nodded toward the counter beside him, not the dining table. Considering what happened there last night, she readily complied, hopping up with her legs dangling over the side. His chocolate gaze took in her attire, his lips curling. "That looks good on you."

"I know." She pulled her hair over to one side and

leaned back on her hands. "Naked looks fantastic on you."

"I know," he replied, repeating her words with a wink. He added some finishing touches to the breakfast platters and set one beside her. "Don't touch that."

She arched a brow at him. "An order?"

"Yes." Balthazar went to the fridge, pulled out a bottle of champagne and a crystal pitcher of what appeared to be freshly squeezed orange juice. A quick study of the kitchen showed a used juicer near the sink, confirming her assumption. He plucked two flutes from the cupboard, handed them to her, and popped open the bottle.

"Mimosas." She approved. "Where did the glasses come from?" Because she was sure the hotel—although nice—didn't come equipped with all of these fixtures.

"Jacque," he replied.

The Hydraian teleporter. Made sense.

He finished assembling their drinks, then took one of them from her and clinked the glasses together. "Cheers, Lee."

"Cheers," she murmured before sipping the bubbly fruit. "Wow, this is good."

He smirked, taking a swallow of his own. His sensual gaze simmered with intent as he traded his mimosa for the plate. The stacked pancakes had her mouth watering for a taste that he only intensified by slowly slicing off a bite with a fork. "Open."

She parted her lips, ready. He slipped the metal prongs into her mouth, and her senses exploded with flavor. Berries, maple syrup, vanilla, chocolate chips, and, of course, pancake.

Leela savored every delectable ingredient, her eyes closing on a moan. *Oh, sweet lover.*

Another bite followed, her tongue rejoicing at the contact as she chewed and swallowed. "Seduction by food," she whispered. "I approve."

"Whole package," he said, repeating his words from the night before. "And more."

"Yeah?" She opened her eyes to find his gaze on her mouth. "What's *more?*"

He merely smiled and fed her another piece of the pancake. Ambrosia—food of the gods. Somehow Balthazar had perfected it, and dear heaven, it was amazing. Leela always loved pancakes. She only told him she preferred waffles yesterday because she knew it would provoke him—the breakfast debate in Hydria was a frequent one.

His thumb brushed her lower lip. "Such a beautiful mouth."

Her pulse kick-started, thrumming energy through her veins and heating her lower abdomen. She should not be this turned on, not after everything they'd done to each other. The male held a persuasive pull over her unlike any other. She'd expected it to be good between them, but this… *this* she couldn't define.

He smiled. "Want more?"

"Yes."

He brought another bite to her mouth, which wasn't what she had in mind, but she accepted it anyway. Then he set the fork aside and placed his hands on the counter on either side of her hips. "Waffles or pancakes?"

Her lips twitched. "I thought you had moved on to a new challenge."

"I have, but my competitive side has to know so I can relay the verdict back to Luc."

She chuckled to herself. Immortality was a strange beast. Some chose to lose their humanity, most slept eternally from boredom, and yet these Elders, as they were called, chose to indulge in humorous games over breakfast foods. No wonder they all still smiled. They truly enjoyed being among the living. Her Seraphim brethren could learn a thing or two from them.

"Well?" he prompted, a single eyebrow arched.

What now? Did she tell him that she'd lied originally or allow him to think she changed her mind? "Your pancakes are phenomenal," she said slowly, drawing it out while she considered. "I think you could convert me into a pancake lover."

"Think?" he repeated. "Have I not proven the versatility pancakes allow? Because you can't stack a waffle nearly as successfully, despite how hard Luc tries. It's not the same."

"I wouldn't know, as I've not tried his version, but yours is delicious." And she couldn't believe this was what he chose to talk about with his hard cock so close to her sex. She grabbed his biceps and ran her palms up to his shoulders and then to his neck. "If I tell you I now prefer pancakes, can we make breakfast more interesting by eating it off each other?"

His eyes twinkled. "Oh, Lee, you truly are a Seraphim after my own heart."

She started to grin, then his words registered.

Seraphim.

Wait...

"Do you always go into an ethereal state when you orgasm, or was that something I caused?" he asked, his expression curious.

She swallowed—or tried to, anyway. Her throat reminded her of a giant boulder, refusing to budge. *He knows.* What now? Oh, Vera, of course. Chills skated down her spine at the verdict. What sounded so simple yesterday suddenly didn't *feel* all that easy. One phone call, a mind wipe, and he'd forever remain in ignorance. While she would remember the best night of her very long existence.

No. She couldn't think that way. This wasn't about her but about the fate of the future. Any alterations from this path could lead to catastrophic results.

But what if he could help? some small part of her wondered.

With what? the practical Seraphim in her replied. *Telling Stas her fate and ruining everything?*

"You clearly know who we are," he continued when

she didn't speak. "I've mentioned Jacque and Luc today, and you didn't react at all. You even knew my challenge was about waffles and pancakes, yet I'd never expressly stated it. And you've claimed to know me from the beginning."

The heat of his body seeped into hers as he drew closer, his hands going to her hips to slide her to the edge of the counter, his cock flush against her sex. She shivered at the contact even while her heart hammered in her chest.

This had to end.

She knew that going into it; she just hadn't expected to second-guess the decision.

One of his palms slid to her lower back while the other ventured up her side, grazing her breast and ending at her neck, where he wrapped his palm around her nape. She arched into him, luxuriating in the serenity of his control. Never had her body responded to someone this strongly.

Not a good enough reason to ignore fate…

Fine, but one more day wouldn't kill anyone, right? She could tell him what he wanted to know since Vera had to erase his thoughts anyway. Might as well enjoy a few more hours, get whatever compulsion this was out of her system, and move on. Balthazar would be none the wiser, leaving her to bear their memories alone.

I can live with that, she thought. *It's only sex*. Really fantastic, mind-blowing sex, but she existed in a world of pleasure.

"Leela," he murmured, squeezing her neck. "I might not be able to read your mind, but I can sense your conflict. Talk to me." He ran his nose along her cheek, and just that small touch felt so, so good. She could mist out of his reach, put some much-needed space between them, but she didn't want to.

Right and wrong were two fickle sides separated by a thin layer of uncertainty. Leela existed in that layer.

"You're not supposed to know," she admitted. "You weren't supposed to know."

"Maybe not, but I do." He laid kisses along her jaw, so sensual and smooth. She melted into him, unable to ignore his seductive touch. Her hands caressed his muscular back, memorizing the feel beneath her fingertips. This feeling inside, so foreign, urged her to *keep* him. He barely knew her. She only knew what she'd observed of him. Granted, those observations told her almost everything about him, and last night, well, it left nothing to the imagination.

Still, he didn't know *her*.

I could change that.

For a price.

But perhaps it's worth it?

There was only one way to *know*.

She licked her lips. "All right." She'd tell him a little and see how he reacted, and go from there. "I am a Seraphim, and I told you the truth about where I'm from."

"The South Pacific."

"Yes. A cluster of islands humankind will never discover, thanks to powerful runes—"

"Like the one on your hip."

She scoffed at that. "No, they are far more powerful than that little thing. I etched it into my skin centuries ago with angelfire. Very simple."

"Angelfire," he repeated, his voice low and hypnotic. "Never heard of it."

Her lips curled. "No, I suppose not."

His palm moved in soothing circles against her back while his other remained around her neck, his thumb massaging a tender spot below her ear. The man truly knew how to play a woman's body with the subtlest of touches. She wanted to rest her head against his bare chest and close her eyes.

"So there are more of you?" he asked.

"Yes," she said, slightly drowsy from his intoxicating touch. "Many more."

"And you're not all stoic." Not a question.

"The High Council believes emotion is irrelevant, and

they pity those like me who have a gift tied to humanity. Pleasure, in their opinion, is a waste of energy." She sighed, giving in to the impulse to fully relax against him, her forehead hitting his sternum. "It's complicated."

"Do they all know about us?"

She nodded. "The abominations are well known."

"Abominations?"

"The Seraphim of Resurrection created you all against the rules, hence the term assigned by the High Council. It's a bit harsh, I know." She pulled back to meet his chocolate eyes as she playfully added, "I prefer to call you all wannabe immortals."

He arched a brow. "Wannabe immortals?"

"You can die. I cannot. Therefore, it is appropriate."

"Ouch." He didn't appear all that wounded, not with the amusement radiating off him. "So the Seraphim are watching us and know all about our lives? Like the waffles and pancakes debate?"

She snorted. "Hardly. Your lives would bore them."

"Yet, you know all about us… ?"

Yeah, that. Leela had already said far too much, but it felt good to be honest with him. Even if she would have to wipe his memory later. Her heart pinched at the thought, while her mind rumbled its approval. *The practical way.*

"I'm not a normal Seraphim," she said by way of explanation. "And I think my gifts suit with your natural strengths."

His gaze heated. "You sought me out."

She considered reminding him that *he* sat beside *her*, but this provided a reasonable distraction. Leela would much rather spend their limited time together in the throes of passion, not discussing the complexities of their worlds. Her lips curled as she engaged their new game. No, she hadn't sought him out, but she didn't regret Ezekiel sending her here either.

"Are you disappointed?" she asked, purposely not answering his accusation.

"Hardly." The hand at her back flattened, his cock pulsing between her legs. "Still hungry?"

"Depends. Are you taking me up on the offer to make breakfast more interesting?"

Mirth taunted the edges of his mouth. "The maple syrup is still warm."

"Is it?"

"Hmm, yes." His hands went to the shirt covering her torso to gently slide it apart to reveal her breasts. "I haven't eaten yet, Leela. And it's such a shame with all the delicious toppings lying around. Cream, berries, chocolate sauce…"

"That sounds appetizing," she whispered, arching against him. "You should use me as a base."

He pressed his lips to hers, chastely, tauntingly. "It's like you read my mind, Lee."

"If only you could read mine," she teased.

"I don't need to, love. Your body speaks to me plenty." He punctuated the point by sliding his shaft through her slick folds. "Now don't move. I'm going to decorate you and devour you until your throat is raw from screaming my name."

Her stomach somersaulted. How could she refuse such an offer?

One more day.

Yes.

Then back to work.

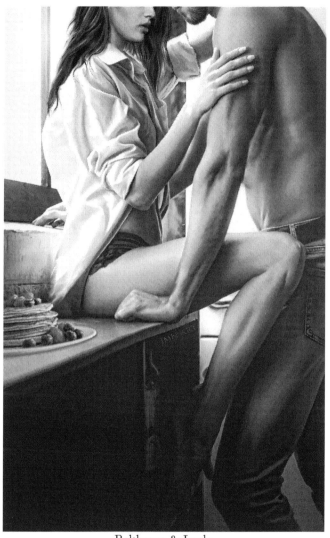

Balthazar & Leela
Brazil
Date Unknown

CHAPTER SEVEN

Leela

Balthazar resembled a god even while he slept. His long dark lashes fanning his cheeks, his lips slightly parted, his defined chest rising and falling with each soft breath.

Leela studied him, memorizing him, her heart fracturing with every exquisite detail.

It has to be done.

But fuck, it hurt.

She didn't want to erase this from his mind. Two days of bliss unlike anything she'd ever experienced. He took her to new heights, introduced her to sensations that she'd never forget. But he would.

Once Vera arrived, he'd never know Leela existed. This whole weekend would be replaced with a new memory, the one of her washed away forever.

Her vision blurred.

This shouldn't matter. It was only *two days*. So what if he awoke a new life inside of her. That type of infatuation was temporary, right?

She bit her lip to keep it from trembling. Why did this hurt so badly? Why should she care if he forgot her? This was never supposed to be more than an experience. Their fate was determined from the beginning. He never should have even *met* her.

Leela pinched her nose, her eyes closing as a single tear fell. Maybe someday in the future… No. She knew that wasn't possible either. God, she'd told him so little about the war to come and the fate of his kind.

It was almost cruel, leaving him in the dark. Yet, it protected him. For him to know was dangerous. Knowledge changed everything; she knew that better than most. And she owed it to Caro and Sethios to see everything through. For Stas too.

Already she'd dallied too long, had mentioned too much. This was her punishment—making him forget her.

I don't want him to forget me. I want to stay here, with him, in this moment forever. This was the first time she'd truly *felt* in so long. Pleasure, yes, but Balthazar touched her on a level she nearly forgot existed. And now she had to give him up.

He'll never know me, not like I know him.

The consequence of her task. Oh God, she hated this.

He can't know.

I know. She swallowed. *I know.*

Her hand tensed around her mobile. She'd misted to her room to grab her bag earlier, knowing this moment would arise sooner rather than later. And now was the best time, while he slept.

She opened her eyes to take him in one last time. His face soft with sleep… she would remember that always. And his lips, the things they did to her, said to her, evoked from her… Always. A dream to cherish and revisit later. And she could visit him whenever she wanted, just without his knowledge.

Which would only hurt more. Because he wouldn't even know she was missing.

Because I'll be nothing…

Her throat worked, another tear falling.

God, what have I done?

She slid her fingers over the keypad without looking, the words too much for her to bear. Enticing him on the beach… at the bar… on the dance floor… she knew better. She deserved this for being so foolish. Of course dallying with Balthazar resulted in consequences. That's why she'd avoided it for so long.

She typed the address and location to Vera, then tossed her phone aside to lie beside him once more. "I hope one day you'll forgive me, B," she whispered. "Assuming I can even tell you."

Vera appeared at the end of the bed, wearing her trademark scowl. "Seriously?"

Leela wiped away the evidence of her emotion and sat up with a forced smile. "Sorry?"

Her best friend's frown deepened, her gaze pensive as she took in the scene. "How many days?"

"Best to do a little over two," Leela said, her voice cracking a little. *Goodbye, B.*

Vera nodded, walking around the side of the bed to lay her palm over Balthazar's heart, her power already flaring.

Leela bit back the urge to stop this, her own heart beating a mile a minute in her chest. Oh, how fast she would be erased from his mind.

"What story should I weave in replacement of all this?" Vera asked, her voice softer than it was before.

Leela cleared her throat. She told her about the challenge, her pulse thrumming in her ears the whole time. At the end, she closed her eyes and added, "Make sure he wins. He deserves at least that."

Vera nodded, her power weaving through the room and breaking Leela inside.

My punishment to bear. Always.

It would be so easy to ask Vera to do the same to her, to have her remove the memories that she knew would haunt her for a lifetime, but that would be selfish. Someone had to remember. It was too beautiful not to.

Oh, Balthazar.

But he'd never know.

She watched his lips curve at whatever Vera was programming in his mind. Her own responded in kind, but for an entirely different reason. Because that smile didn't match the ones he gave her. Those would forever be hers to cherish, and regret.

"I'll need to do the others," Vera said flatly. "He mentioned you to Alik and Lucian before your erotic dance."

She's already back that far? Leela thought. *So fast… too fast.*

"He didn't realize what you were by that point, just that you were different." Vera's brow creased. "From what I gather from the feelings, he chose another night with you over reporting back to his friends. He wanted to keep you to himself for another day. Interesting."

Leela's angelic soul shifted with discomfort. He had to feel obligated to give the details to his friends. *He chose me over duty.*

"At least I won't have as much to alter in their memories, but you still owe me for this, Lee."

"I know," she whispered. "Sorry."

Her best friend removed her hand, her blue-green eyes flashing with knowledge. "It's a shame, though."

"What do you mean?"

"He's clearly your other half, and now he'll never know how you met." She sounded almost sad, but she shrugged and disappeared in a flash, off to complete her task.

Leela sat on the bed, shaking.

And now he'll never know how you met.

Even if she told him in the future, he'd never remember. Because of her. Because of this moment. Because of her vow to protect another.

"One day," she whispered. "One day I'll make it up to you. I promise."

He stirred beside her, his arms flexing as he stretched.

"Goodbye, B," she murmured, misting as his eyes opened. *I'll see you again… but you won't see me.*

WAFFLES VS. PANCAKES
READER DISCUSSION

"We sort of took over their book…"

—Leela

Vera: *That's what happens when you play with people's minds, Lee.*

Stark: *Yeah, but it can be undone.*

Vera: *I'm not a toy to be called upon for fun when you all need a memory alteration.*

Stark: *I was referring to Stas.*

Vera: *Oh, well, yes, that is entirely different.*

Ezekiel: *Can we get a move on that sooner rather than later? Because this whole game of interfering has really lost its allure.*

Stark: *Her twenty-fifth birthday is fast approaching. Almost time.*

Leela: *And then what?*

Stark: *That's up to Stas.*

Vera: *I'm out. Tap me if you need me.*

Leela: *We should give them their book back now.*

Stark: *Agreed.*

———

B: *And once again, you all see why pancakes are better than waffles.*

Luc: *I'm picking the location for the next round.*

B: *Won't change the outcome.*

Luc: *Yeah? Belgium would disagree with you.*

B: *Oh, that sounds like a challenge I would enjoy.*

Alik: *No.*

Jay: *You'll need a new wingman, B.*

B: *True. I need to groom someone.*

Alik: *Yeah, go ahead and take a decade to work on that. Or better yet, a century.*

B: *Well, at least a few months. I have some parties to plan, starting with Jay and Lizzie's engagement party. Which reminds me, we missed an important October holiday.*

Luc: *You thinking what I'm thinking, B?*

B: *Halloween-themed engagement party?*

Luc: *It's like you pulled the idea from my thoughts, B.*

B: *Imagine that.*

Issac: *I'd rather not.*

Jay: I should probably ask Lizzie about this first.

B: Already in the works, Jay. Trust me.

Luc: Always.

Alik: You realize Osiris is a major player right now, yes? Jonathan? That Stark guy? Any of this matter to you all?

B: Of course, but we're not going to stop living because there are a few threats lying around. Right, Luc?

Luc: Yes, these events are important for morale and bonding. It's what makes us stronger.

B: Exactly. All right, party time. Flip the page.

A HALLOWEEN ENGAGEMENT

"Jay missed one of my favorite holidays.
Time to rectify that."

-B

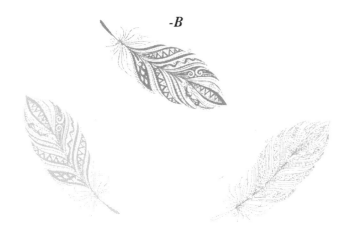

INTRODUCTION

"I need to prep. Who wants to lead?"

—B

Luc: *I think Stas needs to take over.*

Stas: *I'm good.*

B: *I agree with Luc. We'll be far too busy entertaining for this one. Go for it, sweetheart.*

Stas: *Seriously, I'm fine to just let this whole "book" be yours.*

Luc: *I'm off to find a proper costume.*

B: *Me too.*

Silence

Stas: *All right. Guess it's my turn, then.*

CHAPTER ONE

Stas

"I can't wear this." The white fabric cut down to Stas's belly button and the back practically didn't exist. Not to mention the slit up her right thigh. "Nope. Not happening."

Lizzie finished brushing her dark red hair and raised one perfectly sculpted eyebrow. "I'm pregnant and wearing seashells with a miniskirt. You can wear a floor-length gown."

"Is that what it's called?" Because it felt like wearing a revealing sheet. "I can't even wear a bra with this."

"And I can?" Lizzie gestured to her ample breasts. "I barely fit into these cups and"—she pointed to the slight bump in her abdomen—"I'm fat."

Stas grinned despite her best friend's petulant tone.

"That wasn't meant to be funny!"

"Oh, come on. You're hardly showing, Liz." Technically, she shouldn't be showing at all, but nothing about this pregnancy could be considered normal. "I think you're gorgeous," she added with a side hug.

Lizzie would make a beautiful mom. Already she demonstrated a sense of protectiveness over her belly, one her future husband seemed to share. Jayson barely let the woman out of his sight. It was a miracle he'd allowed the two of them to get ready for the party alone.

Pink painted her best friend's cheeks as she returned the smile. "You're right. I know you're right." She palmed her stomach and giggled with a shake of her head. "We both look ridiculous. Why did B decide on a themed engagement party?"

Oh, it was more than "themed." He'd gone all out and rented an entire hotel in Miami. All thirty-three floors. Everyone had their own room, with Lizzie and Jayson staying in the honeymoon suite—their current location—and the floors not being used for sleeping were for the festivities.

"You like dressing up," Stas reminded. "And apparently, so does Jay." Because when B announced his plans, Jayson's eyes had lit up like a Christmas tree.

"Of course he does. He put me in a mermaid costume."

"Because you're the perfect *Ariel*," Jayson announced from the doorway. He must have heard his name.

Stas checked the clock. "You lasted thirty minutes. I'm actually kind of proud."

He grinned as he wrapped his arms around Lizzie's waist. "It helps being only a few feet away."

Lizzie huffed at that. "I'm not dying."

"No, you're just a little over a month pregnant." He palmed her belly as he bent to kiss her on the mouth. "And positively gorgeous."

"You're only saying that to sweet-talk me out of these shells," Lizzie accused.

"Sexy as fuck," he continued as if she hadn't spoken. He started to walk her backward toward the massive hotel bed, giving Stas her cue to leave.

Maybe I can find a new outfit in the living area.

Not likely, but a girl could try.

She closed the bedroom door softly just as Lizzie giggled from being tossed onto the mattress. Such a bittersweet sound that elicited a pang of happiness followed by a hollow ache inside of Stas's chest.

She missed that—the butterflies and the excited race of her pulse. Lately, all she'd felt was uncertainty. And the reason for that uncertainty stood in the foyer with one shoulder propped up against the wall. Waiting.

Issac's sapphire gaze burned her exposed skin as he took in her revealing attire. Admiration curled his lips, his attraction to her as evident as always despite their difficult situation.

And the feeling was definitely mutual.

"A soccer player?" she asked, surprised by his costume of choice. He sported white gym shorts, black socks up to his knees, cleats, and a red jersey with gold writing on it.

Manchester United.

And here she thought he only owned tailored suits.

"Football," he corrected as he sauntered toward her. "Athena would know better."

"Yeah, well, I'm an unwilling version of the Goddess of Wisdom." When Lizzie had recommended a Greek-themed costume for the party, Stas hadn't thought much of it. Now that she was braless beneath a sheet of white, she regretted that decision.

Issac stopped an inch away from her and fondled the golden chains holding the fabric together over her shoulder. "I'm going to enjoy playing with these later."

Her blood heated at the very real promise in those words. They hadn't been intimate since her rebirth. A few kisses here and there, and most nights she slept beside him, but nothing happened beyond a few chaste touches.

Because one bite would end his life.

I'm poison.

She slammed the door on that thought.

No.

Tonight was meant to be a celebration of happy events. They all needed a break from reality, and Balthazar had gloriously provided it in the form of a belated Halloween-themed gathering.

"You look amazing, Aya," Issac murmured as he wrapped his arms around her.

God, she loved this feeling.

He radiated strength and tenderness. Her soul rejoiced at the bond between them, refused to let him go even though they both knew she should.

Love.

She'd only said the word out loud once, and may never say it again, but it didn't matter. Titles and frivolities weren't important.

He pressed his lips to her temple as she hugged him back. Beneath the heat of his embrace lay a hint of hesitation neither of them could ignore.

Death lurked between them.

A single wrong move. One drop of her blood against his lips and he'd collapse. Forever gone. Because of her.

Stas winced. *I just decided not to think about that.*

But it existed at every turn, glance, and touch, all tainted by their new reality.

Issac sighed. "I hate it too, love." His words only further confirmed their bond. He knew exactly where her thoughts had gone and why without her ever having to say a word. That level of understanding almost hurt, the intensity of it singeing her being for eternity, marking her forever as belonging to the one man who could never truly have her.

So they continued this charade of a relationship because their hearts refused to let go. No, it went deeper than that. Her soul connected to his on some inexplicable

227

level, fusing them together even in the most dire of circumstances.

Yet, she knew this wasn't maintainable. Not forever. Not when Issac still needed to *feed*.

No more.

Forget. Just for one night.

She slid her palms to his lower back and lifted her gaze to his, determined.

"I don't want to think anymore," she said softly. "I want to pretend everything is normal, or as normal as it can be with Balthazar playing host in a hotel party." Her passive attempt at a joke seemed to ease some of the tension between them, but not all of it.

Issac's full mouth tilted upward. "Seventeen themed floors. I suggest we avoid a few of them based on what I'm seeing."

This subject she could explore. It even sparked a note of curiosity, something she so badly needed right now. "Do I want to know?"

He shook his head, amusement radiating from him. "No. You really don't. Though, I wouldn't mind you joining the water volleyball game outside."

She raised an eyebrow. "Why doesn't that sound as innocent as it should?"

"Because you're learning that nothing where Balthazar is concerned could possibly be as modest as it sounds."

"Truth," Jayson agreed as he exited with an arm around a blushing Lizzie. He wore a pair of green board shorts and flip-flops. No shirt.

"Are you supposed to be a beachboy?" Stas asked incredulously as she moved to Issac's side. "Or is that your version of a merman?"

"I'm a more appealing version of the male character from that cartoon mermaid movie." He grinned. "But I can go nude and pretend to be a merman who washed up on the beach, if you think that's more appropriate."

Lizzie turned impossibly redder. "Maybe later."

"Definitely later." He kissed her temple. "We'll go make a quick appearance to appease the host, then head back up here."

That turned Liz from blushing bride to perplexed fiancée as her brow crinkled. She faced her husband-to-be and put a hand on her hip. "It's our party, Jayson." Softly spoken but underlined with meaning. The poor guy didn't stand a chance.

"Which is why we can leave whenever we want."

"No. It's why we have to attend the whole time." Lizzie gave him a look that begged him to argue, and his smile faded.

Smart man, Stas thought. She'd been the recipient of that expression a few times in her past and knew better than to say anything.

But Jayson, of course, didn't. "Seriously?"

"Seriously." Lizzie folded her arms and somehow managed to affect the perfect mom pose. How appropriate. "It's rude to leave a party early when it's being held in our honor."

"Balthazar is going to be too busy to notice, nor will he care."

"That's not the point," she chastised. "He's gone through a lot of effort to put all this together, and we should support him."

Jayson gaped at her. "This is B we're talking about, right?"

She merely stared at him, waiting.

He rubbed his jaw, his shrewd gaze heating as he glanced over her—no doubt weighing the benefits of appeasing her. Or perhaps deciding what would happen if he marched her back into the bedroom right now.

Lizzie held his gaze without flinching, but another flush crept its way up her neck. His open appraisal seemed to be having the impact he desired, because his dimples flashed in response.

To think, Stas hadn't approved of this relationship only

a month ago. But these two clearly adored each other. Perhaps a little too much.

"Alik is requesting your ETA," Issac said, his expression artfully blank. "Shall I respond with an image of the current time, or shall I add a few minutes to it? I would imagine it's rude to keep the guests waiting, but I'll leave that judgment up to Elizabeth."

The latter was said with a touch of humor that only Stas seemed to hear. Her lips threatened to curve. The urge only worsened as Lizzie turned a shade of purple.

"Oh! You're right. We need to go, Jay. Right now." She grabbed his hand and dragged him toward the door. He met Issac's gaze on their way and shook his head.

"Jackass," he muttered.

Issac affected a guiltless expression and tone. "I'm merely the messenger."

"Right." Jayson didn't get a chance to add to that as Lizzie yanked him through the threshold.

"We'll meet you down there!" she called, not bothering to wait for confirmation.

Stas laughed as the door closed.

Issac blinked innocently down at her. "Something amusing, love?"

"Alik didn't ask about them at all, did he?"

He shrugged noncommittally. "Jayson's imagination had started to wander, and he needed a nudge to steer him back to the proper course."

"Like reminding the guest of honor that she was late to her own party?" Stas smiled at her wicked demon. "That was cruel."

"I prefer *brilliant*." He dipped his head to brush his mouth softly over hers. "Shall we follow or head over to our suite?"

"Our suite?" she repeated. "You sound rather sure of yourself."

"We both know you'll end up in my bed by the end of the night, Aya." He kissed her again, this time with a little more force. His sapphire eyes glimmered with arousal as he pulled back. "I've been without you beneath me for far too long."

She swallowed. *Me too.* But sex complicated things between them, inspired lusts that couldn't be ignored. If he lost control with her, she'd never forgive herself. Losing him wasn't an option.

What if he fed first? she wondered. From what she knew, he hadn't bitten anyone since her turning. And he'd once told her he required blood weekly.

He had to be hungry.

Maybe he could find someone to satisfy his thirst, then they could sate their physical needs together afterward.

Issac nuzzled her nose, her cheek, and her neck. "I miss you, Aya," he breathed against her ear, showering goose bumps down her neck. "Let's go enjoy the party and pretend things are normal—just as you said—and see where it goes?"

God, how could she refuse him when he spoke to her in that voice? The one underlined with desire and command, with just a hint of a plea.

Stas melted on the spot, her body giving in before her mind could interfere. Risks be damned.

"Okay," she whispered.

Except she knew it wouldn't be okay at all, or normal. Because even now, in this moment of intimacy, he held her as if she could break at any given moment. Not because he was afraid to hurt her, but because of his fear that *she* could hurt *him*.

But if he wanted to try, she'd try. Because that was all they had left—devotion.

"Always," Issac murmured against her neck. "You know that, Aya."

"Always," she repeated.

CHAPTER TWO

Issac

Torture. That's how Issac described Astasiya's dress. He wanted to peel it off with his teeth, but instead he stood quietly beside her in the reception area of the hotel.

Two hours, he promised himself. That's how long they needed to attend this party without anyone causing a fuss at their absence.

Then, Issac would figure out how to make this work with Astasiya. Because the chaste behavior could not continue. Her blood was the issue, not her mouth, or her body or hands. So long as he didn't bite her, they would be fine. It wasn't as if he possessed an aversion to control. He just had to be a little gentler than usual.

"Remind me why we came down here," Astasiya whispered as she took in the haunted interior of the lobby.

Cobwebs adorned various fixtures, faint lights cast a

ghostly appeal over the plush carpet, and splatters of fake blood decorated the walls. Balthazar had certainly gone all out, as he always did in these circumstances.

"For the experience," Issac replied, amused.

They were waiting for the elevator to arrive that would take them to the true start of the party on the second floor. The lobby was just for show, and also shrouded in discreet security. Issac normally didn't play along with Balthazar's theatrics, but Astasiya had never attended one of his infamous events. Best to give her the full tour.

"Okay, but why?" she asked softly.

He stepped behind her to wrap his arms around her waist and hug her back to his chest. "Nervous, love?"

"No." Her shiver betrayed the lie. "I just don't understand why we're down here."

"You've never experienced a Balthazar production," he murmured against her ear. "You require a proper introduction."

"You don't even like him," she pointed out. "And this isn't really your scene, Mr. Billionaire Gala Extraordinaire."

He chuckled. "Perhaps not, but I'm willing to make exceptions." This occasion being one of them. "You wanted normal. I'm giving you normal."

"In a haunted lobby, waiting for a spooky-as-fuck elevator?" She snorted. "Yeah, that's normal."

"You almost sound scared, Aya." He nuzzled her neck. "Don't fret, darling. I'll protect you."

"That makes me feel better," she deadpanned as the elevator dinged. Her spine stiffened as it opened to reveal a person dressed in all black. *Jeremy.* One of Jayson's Guardians. They were probably all in attendance with the purpose of protecting Elizabeth and her unborn child, on Jayson's orders.

Issac nudged his goddess forward when she didn't move. "Come on, love. Let's play the game."

"Something is seriously wrong with all of you," she muttered, her feet moving. She turned upon entering, and he backed her up into the wall, his hands on her hips.

"You can face off against Osiris, and yet, it's a haunted hotel that scares you?" He chuckled at her piqued expression. "How charming."

"The difference is having a reason to stand up to my fears versus purposely putting myself in a situation where the aim is to make me scream."

He ran one hand up her side as the elevator began to move. "Would you prefer a different situation that results in screaming?"

A lovely shade of pink caressed her cheeks. She licked her lips. "Don't make promises you can't keep."

"Is that a challenge, love?" Because he had every intention of fulfilling that promise tonight. No more of this tiptoeing around each other. *I will find a way for this to work.*

The door dinged before she could reply.

"Proceed at your own risk," Jeremy advised, his pun unoriginal. None of the Hydraians approved of this relationship between Issac and Astasiya.

"I shall," Issac replied, catching the other man's hazel gaze. Despite his status of Guardian, he was the first to look away. Jeremy's affinity for manipulating the earth was impressive, but Issac's visual talents were renowned. His age and status helped as well.

"Enjoy your evening, Jeremy," he murmured, placing his hand against Astasiya's back to escort her out of the elevator.

"You as well," the Hydraian replied, his tone holding a hint of defeat.

Astasiya shook her head as the doors closed. "You know they're just worried about you."

He snorted. "No, Aya, they are concerned that their newest asset has ties to the Ichorian community." He gazed sideways at her. "A war brews on the horizon, love. Everyone, including me, can feel it."

"I agree, but they know you're on their side, Issac.

You've more than proven your allegiance."

"Yes, it is not my loyalty they question so much as my influence."

She frowned. "Over what?"

"You, darling." He pulled her closer and kissed her forehead. "They worry about your reaction should something happen to me."

Her shoulders tensed. "Issac—"

"Shh, it's a moot concern, love. I fancy being among the living and intend to remain here. With you." His lips brushed her temple. "Now, you wanted an evening of normalcy. I suggest we follow that sign and see where we end up."

Her focus shifted to the wall. "You mean the one that says 'Enter If You Dare' in blood?"

"That would be it," he replied, grinning. "Unless you're too afraid?"

"It's not about fear but about purpose," she growled. "I'm not scared, just not all that eager to have things jump out at me."

"That's half the fun, love."

"I can't believe you actually want to go through a haunted, uh, whatever you call this. Floor, I guess."

His lips threatened to curve at her skepticism. Because she was right. He normally would have no interest in such an activity, but Astasiya had changed him on an irrevocable level. She encouraged him to live in a way he never appreciated previously. Including venturing into a maze of horrors.

"The seven floors of hell," he corrected. "And actually, I'm quite intrigued. I rather enjoy hearing you scream."

She narrowed her gaze. "You may take that back soon."

He fondled a piece of her blonde hair hanging loosely against her breast. "No, I don't think I will." Issac gave the strand a tug. "Are you finished stalling, or do you require more time?"

"I'm not stalling."

"Whatever you say, love." He purposely laced his tone with doubt, knowing it would force her into action.

The fire lighting her gorgeous eyes confirmed that it worked. "Fine." She wove her fingers through his and started in the direction of the festivities. "Osiris is a real threat, but sure, let's go scare ourselves for fun."

He chuckled. "That's the spirit, love."

"Who are you and what did you do with my Issac Wakefield?" The note of confusion in her voice was belied by the mirth dancing in her gaze.

"Right here." He squeezed her hand just as a chainsaw revved and appeared out of nowhere in front of them. Astasiya leapt backward with a yelp while Issac chuckled. He may have seen that coming.

"Shit!" Astasiya was not nearly as amused, her free hand covering her heart.

"We've not even entered yet, and already you're screaming." This would be quite fun indeed, especially if she continued to clutch him in the way she did now.

The lights flickered overhead.

Time for the initial show, Issac thought as darkness swept over the hallway. The sound of a clock chiming rung overhead, another chainsaw revving ahead.

"Issac?"

"I believe the goal is to find our way to the next level." From what he could see, this activity spanned the first three floors. "Lead the way, love."

"You're the one with an aptitude for vision," she muttered.

"That would be cheating."

"Like that has ever stopped you before."

He smirked. "Are you stalling again?"

"You're enjoying this far too much." She started forward cautiously, her hand holding his in a death grip. "And where are all the other people?"

"Scattered throughout the hotel, preparing for the

humans to arrive."

She stopped. "What?" He sensed her gaze seeking his out in the dark, but he couldn't *see* her. How he longed to find a way to undo that rune at the base of her spine and manipulate her sight just once. Especially in her dreams. "Issac, what do you mean about the humans?"

Right. Explanation. "Do you think Balthazar organized all of this just for the Hydraians?" He paused. Her silence indicated she required more. "The primary purpose is to celebrate Jayson and Elizabeth's pending nuptials; however, Balthazar does not throw parties in this elaborate of a manner just for the immortals. He's invited the public—for a fee, of course. Afterward, he'll anonymously donate the proceeds to a charity in need." Giving back to the community was one of the Elders' ways of maintaining positive relationships with humanity. Osiris could learn a few things from them.

"Okay, then where are all the other Hydraians? Jacque brought, like, everyone over."

Not everyone. At least a hundred were left behind to guard Hydria. "Several are going through the haunted floors—which you would know if you stopped delaying the inevitable—and others are upstairs celebrating in the main rooms."

"While we're here in a dark hallway listening to a clock chime incessantly."

"Because you stopped moving," he added. "Indeed."

"Okay, I'm not afraid, Issac." She started walking again. "I just think this entire—"

The sound of an engine turning over came from the side, paired with headlights, causing Astasiya to jump several feet forward on a shriek. Eerie music soon followed as a dusting of stars illuminated the hallway overhead, bathing them in subtle light.

"Not cool," she grumbled.

"You were saying?" he asked casually.

"That I'm going to pay you back somehow for all of

this? Yes." She kept moving, this time faster, and masterfully ignored a few props that leapt out at her along the way.

Until they stepped onto a moving floor.

She fell backward, and he caught her with ease, smiling. "Having trouble?"

"How? *How* have they added these effects everywhere?!"

"Welcome to life as an immortal, love," he whispered into her ear. "Now keep moving." He nudged her onto the shifting surface instead and helped her navigate through the awkward tunnel to the stairwell. Faint red light illuminated their path upward, and they came face-to-face with a pair of twin clowns.

"Cute," Astasiya muttered before wandering past them.

Issac shrugged at the two Hydraians who seemed quite disappointed in her lack of a reaction. They would hopefully have a better time entertaining the humans being let in downstairs. At least two hundred minds, from what his senses told him. Perhaps more. He closed off the majority of their visual receptors in his mind, only allowing in a few key players throughout the building as a sort of security measure. He could never be too sure with all the threats lying in wait.

Stas froze at the ice wall before them. It was illuminated by a faint blue bulb that rivaled the others around them. There were trails on either side. Astasiya chose left, leading them to another icy brick. "A maze," she said flatly.

"It would appear that way," he agreed. "Where to, love?"

She responded by heading back the way they came and taking the other path. Several twists and turns later, with a few surprises along the way that didn't faze Astasiya, landed them in yet another stairwell. It seemed the winter wonderland part of the journey wasn't nearly as interesting as the first level, at least to his goddess. If she realized a water elemental had crafted the scene, changing ice layers as they moved through it, she may have been more impressed.

"This is getting old," she grumbled as they reached the top.

Strobe lights streamed through the entrance, matching the thudding beat of hard metal. Cries for help littered the air as they stepped through the threshold, causing Astasiya to move into Issac's side.

She crept forward while keeping a death grip on his hand.

Issac sensed the Hydraians up ahead but said nothing as she wandered right into their trap. They leapt out at her with chainsaws, sending her skipping several steps with a curse.

He chuckled as he followed, shaking his head at the two idiots in masks. The humans, of course, would enjoy all of this. Astasiya just seemed irritated. She eyed the checkered walls and floors ahead of them and sighed. "A butcher's kitchen? This is ridiculous."

"Take it up with Balthazar, love."

She muttered something uncomplimentary under her breath while walking through the fake slaughter, blood, and gore. When another actor in a mask greeted her, she flipped the male off and continued on her way.

"Tell me this ends soon," she said.

"Three down, four to go. However, I do believe we've caught up to some of the others finally." There were several parties of two and four that went through before them—all testing the layers before the public entered.

As Astasiya and Issac reached the next level, the door closing firmly behind them, he understood why.

No light.

Overwhelming electronic bass.

A slithering maze of insanity, pitfalls, dead ends, and more.

"Right, then," he murmured. "The other levels were all

a warm-up for the next four floors."

"Great," she whispered back at him as someone screamed up ahead. "Just great."

CHAPTER THREE

Stas

Spiders, pools of blood, fire, and monsters that appeared far too real. By the time Stas finished with it all, she wanted to retreat upstairs for a long bath. "I can't believe you made me go through every floor." She shivered while her demon chuckled.

"Full experience, remember?"

"One I could live without."

"It's all glamour, darling." His lips curled into one of his trademark sinful smiles. "I still can't believe all of those things frighten you, but Osiris does not."

"Oh, he scares the shit out of me. I face him out of necessity. That"—she pointed to the stairwell they'd just escaped from—"is pointless horror that causes heart attacks for no viable reason."

"You don't approve of my theatrics?" A sensual voice

asked from up ahead. "Perhaps you should take her to level thirteen, Wakefield. Might be more her speed."

Stas met Balthazar's warm gaze and cocked a brow. "Is it more blood and gore?"

"Only for those requesting it," he murmured, a sinful note to his tone. The Hydraian Elder oozed sexual energy, even now, in a darkly lit hallway leading to who the fuck knew where. "The heart of the party, sweetheart."

Always listening to my thoughts, she said to him, smiling. Issac wasn't a fan of Balthazar's mind-reading ability, but it didn't bother her. Balthazar always kept her confidence, never sharing her feelings or words without permission. He treated everyone in a similar manner, except for maybe her demon. Though, she suspected that was part of their rivalrous friendship.

"As for floor thirteen, feel free to venture upward to find out," Balthazar added with a smirk.

"A fetish-themed arena." Issac's palm slid to her lower back, branding her skin. "We intend to skip that portion of your party."

Balthazar shrugged. "To each his own." He pulled a phone from the pocket of his jeans and read something from the screen. Aside from the mobile and pants, he wore nothing else.

"As the party host, shouldn't you be in a costume?" she asked.

He cocked a brow. "Who says I'm not wearing one?"

She eyed his chiseled physique. "Yeah, okay, I'll bite. What are you supposed to be?"

"I'll give you a hint instead." He slipped the device back into his pants, his dark eyes sparkling with intent. "I was fully dressed this morning. However, several guests are now wearing articles of my clothing. Keepsakes, if you will. What am I?"

Uh… Stas glanced at her demon, who just shook his head with a small smile. "I have no idea," she admitted.

"He's sex," Issac murmured.

"Sex?" she repeated.

"Yes. He's indulged significantly today, granting each of his conquests a keepsake to remember him by, and lost his attire in the process. I presume he'll spend the rest of his evening sans clothing once he finds a final partner."

"That's…" Yeah, she had no words.

"Well done, Wakefield." Balthazar pushed off the wall with a charming grin. "I would reward you with my final piece of clothing, but I'm needed in the pool outside. Feel free to join us later."

"Water volleyball?" Stas asked, remembering what Issac had mentioned earlier.

"Among other things," Balthazar replied, his alluring gaze swirling with innuendo. "Lizzie and Jay are dancing. Perhaps have a whirl and then come down for a dip." He winked at Issac before disappearing through the stairwell.

"Are they swimming in blood?" she asked, baffled.

Issac chuckled. "No. However, Tristan would certainly enjoy that."

She snorted. Issac's best friend and progeny was not her favorite Ichorian. "I'd like him to swim in a vat of his own blood."

Her demon laughed outright as he shook his head. "Come on, love. Let's have a dance and then decide how to spend the rest of our evening. There are still eight floors of madness left unvisited beyond this one."

She glanced up at him. "We don't have to see them all, right?" Because the levels of hell had been more than enough to satisfy her Halloween inclinations for at least a decade.

He pulled her closer, his lips brushing her ear. "Our suite is the only room in this entire building that truly matters to me."

Butterflies took flight in her lower belly at the suggestion. "We could just go there?"

"After we make an appearance," he whispered. "Or Elizabeth will be very disappointed in us, and I, for one, do not wish to be reprimanded."

Fair point. "Okay. We go dance for a little while, then escape." Which was what they should have done to begin with, but for reasons that remained elusive to her, Issac had wanted to go through the haunted floors.

Normalcy, my ass.

She shuddered just thinking about the too-real snake pit from the final level. Dancing sounded far safer.

Issac guided her toward the soft buzz of music coming from a room up ahead, and they paused at the threshold. A handful of Hydraians she recognized were line dancing throughout the suite.

Where did they put all the furniture?

"Hmm, right, let's try the next room," Issac murmured, his palm against her lower back.

The new one seemed to be a techno rave. Jacque was popping around the room—literally—in a classic chauffeur's outfit. "How appropriate," she mused.

"Indeed," Issac replied, leading her to the next suite— salsa music.

"Okay, this is creative," she admitted. "As was finding ways to repurpose hallways and adjoining rooms below."

"Blueprints," Luc said as he joined them in the hallway from their next stop. How he heard them over the mosh pit thriving behind him was beyond her. He shut the door, quieting the corridor to a dull hum.

"What are you?" she asked, taking in his jeans, button-down shirt, and artfully placed ruler in his belt.

"The architect of this party," he replied, pushing a pair of fake glasses up the bridge of his nose.

Is that a calculator in his other pocket?

"You and Balthazar certainly outdid yourselves," Issac said, his arms circling Stas's waist as he laid his chin on her shoulder. The movement struck her as territorial, done not out of jealousy but as a way of confirming his place at her side. While Luc had yet to outwardly say anything, everyone knew he didn't approve of this relationship. No one did.

"I designed the maze," Luc said, his dimples appearing briefly. "The mortals are going to love it, assuming they make it to the end."

And that was the entire point. There were exits on each floor—something Stas noticed a few times on their way up—for those to depart if the horror became too much.

"That's why there's a pool party going on downstairs," she said, finally realizing the whole point. If the humans reached the end, they could party up here with the Hydraians. Otherwise, they returned to the lower level to join Balthazar in the swimming area. "Brilliant."

"Yes, the only way to reach this floor and the one above us is through that specific door." Luc pointed down the hall to the one she had no desire to go back through again. "Unless you have a specific key card that grants you access via elevator, which only our true guests possess."

"Allowing the mortals access to the other floors as well, should they choose to enter," Issac mused. "As always, your genius impresses me."

Luc shrugged. "It provides a diversion that my people require. Especially now." A solemn air settled around them, one that prickled her skin and sent a foreboding shiver down her spine. "Enjoy the evening, both of you. We'll need to discuss soon what the future holds for us all, but not tonight. Tonight we celebrate life and love, and the pending nuptials between an old friend and a new one."

"Cheers, Lucian." Issac hugged Stas harder. "You enjoy your evening as well."

"Oh, I intend to. I'm on my way to play naked water…" His gaze went to something behind them. "What the hell are you doing here?" he snapped. "I specifically ordered you to stay in Hydria."

"And I specifically ignored that command," a feminine voice replied with mock sweetness.

Stas shifted and found a familiar brunette wearing nothing but fig leaves. Eliza dressed as Eve, and wow, did she pull it off. Not that Luc seemed all that impressed by it.

"How did you convince Jacque to teleport you here?" The Hydraian King demanded.

"I have my ways," Eliza replied. "Not that it's any of your fucking business."

His blond eyebrows shot up. "Any of *my* business? Do you have any idea whom you are talking to?"

"Oh, sorry, you're right. Not that it's any of your fucking business, *Your Majesty*." She curtsied low, her dark eyes mocking. "Better?"

Luc looked more flustered than Stas had ever seen him. "You're going home. Now."

Eliza laughed. "Yeah, good luck with that." She turned on her four-inch stiletto heels and started down the hall. "Toodles."

"You think this is a joke?" he demanded, following her. "This is *your* life, Eliza."

She rounded on him. "Exactly. So stop telling me what to do."

Tension vibrated through each step as he approached Eliza. Most Hydraians would cower. She met him head-on, hands on her hips, expression challenging. Such a strong woman, especially after everything she'd endured. And stubborn as hell, from what Stas had gathered.

"I'm trying to protect you, something you would realize if you ceased all this childish behavior." Luc sounded so patient, yet his irritation was palpable.

"Childish?" She scoffed. "*You* are the one treating me like a child."

"Because you insist on acting like one," Luc replied. "You're going back to Hydra. Now."

"No." She folded her arms and glowered up at him.

"No," he repeated, his voice calm and steady. "You continue to defy me at every turn despite everything I've offered you. Fine, Eliza. Endanger yourself. But when your rebirth occurs too early, do not look to me for answers."

He left her glowering after him as he disappeared through the stairwell.

"Thinks he knows me," she muttered. "I'll show him." She marched off after Luc, hands fisted at her sides.

"I've never seen Lucian lose his temper," Issac said as the door slammed behind Eliza. "Fascinating that the young fledgling brings it out of him."

"That was Luc losing his temper?"

Issac gazed down at her. "Well, yes. He left."

She considered his words and frowned. Luc always maintained a nonchalant, yet calculative, persona in her presence. He also debated her at every turn, especially when he felt his point needed to be heard. And, admittedly, the Hydraian King was usually right, hence his position of leadership among the immortals.

Yet, he walked away. "Huh." She blinked. "You're right."

"I usually am," he murmured, his arms coming around her again. "Now, what do you say we continue meandering along this dancing hall, make our presence known in the final room, and then venture upstairs?"

She gazed up at him over her shoulder. "I like the sound of that."

His sapphire gaze lit up. "Look at that—I'm right again."

"You wear arrogance so well," she whispered, brushing her lips against his. "Now let's get this socializing over with." *And maybe find you a blood drink to help quench your thirst.* Her stomach somersaulted at the thought. She'd forgotten about that being a necessity for the evening.

The only way they could enjoy each other later was if his other needs were met, and Issac only drank fresh from the source. Which meant they needed to find a donor.

"I'm quite sure I don't like that look." Issac turned her in his arms, his head cocked to the side. "What has you perplexed, Aya?"

Damn him for reading her so well. "Um…" She

cleared her throat. "Well, I was just thinking that you should, maybe, drink from someone before we head upstairs."

All the playful energy between them died as his body tensed against hers. "You think my control will slip?" The edge in his voice sent a chill down her spine. "That I'll bite you in error?"

"No, it's not that." She wasn't explaining this right. "I just meant, you need to feed."

His eyebrows shot up. "Do I?"

"Well, yes. You've not fed since…"

"Since when?" he prompted, letting her go and taking a step back. "When was my last feed, Astasiya?"

The day of my rebirth. Three weeks ago.

Yeah, so much for their "normal" evening. She ran her fingers through her hair, her back hitting the wall. "Don't make me say it." Her heart couldn't take it. Not after everything they'd been through. "Please."

He sighed, "Aya." He pulled her into his arms again, and she collapsed against his chest.

"I'm sorry. It's just, I know what you need, Issac. I can't ignore it."

His strength rolled over her in waves of warmth that caressed her senses. Peppermint and sandalwood—two scents she always associated with him. She breathed deep, taking him into her lungs while allowing his presence to soothe her in ways no one else could. Her heart beat in time with his, her soul rejoicing at having him so near, while her mind remained uncertain.

She hated this. It wasn't fair. All she wanted was the one thing she could never really have. She wanted to scream, to cry, to hide.

"We promised to fight," he whispered.

"I know," she replied. "I am." Why else would she suggest he feed from someone else? He had to know that it would hurt her on a fundamental level to see him with another person. To watch his lips caress a neck that didn't

248

belong to her.

"I've been alive a long time, Astasiya. I know my body, and I will tell you when I require blood."

She shook her head. "But I don't understand. It's been weeks."

"A detail that has me troubled as well, but I feel fine." He grabbed her chin and forced her to meet his gaze. "I need you to trust me, Aya. This will never work without your faith in me."

"Of course I trust you, Issac." She wouldn't be standing here with him if she didn't.

His midnight-blue eyes searched hers. "Then why doubt me on this?"

"It's not doubt. I'm just… I *miss* you, and I thought… I thought it might help." She tried to look away, but he held her with ease.

His pupils flared. "We'll socialize as expected, then we're going upstairs to continue this conversation. Naked. Understood?"

She swallowed, her mouth going dry. "Y-yes."

"Brilliant." His lips touched hers, sealing their vow. "Let's go celebrate."

CHAPTER FOUR

Issac

Thirty minutes. That's how long Issac promised to remain in this room before he dragged Astasiya upstairs.

Then his sister intervened by asking him to dance. He could never refuse Amelia anything, especially this. After all, it was she who taught him the Baroque style, as well as numerous others. Not that they were following any rules now. The room wasn't big enough, nor were there enough participants who knew the format. Instead, they followed a more contemporary style with their own improvisations.

"I've quite missed this," she said after a soft spin.

"Thomas doesn't dance with you?" Issac found the blond male in question. He stood beside Astasiya, laughing at whatever she just said to him. "I can happily fix that for you."

"Be nice," Amelia said, her blue gaze sparkling with

mirth. "And I'm sure he would; I just haven't asked him."

Issac shifted his focus back to his sister. "Why not?"

"I wasn't sure if I would still enjoy it."

"Ah, I see. You used me as a test." He twirled her before she could respond, causing her to laugh as he caught her. "An excellent choice, by the way."

She shook her head. "Show-off."

He smirked, glancing at Astasiya. The feminine approval in her green eyes lit his soul on fire. *Mine*, his soul whispered. Fuck the rules, the expectations, and those who said it was impossible. He would find a way.

"I've never seen you so taken by a woman," Amelia murmured, her attention following his own. "It's lovely."

He held Astasiya's gaze for a beat longer before looking down at his sister. "You don't disapprove?" Everyone else had made their sentiments known, including his maker, Aidan. *It's not practical*, they all said. *It's dangerous.*

"I'm concerned," she admitted. "But I've always trusted your judgment, and there's something different about her."

On that, he agreed. Osiris had referred to her as his "granddaughter." Did he mean that in the sense that his Ichorian progeny had created her? Or was it meant to imply something else? That he didn't require blood after sustaining himself on hers for so long was a significant mystery. As well as the other details he'd noticed that may, or may not, have been a figment of his imagination.

Like his suspicion that his powers were growing.

He cleared his throat and whirled Amelia once more, his eyes once again traveling to his Aya. She wore that white gown so well. It had taken significant restraint not to play with the low cut across her breasts or to explore the slit up her thigh. Her constant bumping up against him in the haunted floors only deepened his need. The smile flirting with her lips now said she more than shared his desire.

Issac sent a mental vision to Thomas—a subtle

suggestion that the former Sentinel received loud and clear. He excused himself from Astasiya's side and started toward them in his army fatigues. Amelia had worn a similar outfit of camouflage pants and a matching tank top. She even had her hair in a ponytail.

So different from the sister I lost nearly seven years ago, and yet, so much better for it. He loved this stronger, more confident version of Amelia.

"Can I cut in?" Thomas asked, right on cue.

"Of course." Issac kissed his sister on the cheek. "Thank you for the dance, love. Good luck teaching Thomas the proper steps."

"I know how to dance, Wakefield," the former Sentinel replied, taking Amelia's hip as Issac spun her into his waiting arms. "It was part of my high-society training. Just ask Lizzie."

Issac's lips twitched. "Then you should have no trouble keeping up with my sister."

Thomas's gaze narrowed. "Why does that sound like a challenge?"

"Because it is," Amelia replied, grinning. "Let's see what you can do."

His blond brows lifted. "Oh, is that how this is going to go?"

"Intimidated?" she taunted.

He dipped her so low her head nearly hit the ground. "Not at all."

Excitement shone bright in her gaze. "Arse."

"Asset."

Right. Time to leave.

Issac excused himself with a slight bow before going in search of the woman he wanted to dance with—preferably naked. She stood waiting by the door, her shoulder braced against the wall, arms folded, expression expectant.

"Ready?" she asked as he approached.

He tangled his fingers in her hair and pulled her to him, his lips brushing hers. "I should be asking you that question, love."

A lovely flush crept into her cheeks. "Let's go."

He sent a visual image of their departure to Jayson, so that Elizabeth wouldn't come looking for them later, and guided Astasiya toward the elevator with his hand against her lower back. Thankfully, the car that arrived for them was empty.

Twenty-three flights. Plenty of time.

He used his key card to select the floor they needed, then backed Astasiya up against the wall. Her green eyes flashed, sending a jolt of electricity through his veins.

"Don't move," he whispered, his hand circling her throat.

Trust stared back at him, something he required for this to go as he desired. He gently pressed his lips to hers, his senses firing. Ichorians could sense blood, especially that of a Hydraian, and while hers sang to him as it always had, he didn't feel overwhelmed by it.

As an immortal, she healed quickly. Unless she'd bitten herself in the last several minutes, she posed no risk to him. And he'd smell the fresh blood if she had.

The true test.

A kiss.

He traced the seam of her mouth with his tongue, resulting in a gasp from her. *Technically moving...* He'd take that up with her afterward, because fuck, he needed this. Craved it above all else. He missed the intimacy; he missed *her.*

His grip tightened, his other hand going to her hip, holding her in place. He required the control in order to proceed with the next step.

Oh-so slowly, his tongue parted her lips and dipped inside to find hers. She didn't move or reciprocate—her entire body frozen against his—as he explored her to his liking. The sound of the elevator's arrival had him pulling back to find her staring up at him with unveiled arousal.

"Takes effort not to react, doesn't it?" he asked softly,

releasing her neck.

She swallowed. "Tell me I can do that to you."

"We'll see," he murmured, linking his fingers with hers. "I want you naked first."

Astasiya followed him into the hallway. "The feeling is very mutual." The raspy quality of her voice appealed to his masculine pride.

He wrapped his arm around her, needing her close, and opened the door to their suite. His instincts dared him to take her against the door, while his mind urged caution. They had to proceed carefully, a challenge that fascinated him. *Something different.* Issac rather liked the prospect of that, even if it meant ignoring some of his natural urges.

"I'll meet you in the bedroom," he murmured, setting his key on the counter.

Excitement flared in her gorgeous eyes. "Okay."

She toed off her heels, taking two steps before he added, "And, Aya?" She glanced over her shoulder. "Lose the dress."

Embers flickered in her pupils. "Yes, sir." She slid the gold chains from her shoulders, causing the fabric to fall to the floor around her. "Better?"

He ran his gaze over her as if seeing her for the first time. Perhaps because he hadn't seen her naked since her rebirth. Too much temptation, and now he remembered why.

Flawless. Every inch of her. And she'd worn nothing beneath that dress all night.

Tease. "You're gorgeous, love."

A faint blush touched her cheeks at the praise. "I'll be in the bedroom." She turned and sauntered off, his gaze on her ass the whole way. He wanted to grab her and fuck her against the wall, which he couldn't do.

I need a distraction.

Issac turned toward the cabinets and found the red wine he'd brought with him from Hydria. His original intentions of enjoying a few glasses with Astasiya melted into a new plan, one they would both thoroughly enjoy.

He uncorked the bottle, selected a single glass, and started toward the bedroom.

Right. His football boots had to go. As much as he enjoyed a good match, dressing as one of the players was not high on his repeat list. He kicked off the shoes— Astasiya would remove the rest.

She sat waiting for him on the bed, lounging in the pillows. Such a regal pose and well deserved. "Now you resemble Aphrodite," he mused, pouring wine into the glass and setting the bottle on the nightstand beside her.

He took a sip while taking in every inch of her gorgeous form. Long legs, slender waist, shapely breasts, and virescent eyes. *All mine.*

"Come here." He pulled more red wine into his mouth. She went onto her knees before him, her hands on his shoulders as he wrapped her long, blonde hair around his free hand. *Now for some fun.*

He pressed his lips to hers. She opened automatically, allowing him to pass the liquid into her mouth for a taste. Her groan of approval hit him right in the groin, but he was nowhere near done yet.

Issac angled her head and kissed her again, his tongue seeking hers. She met him halfway, her nails digging into his shoulders while he set the smooth pace. One wrong move, just the nick of his teeth, and everything would end. The danger of it added fuel to the effervescent flame between them, heightening the intensity of the act.

He set the glass aside to better hold her. She moaned against him, her body trembling beneath his touch.

Restraint—oh, what a beautiful, addictive sensation. *More.*

He nudged her onto her back, kneeling between her parted thighs, and bent to continue their kiss. Slow, tender, teasing, and unlike any embrace they'd previously shared.

Her hands went to his shorts, her eager fingers working the drawstring loose. He smiled against her mouth, wishing so badly he could bite her in reprimand.

"Take them off," she said, her voice underlined with power.

"Aya," he growled, complying. "Are you going to make me gag you, love?"

She raised a blonde brow, her lips curling. He didn't understand until his jersey joined the pile on the ground. She'd truly come into her gifts these last few weeks, being able to persuade mentally and not just verbally. It set his soul on fire, stirring a depth of desire inside him only she could sate.

Mine.

"The socks can stay, if you want," she said, her gaze roaming his chest and abs and pausing at his black boxer briefs. "Those—"

He silenced her with his mouth, his tongue more forceful than before, but not nearly as hard as he wanted. "Persuade me again and see what happens." This game between them was one of his favorites. His groin ached with need as he settled between her thighs—the only barrier between them a thin layer of cotton. "You fancy yourself in charge, do you?" he asked, his lips barely touching hers.

Astasiya's hands slid up his bare back, her hips bucking against his. "Fuck me, Issac." This time her gift didn't register, only a plea in her voice to move this along. So many weeks without each other had taken its toll on them both.

He pressed his forehead to hers. "We have to be careful."

"I know."

The trust required to truly do this spoke volumes about why they couldn't stay away from each other, why they had to try this, why they had to find a way to make this work. He knelt again, pulling off his boxers and socks, and went onto all fours above her. "This won't be like all the other times, Aya."

She nodded. "Different isn't bad."

"Certainly not." He nudged her thighs wider. "If anything, it'll be a new experience."

"I like new."

"I do too." He grabbed her hips, letting her think he meant to fulfill her wish. But she required a reminder in who dominated whom in this room. "Now try not to move." He bent to take one stiff nipple into his mouth and gently nibbled.

She hissed his name, her muscles locking in place as he nipped her again. Not too hard, but enough for her to feel it and excite the risk between them.

"They say fear can be an aphrodisiac," he whispered, switching breasts. "I think they might be right." Another graze of his teeth against her skin elicited a sheen of sweat. "Is it hard staying absolutely still?" he asked her, taunting. "I imagine it takes great self-discipline." He spoke against her stiff peak, stirring a moan from her throat.

Issac smiled, his lips running down her flat stomach to the alluring slickness waiting for him between her thighs. "Can I trust you, Aya?" he whispered against her damp folds. "Can you remain completely still?"

She shuddered, her hands fisted in the comforter. "Y-yes. Please."

"Mmm." He nuzzled her clit as a test. She didn't shift or react, but a look at her face showed clear restraint. "Don't bite that lip too hard, or I won't be able to kiss you, love."

"You're killing me," she said on a gasp. "Oh my God, I'm ready. Just fuck me."

He chuckled, dipping his head to continue, this time with a lick that resulted in a near scream from her. Such a beautiful sound. He encouraged another with a deeper probe of his tongue and tightened his grip on her hips.

"Issac," she whispered. "I c-can't."

"Can't what, darling?" He sucked on her most sensitive point, not nearly as hard as he wanted but enough to garner a vocal reaction from her. Her limbs shook wildly on either side of him, her chest vibrating with a combination of determination and desire, and her expression was one of pleasure-pain. He recognized the limit and sat up slowly, knowing she would combust if he pushed her any further.

Too bad, really. It would have been a sight to behold.

"Please," she begged. "Please, Issac."

He bent her knees while keeping them spread wide and aligned his cock with her entrance. "Tell me if it's too much," he said, sliding into her wet heat. Her thighs squeezed him, a sound of approval falling from her lips. He went to his elbows on either side of her head, his gaze on her mouth. "Did you bite yourself?"

"No," she whispered, shaking her head. "But I want to bite you."

"I might enjoy that, Aya." He kissed her far too softly for the moment, his soul requiring more. The need burned inside of him, creating a maelstrom of emotions mingled with fear. *One wrong move…* "Command me to stop if I start to lose myself."

Her hands went to his face. "I will," she vowed, holding his gaze. "Make love to me, Issac."

"Always," he brushed the word against her mouth.

"Always," she repeated, completing him on a level no one had ever accessed.

She owned him completely. There would be no other, and he showed her that with his body. With every thrust, every kiss, every moan, he promised her that this was their beginning, not their end. Fate be damned, they would find a way to be together. They would solve all the puzzles, defy all expectations, and they would be together.

For there was no other option.

Astasiya was his forever.

Always.

A HALLOWEEN ENGAGEMENT READER DISCUSSION

"Okay. I'm done for now."

—Stas

B: Not bad. I give Issac's performance a seven point three. Points deducted for wearing boxers.

Issac: Fuck you.

B: Happily.

Luc: Hey, it's time for the bachelor party, right?

B: Next book.

Luc: Damn. I was looking forward to that.

B: It's coming. Pun intended.

Jay: I've been thinking about maybe sitting that one out.

B: That's cute. No.

Alik: If he doesn't have to go, then I don't have to go.

B: Again, no. You're both coming, plans are set, and we leave New Year's Eve.

Stas: *Um, that's… Yeah, never mind.*

Issac: *What?*

Stas: *No, it's fine. You all have fun.*

Lizzie: *Her birthday is January 1st.*

Stas: *Lizzie!*

Lizzie: *What? It's your twenty-fifth, or would be, if you hadn't… uh, yeah.*

Issac: *Then I'm staying with Aya.*

B: *Right, again, no. You're all attending, and I'll have you back for her birthday the next day.*

Luc: *Perfect. Well, I do believe our work here is done.*

B: *Yep. I thought it went pretty well.*

Luc: *Me too. Until next time, readers.*

B: *Much love to you all.*

Jay: *Thanks for hanging around.*

Lizzie: *Bye, everyone.*

Issac: *Cheers.*

Stas: *See you all soon.*

———

Leela: *How long until she realizes Issac can bite her?*

Stark: *Hopefully, not anytime soon.*

Leela: *Spoken like a true—*

Stark: *Don't say it.*

Leela: *Why not?*

Ezekiel: *Spoiler, obviously. Let them figure it out themselves.*

Leela: *Ugh, it's taking too long.*

Stark: *Then stop talking so our creator can continue with the next book.*

Leela: *Huh, fair point. All right, I'm out.*

Stark: *Likewise.*

Ezekiel: *Peace.*

EXTRA STUFF

"Because we can."

—*B*

IMMORTAL CURSE RECIPES

Alik's Sandwich

Ingredients:

- bread
- meat
- cheese
- lettuce
- condiments, if you feel it's necessary

Directions:

Assemble. Eat.

Optional Commentary:

B: Well, we've never called you inventive, have we?

Amelia's Hot Chocolate

Ingredients:

- 16 oz whole milk
- 12 oz Argentinian dark chocolate
- 2 peppermint sticks
- Balthazar's homemade whipped cream (can be found in his fridge on Hydria)

Directions:

Warm milk on stove over medium heat while stirring constantly. Once it starts to boil, add chocolate and continue stirring until chocolate is fully melted. Can add more or less chocolate depending on taste.

Serve in two mugs. Add peppermint stick to each. Top with whipped cream. Serve. Enjoy.

Optional Commentary:

Tom: It's delicious, as is Amelia.

Balthazar's Pancakes

Ingredients:

- 1 1/2 cups all-purpose flour
- 3 1/2 teaspoons baking powder
- 1 teaspoon salt
- 1 tablespoon granulated sugar
- 1 1/4 cups whole milk
- 1 egg
- 3 tablespoons of melted butter
- 1 bag powdered sugar
- 1 bottle pure maple syrup (no corn syrup allowed)
- chocolate chips, chocolate sauce, chocolate fudge—all acceptable toppings
- fresh fruit
- fresh whipped cream (from my personal stash)
- other toppings as desired

Directions:

Sift the flour, baking powder, salt, and sugar in a large bowl. Create a hole in the center of the bowl and pour in the milk. Crack egg into mixture and add melted butter. Chocolate chips are optional additions, or can be used later as toppings.

Beat mixture until the texture is smooth. This activity serves as great exercise, especially when using your other hand for more creative assembly in the kitchen.

When finished with both tasks—pleasuring your partner(s) and mixing to a smooth texture—place a griddle or frying pan over medium heat. Lightly oil the surface, and perhaps those around you (if interested), then pour or scoop the batter onto your pan. For each pancake, 1/4 cup is adequate. Brown evenly on both sides.

Dust pancakes with powdered sugar. Bonus points awarded to those who use sugar creatively on their guests.

Balthazar's Pancakes

Add toppings as desired. Strongly suggest use of whipped cream, fresh fruit, maple syrup, and chocolate, either on pancakes or partners.

Multiply recipe as appropriate for after-party care.

Eat. Hydrate. Enjoy.

Optional Commentary:

Luc: I approve of your use of maple syrup.

B: I thought you might.

Issac's "Where to Bite" Guide

Ingredients:

• Astasiya

Directions:

Mine.

Optional Commentary:

B: Seriously?

Issac: You tasked me with the above. I answered.

Stas's Coffee

Ingredients:

- black coffee
- 2 teaspoons brown sugar

Directions:

Put sugar in coffee. Stir. Cool. Drink.

Optional Commentary:

B: You're almost as bad as Alik. Almost.

Jay's Pizza

Ingredients:

Sauce:
- 2 tablespoons olive oil
- 4 cloves fresh garlic
- 1 sprig fresh basil
- 2 sprigs fresh oregano
- dried crushed red chili, to taste
- 800 grams San Marzano tomatoes, peeled and crushed
- salt, to taste
- fresh-ground black pepper, to taste

Crust:
- 1 teaspoon active dry yeast
- 3/4 cup water, lukewarm
- 2 cups tipo 00 flour, plus a bit extra
- 3/4 teaspoon salt
- 2 teaspoons olive oil

Directions:

If you have a proper wood-fired brick oven, get a fire going and heat it to about 450°C (850°F). If you do not, preheat your modern oven to 235°C (450°F) with a baking sheet or pizza stone inside on a low rack.

Heat the olive oil in a saucepan over a medium-low flame. Peel and finely chop up the garlic, crushing it with the flat side of your knife afterward. Mince the basil, both stem and leaves. Strip the oregano leaves from the stem and dice them; discard the stem.

Jay's Pizza

Cover dough and let rise for 10 to 15 minutes.

Divide dough in half. Stretch and flatten each half into a thin, round shape; you may use a rolling pin if desired. If the dough shrinks back when rolled, let it sit a few minutes longer and try again.

If using a modern oven:

Remove stone or baking sheet from oven and place on a wire rack. Transfer one pizza crust to your stone or baking sheet. Brush top surface of dough with olive oil, then spread on a thin layer of sauce.

Place in oven for 3 minutes, then remove and add desired toppings. I prefer buffalo mozzarella, Italian sausage, corn, and caramelized onions. Lizzie prefers shredded mozzarella, American pepperoni, and a variety of veggies.

Once done negotiating toppings (clothing optional), return to oven for 8 to 10 minutes. Repeat with second crust.

If using a wood-fired brick oven:

Dust a wooden pizza peel with cornmeal or flour; place dough on peel. Brush top surface of dough with olive oil, then spread on a thin layer of sauce. Add desired toppings. See my comments above regarding preferences and negotiation of said toppings.

Transfer directly to stone floor of hot oven; bake for 3 to 5 minutes, rotating pizza 180 degrees halfway through to ensure even baking. Repeat with second crust.

Optional Commentary:

Lizzie: *Removing your shirt usually wins you the best toppings. Just sayin'.*

Lizzie's Chocolate Chip Cookies

Ingredients:

- 1 cup plus 2 tablespoons all-purpose flour
- 1/4 teaspoon baking soda
- 1/4 teaspoon baking powder
- 1/2 teaspoon salt
- 1 stick (4 ounces) unsalted butter, preferably at room temperature
- 4 tablespoons granulated sugar
- 1/2 cup brown sugar
- 1 egg
- 1/2 teaspoon vanilla
- 1 cup semi-sweet chocolate chips (this can also be dark chocolate chips, peanut butter chips, or whatever your immortal is craving)

Directions:

Preheat oven to 350°F. Prepare baking sheets by lining them with parchment paper.

In a medium bowl, combine the flour, baking soda, baking powder, and salt. This is a great task to give a hungry immortal, especially one who has nothing better to do than to ask you for cookies. Daily.

Using an electric mixer, beat the butter, granulated sugar, and brown sugar until creamy. Or, ask immortal to remove shirt and stir mixture for you. Makes for a fantastic show. Otherwise, beat for about two minutes with electric mixer, then add the egg and vanilla, beating well to combine. Gradually add the flour mixture and then stir in the chocolate chips.

Scoop 1 1/2 tablespoon-sized balls—give half to immortal and place the rest on prepared baking sheet.

Lizzie's Chocolate Chip Cookies

Bake for 9 to 11 minutes or until golden brown. Allow it to cool for 2 minutes before switching them to the wire racks to let cool completely. Warn hungry immortal what happens when he eats a cookie too soon. Prepare speech that involves "I told you so" when he ignores you.

Enjoy!

Optional Commentary:

Jay: I love you, Red.

Luc's Waffles

Ingredients:

- 1 1/2 cups fresh whole milk, lukewarm
- 1 1/2 tablespoons white sugar
- 7 grams active dry yeast
- 3 fresh eggs, yolks and whites separated
- 1 1/2 cups sparkling water, room temperature
- 3 1/2 cups finely milled, unbleached flour, thoroughly sifted
- 1 tablespoon plus 2 1/4 teaspoons baking powder, sifted in with the flour
- 1 generous pinch salt, sifted in with the flour and baking powder
- 10 1/2 tablespoons unsalted Irish butter, melted
- a bit extra butter, for greasing iron and for topping
- pure east Canadian dark amber maple syrup

Directions:

Combine the milk, sugar, and yeast in a large bowl; allow to bloom for ten minutes.

Lightly beat the egg yolks and incorporate into the milk-yeast mixture, then gently stir in the sparkling water until thoroughly combined. Add the flour mixture through a sieve, then beat until smooth (you can use a mechanical or electric mixer if you lack the forearm strength to do this by hand).

Gently fold in the melted butter. Beat the egg whites until they form soft peaks, then fold into the batter by hand.

Allow the batter to rise for about a half hour.

While the batter is rising, heat your waffle iron. My preference is the traditional cast-iron heated on a wood stove, but the electric irons invented a century ago work equally as well. This is essential for your waffles to have a crispy exterior. Grease the iron well (even if it has that blasphemous purported "nonstick" coating); butter or ghee will work best.

Luc's Waffles

Once your iron is hot and your batter is bubbly, you are ready to bake. Pour about 1/3 cup of batter into your iron and bake until it has browned completely. Repeat until you have used all of your batter (enough for about seven waffles).

Use maple syrup as appropriate (both in the bedroom and on the waffles).

Serves one immortal being with large muscle mass and high calorific needs; alternatively, serves four or more mortals (you may need to double or triple the recipe).

Optional Commentary:

B: I will begrudgingly admit that this sounds edible.

A BONUS STORY

"I recently took over Lexi's reader group on Facebook. Here's a copy of the story I told them. Consider joining us in the future in case I decide to take over again."
—*Issac*

A note from the author: This story takes place after the events in *Blood Heart*; however, it does not fit the chronological timeline. It is included in the "extra stuff" because that's exactly what this is: a fun tidbit offered to my reader group that I wished to share with those who might not be on social media. I hope you enjoy it.

A "SURPRISE" BIRTHDAY PARTY

Issac

Part I

Balthazar.

Naked.

Issac sat bolt upright, causing the blonde using his shoulder as a pillow to groan. An apology sat unused on his tongue as the images continued to assault his mind.

I'm going to kill you, Issac vowed, knowing full well the mind reader in the other room could hear him.

His response was a well-placed birthday cake. Over his groin.

"Issac?" Astasiya mumbled, her gloriously nude body lost to the visions clouding his thoughts. Most days he loved his gift for visual manipulation, but not when they woke him in a sexual nightmare.

He mentally punched Balthazar in the face and turned

the cake into a sharp object that the man immediately dropped. Which, of course, only worsened the entire image.

A hand on his thigh switched his focus to a pair of curious green eyes. She raised one brow in question.

"Remind me why we decided to move in with Balthazar," he said in response.

"Because he owns one of the largest properties on Hydria and offered us a place to stay." Her lips curved. "Is he bothering you?"

"That amuses you?"

"Yes." She didn't even hesitate, the bloody woman. She even added a giggle. "What's he doing?"

"He's attempting to offer me a birthday gift I have no intention of unwrapping."

"Birthday gift?" Now she sat upright. "It's your birthday?"

"You sound surprised."

"Because I am. How could you not tell me it's your birthday?!"

Issac gaped at her. "Why would it matter? It's hardly something I celebrate, Aya."

She rolled out of the bed—the precise opposite action Issac had in mind—and grabbed her robe. "Don't move."

Part II

Issac glowered at the ceiling. Astasiya had compelled him to stay. Like a dog. On his birthday. When she returned from whatever she'd run off to do, he would have a stern word with her about using her gifts inappropriately. There were so many more enlightening ways to persuade someone.

Undress.

Fuck me.

Harder.

"Don't move" was not on his list of ideal activities. At

least Balthazar had left him alone.

Issac sought out the mind reader's gaze, curious to see if Astasiya was nearby. Sure enough, she stood in the kitchen beside him, flipping a pancake.

Ah, she wanted to cook him breakfast in bed.

All right, he could forgive her for that. But she could have allowed him to move.

She glanced up at Balthazar, her green eyes grinning at whatever he'd just said to her. Unfortunately, Issac's gift didn't extend to sound unless in a dream state.

He sighed—his chest moving—but his arms and legs remained locked. Astasiya grew more powerful by the day. She'd told him not to move, then altered the command with her mind. Fascinating.

If only they could determine her secondary gift.

The door opened as his Aya sauntered in holding a tray.

He attempted to move his jaw and found it free. As was the rest of him now that she'd returned. He sat up again and leaned against the headboard. "You realize, love, that I would have preferred you to stay in bed and indulge in something else for breakfast, yes?"

Her cheeks flushed as she set the tray down on the nightstand. "That can be your dessert."

"Oh, I believe it will be *your* dessert," he corrected. "It is my birthday, after all, and since you seem so keen on celebrating, then that is what I want."

She licked her lips. "After breakfast."

He narrowed his gaze. "Before."

"Issac, people are coming over—"

"Is it my birthday or not?"

"You're impossible."

He grinned. "You adore it."

She crawled onto the bed, losing the robe along the way. "Fortunately for you, that's true. Now lie down again."

Ah, now that was a command he didn't mind

following.

Part III

"Remind me to celebrate my birthday more often," Issac murmured as he wrapped a towel around Astasiya's shoulders. Her lips were beautifully swollen and her eyes drowsily sated. "You're gorgeous, love."

"Sweet talker." She grabbed a towel for him as well and took great care in drying his chest and abs.

He grinned down at her. "And you call me insatiable."

"What? A woman is allowed to admire." She kissed him carefully on the cheek before stepping away. "Now that your breakfast is cold, let's go make another one."

He caught sight of Balthazar still in the kitchen. "Our host is already working on it." And it seemed she was right about having guests. Alik and Lucian were seated at the counter, both with plates in front of them.

Issac pulled on a pair of grey pants and a dress shirt that he rolled to the elbows while Astasiya watched him with a bemused expression. She'd thrown on a pair of jean shorts and a tank top.

"What?" he asked at her continued look.

"It's over ninety degrees outside and you're dressed for work."

He pulled a pair of shoes from the closet before saying, "This is how I dress."

"Do you own a pair of shorts?"

"Actually, yes. I do." He set down his shoes and opened a drawer to show her his beach attire. "Happy?"

"I'll be happier if you put those on with a pair of sandals."

He grimaced at the wardrobe choice. "No."

She wrapped her arms around his waist. "Please?"

Issac couldn't believe *this* was what she chose to beg him on. "You wish for me to dress casually?"

Astasiya nodded, her green eyes imploring. "Please?"

she repeated.

Suspicion trickled into his thoughts. She never cared about his attire. "Why?"

"Because I want you to be comfortable."

"I'm comfortable as I am."

"Right now, but you'll thank me later if you change now."

His eyes narrowed. "Why? What have you planned?"

"Not me…" Her eyes sparkled as she trailed off.

Oh, hell. He knew that look, and it could only mean one thing. "They're throwing a beach party because it's my birthday." The damn Hydraians would use any excuse to celebrate. "Fuck."

Part IV

Issac agreed to the shorts under the condition that Astasiya would remove them later. With her teeth. She'd accepted the challenge, which was the only reason he managed a smile when he met Lucian and Alik in the dining area. He ignored Balthazar on principle.

"I made you a waffle," Lucian said in greeting. He pushed the monstrosity across the counter with a grin. "I even added a candle."

"Why is it covered in melted ice cream?" he asked, disgusted.

"Because it's a birthday waffle that melted while you were busy with Stas." Lucian folded his arms, his disapproval evident.

Whether it was in regard to what Issac had been doing to Astasiya or the disastrous birthday waffle, he didn't know. Everyone had expressed their concerns regarding his continued relationship with Astasiya, but it wasn't their decision. They were working things out between themselves. Everyone else could go hang.

"I told you not to put the maple syrup on it," Balthazar murmured. "It melted the ice cream."

"Birthday waffles are supposed to be served with a scoop of vanilla bean ice cream, warm pure maple syrup, and sprinkles because they brighten up the ensemble. Had I known he planned to dally in the bedroom, I would have waited." Lucian nudged the plate even closer to Issac. "He's going to eat it anyway."

"I am"—he eyed the soggy breakfast and shook his head—"not."

"It's rude to refuse a gift," Lucian advised, his tone stern. If it wasn't for the twinkle of mischief in his emerald gaze, Issac may have taken him seriously. Alas, he knew the Hydraian King quite well.

"Make me another and I'll try it. You may even convince me to update my preference from pancakes to waffles." He added that last part in coercion, knowing Lucian would never be able to refuse that challenge.

"That means I have to make a birthday pancake to go with it," Balthazar mused. "Challenge accepted."

Lucian snorted. "Your flat pastry will have nothing on my geometrically sound brilliance."

"I can't believe you're encouraging this insanity," Alik growled as he stood. "I'll be down at the beach. Enjoy your breakfast."

Part V

Ice cream on waffles wasn't terrible. Issac would never seek it out for a future meal, but he wouldn't refuse it either.

The chocolate chip pancakes, however, were phenomenal. Something he refused to admit out loud, not that he needed to with Balthazar hearing his thoughts.

Astasiya squeezed his hand and bumped her shoulder against his as they meandered down to the beach. "I still can't believe you didn't tell me it was your birthday."

"I stopped celebrating my birthday long ago, love. As you continue to age, you'll understand."

She said nothing for a long moment, her gaze thoughtful. "I suppose you're right. It's weird to think about—the whole living forever thing."

"Yes," he agreed. "But it becomes second nature after a few decades."

"Which will pass you by in no time," Alik said as he joined them on the path. He lived closest to the beach because he considered it an important perimeter to guard. Issac also guessed the Hydraian chose the location for personal reasons as well, but never pried.

"You would know," Astasiya said. "Being over three thousand years old and all."

Alik's lips twitched, almost revealing a smile. "Yes, now four thousand will be a birthday worth celebrating. I'm not quite sure why we're all throwing this party today. Wakefield isn't even five hundred yet."

"Yes, whose brilliant idea was this?" Issac wondered. "Because I can't remember the last time I acknowledged my birthday, let alone celebrated it."

"Amelia," Alik replied softly. "She wanted to do something fun since all of her family is here on the island."

Astasiya frowned. "She didn't mention anything to me."

"She wanted it to be a surprise." Alik glanced at Issac. "It's the first party she's planned since her return."

Issac's heart gave a little pang at the thought of his sister going through all this trouble for him. She was an entirely different woman from the one he knew a decade ago.

So much strength and courage, he barely even recognized her, and yet, he found himself loving her more than he ever had.

"Let's not keep her and the others waiting, then," he said.

It wouldn't be his birthday he'd celebrate, though. Just the beauty of being alive and surrounded by family and his closest friends, and his Aya.

Part VI

Applause broke out with shouts of "Happy birthday!" as Issac's sandals touched the black sand of the beach. Amusement stirred in his chest at the sight of them all cheering over something so inconsequential.

"This is not a milestone birthday," he chided as Amelia rushed to greet him. He released Astasiya's hand just in time to catch his sister in a hug. Her exuberance washed over him, causing him to chuckle.

After years of presuming her dead, this was the best gift she could have ever given him. Life. He hugged her tighter and spun her in a circle, relieved that she was here. Tangible. Well and truly alive.

"Thank you," he whispered, meaning it.

"You're welcome." She kissed his cheek and hugged him again, her shoulders trembling with emotion. "I'm sorry for all the years I missed."

"Never apologize, love." He gripped her tighter. "Ever. Not for what he took from us."

"I know. Of course I know." Emotion shone bright in her sapphire eyes—identical to his own—as she gazed up at him. "It's just harder some days, especially on the ones with the most memories and importance."

He nodded, understanding. "Then let's make up for lost time. I assume there's a cake somewhere?"

Mirth touched her expression. "Why ever would you think that?"

"Because I know my sister well," he replied. Then he remembered that Amelia had pretty much avoided the kitchen since her return. He frowned. "Wait. You did bake one, right?"

"No, but Lizzie did." Her smile grew. "And according to Jay, it's excellent."

His eyebrows shot upward. "He tried my cake before I even knew it existed?" Issac didn't actually care, but he enjoyed this game. Amelia loved formalities, and this was certainly against the rules.

"Perks of living with the chef," Jayson said as he joined their little circle. "Lizzie may have made a second one just for me."

"Isn't Elizabeth pregnant?" Issac asked, knowing full well the female was indeed with child. "Shouldn't you be the one doing all the work around the house, Jayson?"

"What? Are pregnant women not allowed to bake?" A sharp female voice demanded. "I'm just supposed to lounge around and do nothing?"

Issac blinked at the fiery redhead as she appeared beside Jayson. "Yes?" he guessed, uncertain now that he'd been scolded.

She smirked. "I knew I liked you."

"Stop giving her ideas, Wakefield." Jayson wrapped his arm around Elizabeth's shoulders to hug her to him. "I rather like the benefits of her excellent cooking."

She elbowed his side. "I'm not making you more cookies."

He appeared positively affronted by the statement as he rotated her around to face him. "Why not?"

"I think that's our cue to move along," his Aya whispered in his ear.

He reached for her hand and brought it to his lips. "Indeed."

Part VII

An afternoon filled with laughter, love, and friendship. Issac couldn't imagine a better way to spend the day. And as the sun slipped toward the horizon, the party raged on with Jacque managing the DJ stand.

Issac caught Astasiya by the hip and yanked her against him. She laughed as he dipped her toward the sand and righted her again. Despite everything troubling their lives, they all still managed to find happiness. That was the heart of their world, the reason they would overcome the impending darkness.

As he stared into Astasiya's smiling eyes, he knew somehow, someway, everything would work itself out. Because he couldn't imagine a life without this woman by his side. He adored her on a level that surpassed all boundaries and rules.

Their love—which wasn't a strong enough word—was the kind of love that shattered all expectations. Including the ones that declared this relationship between them impossible.

They would find a way.

There was no other choice.

He twirled her into his arms again, his lips a hairsbreadth from hers. "I will find a way to kiss you again, Aya."

She shuddered, her cheeks flushed from their dance and his vow. They'd tiptoed around each other, only engaging in activities they knew weren't a risk, and it only scraped the surface of their lust for each other. He couldn't taste her, not the way he craved, and it left them both yearning for so much more.

"I love you," she whispered, her mouth brushing his cheek. "Always."

"Always," he agreed, nuzzling her cheek. "Thank you for today, love."

She hugged him closer. "It won't be the last we spend together."

"I know."

"Happy birthday," she breathed against his ear.

He smiled. "Does that mean it's finally time to remove these shorts?"

She chuckled. "One-track mind."

"You adore it," he said, repeating his line from earlier.

Astasiya pulled back to gaze into his eyes, her lips curved at the sides. "Yes, luckily for you, I do."

"Mmm, that sounds promising, love."

"Take me back to our room and I'll show you just how

promising it is, birthday boy."

He lifted her into his arms and smiled. "Keep this up, and I might start celebrating my birthday daily."

"Please do," she replied. "And mine too."

"Noted, love."

The end for now...

The Story Will Continue with *Blood Bonds*

IMMORTAL CURSE SERIES
What's Next

Dear Reader,

Well, that was enlightening and surreal—just a glimpse into the chaos thriving inside my head, really. Most of these stories I never intended to share; they were lurking around for my own knowledge and background. Alas, Balthazar insisted on telling them. And, well, could you tell him no? Because I certainly couldn't. Then when Luc joined the mix, I knew I was in trouble. Those Elders sure know how to force me to write!

Up next is *Blood Bonds*. It's a prequel of sorts to the series that is strategically listed as book five due to the myriad of series spoilers inside the text. All those questions running rampant in your head since *Blood Laws* are about to be answered, and so much more. Seriously, *Blood Bonds* is going to blow your mind (I hope).

Thank you so much for reading! I really hope you enjoyed *Elder Bonds*. There are a lot of Easter eggs planted throughout the book that will come to fruition in the not-so-distant future. Including, maybe, more from Leela and Balthazar. ;-)

I'll be back soon with more from your favorite characters. Until then, thank you so much for your continued support. Cheers, and much love to you all!

Love,

Lexi

ACKNOWLEDGMENTS

Okay, so this book very nearly killed me. Writing so many points of views and following a myriad of different stories, on such a tight deadline, really, really made my head spin. I'm so thankful for my friends and family who push me every day to achieve my goals, while also being my sounding board when I'm losing my mind.

Thank you, first and foremost, to my husband, Matt, for putting up with my bizarre sleep schedule, making sure I eat, forcing me to get out of the house, and for the endless glasses of wine that magically appear on my desk. I love you, Dork1.

Allison: Thank you for being such a supportive friend, for convincing me not to delete Brazil (and really the whole book), for providing your amazing input and endless critique, and for always making me laugh.

Tracey: Thank you for providing me with honest feedback, trying to change the spelling of "Leela" to "Tracey," and always being there for me. Your friendship means so much to me.

Bethany: Oh my God, how badly do you want to kill me right now? Thank you for your patience, for letting me send you *Elder Bonds* in pieces, and for working with me over every one of these books. I would be completely lost without you.

Louise & Melissa: Thank you for being my rock stars, for keeping me afloat while in the writing cave, and for taming all the insanity on social media. Your friendships, loyalty, and partnerships mean the world to me.

Barb, Delphine & Pam: My proofreading team extraordinaire… What would I do without you all?! Thank you for always catching my errors, even the ones I've looked at a dozen times and have not noticed. You all complete me. <3

Julie: Thank you for the gorgeous cover and for forcing me to write that final sex scene. It worked! You've become such an amazing friend. I'm very thankful to know you.

Dan: Thank you for representing B on the cover, for convincing me to write Alik's history (yes, that's on you), and for inspiring Vera. I'll explain that last bit later.

David: Thank you for capturing an amazing photo for the cover—it's perfect! And thank you for letting Julie make you a blond.

Famous Owls: Gah, you all keep me alive. Thank you for your constant support, friendship, and laughs. I cherish all of you!

ARC Owls: Thank you for reading and reviewing, and keeping me laughing when I need it.

And to the readers: Thank you for reading *Elder Bonds*. The Immortal Curse series is my heart, and there are moments when I feel like hiding with the voices instead of sharing them. Your support and encouraging words are what convince me to keep writing, and I can never thank you enough.

Cheers, everyone!

ABOUT THE AUTHOR

USA Today Bestselling Author Lexi C. Foss loves to play in dark worlds, especially the ones that bite. She lives in Atlanta, Georgia with her husband and their furry children. When not writing, she's busy crossing items off her travel bucket list, or chasing eclipses around the globe. She's quirky, consumes way too much coffee, and loves to swim.

ALSO BY LEXI C. FOSS

Immortal Curse Series
Blood Laws
Forbidden Bonds
Blood Heart
Elder Bonds
Blood Bonds
Angel Bonds
Blood Seeker
Assassin Bonds
Blood King
Wicked Bonds
Blood Edict

Blood Alliance Series
Chastely Bitten

Dark Provenance Series
Daughter of Death

Mershano Empire Series
The Prince's Game
The Charmer's Gambit
The Rebel's Redemption
The Devil's Denial

Printed in Great Britain
by Amazon